BLEEDING HEARTS
Dark & Twisted Tales Of Love

BY
PAUL KANE

For further information, please visit:
WEB: www.demainpublishing.org
TWITTER: @DemainPubUk
FACEBOOK: Demain Publishing
INSTAGRAM: demainpublishing

DEMAIN PUBLISHING

Short Sharp Shocks!

Murder! Mystery! Mayhem!

Beats! Ballads! Blank Verse!

Weird! Wonderful! Other Worlds

Horror Novels & Novellas

Science Fiction Novels & Novellas

The 'A QUIET APOCALYPSE' Series

General Fiction

Science Fiction Collections

Horror Fiction Collections

Anthologies

Audios

ACKNOWLEDGEMENTS

My undying thanks to Dean at DEMAIN Publishing for taking this one and to Adrian Baldwin for the amazing cover. A huge heartfelt thank you to Barbie for the superb introduction, and thank yous all round to the editors and publishers who took some of these stories in the first place. As always, hugs and big thank yous to all my friends in the writing and film/TV world, for their continual help both now and in the past; people like Mike Carey, Pete & Nicky Crowther, Simon Clark, Michael Marshall Smith, Stephen Volk, Tim Lebbon and oh so many more. You guys know who you are! Lastly, a massive thank you to my lovely better half Marie for everything. Love you to the moon and back.

For Marie, my one, true love

CONTENTS

INTRODUCTION

I first met award-winning author Paul Kane in 2006, when he interviewed me for his ultimate guide to all things *Hellraiser: The Hellraiser Films and Their Legacy*. (I had a small but meaningful role as the Female Cenobite in Clive Barker's classic horror movie, *Hellbound: Hellraiser II*, 1988.)

As many thespians discover to their chagrin, acting eventually left me behind and I began writing serial killer fiction. Paul and his wife Marie O'Regan encouraged me to expand into horror and I subsequently contributed a Female Cenobite story, 'Sister Cilice', to their anthology, *Hellbound Hearts*. And it's because of Paul and Marie, that *Fangoria* ended up calling me 'one of the finest purveyors of erotically-charged horror fiction around.'

I suppose that this gives me a special insight into the subject matter of Paul's latest horror collection, *Bleeding Hearts*.

So what is *Bleeding Hearts* about? Well, it's about love. (And please don't tell me that *Hellraiser* wasn't really about love. Okay, it is S&M love, but that relationship between Julia and Frank is infernally elemental, to say the least.)

They say love is a many splendored thing and who am I to argue with such a glorious cliché? After all, love is all around. It's a drug...that is so, so easy to get addicted to. And it makes the world go 'round, after all.

Love can give us joy, but sometimes, it can go hideously wrong. It can be a gift...or a curse.

We've all been there. Happily going along living our lives and then BOOM! – love comes right up behind you and hits you over the head with an umbrella. If you're lucky, you'll survive. If you're not so lucky, then you'll end up as an incoherent puddle of sloppy (and soppy) emotions, eventually swirling down into a pool of angst, anger and eventually, even madness.

What struck me as I was perusing Paul's masterfully told tales, was how REAL all the characters and their inner thoughts were. I believed in these folks, and their motivations, to the hilt, no matter how warped they were. Even when the plot twists went into strange and unusual places, I was right there beside them, seeing everything in my mind's eye like a movie, which is really a sign of brilliant writing.

What Paul has explored in the following fourteen stories is love taking a wrong turn somewhere: erotomania, frustration, obsession, retribution and more. All the ingredients that make love so interesting, and at the same time, so painful. But with the added frisson of horror: body horror, supernatural horror, erotic horror, etc. All of which makes *Bleeding Hearts* a heady cocktail of love, sex and the macabre.

Barbie Wilde
Actress (*Hellbound: Hellraiser II, Death Wish 3, Grizzly 2)* and Author (*The Venus Complex* [audio book narrated by Doug Bradley], *The Cilicium Quadra, Voices of the Damned*).

A SUSPICIOUS MIND

I'm caught in a trap,
I can't look back.
Because you've taken out my
Eyeballs baby.

Oh why can't you see…
What this is doing to me,
All your hooks,
And spikes, now baby?

We can't go on together,
With your suspicious mind,
And we can't live our dreams,
With your suspicious mind.

When that old friend I know,
Dropped in to say hello.
Nothing happened,
I swear now baby.

There's no need for that.
For the power saw.
Can't we just talk about this,
Now baby?

We can't go on together,
With your suspicious mind,
And I can't live it seems,
With—

THE CURSED

He wished, every minute of every hour of every day.

Wished that he hadn't said those words. But *that* wish would never come true, not now. Wishes weren't as powerful as their opposite number, Stuart had come to realise. Were fuelled by hope rather than hatred, and nothing ever tops that last one – especially in this world. Hopes are dashed all the time; it was how he'd got into this mess in the first place. Living in hope. Besides, a simple wish couldn't undo what he'd done. Those words, a handful of words, but said with such feeling, with such...

Wished that he'd never said them. But he had. There was nothing he could do about it; not now, not ever. Said when he was drunk, and just a little bit high – but said with such conviction that the 'powers that be', the 'forces of whatever' had listened and taken pity on him. That was a joke in itself, because if anyone deserved pity now it was—

Then again, did people deserve pity if they'd got *themselves* into a mess? Willed it into being? However unintentionally, however misguided they'd been when it happened? But these kinds of things didn't come with a rule book, in spite of what you saw on the TV and in movies. The only rule was it had been done, and couldn't be undone. Not that he was aware of, that he'd been told. It didn't stop him wishing, couldn't stop him...hoping.

It had been, of course, about a girl. Always was, wasn't it? The classic tragedies. Romeo and Juliet and all that, star-crossed lovers, fated. Or about love, more accurately. Boy and girl, boy and boy, girl and girl, or whoever could feel that powerful emotional tug. The emotion that had fuelled the fire of so many great mistakes. That had caused people to lie, to cheat. To kill. And Stuart had considered that option, don't think that he hadn't. It just wasn't *him*: murder. Hadn't been back then, wasn't now. Would never be, especially as Stuart was so close to the end himself. He often wondered if all this might continue, once he was dead. Once the cancer that was currently working its way through his body was done with its task. When he succumbed to this delightful little disease, the scourge of our times. Would it just continue, in another place? The torment? Living, dying, dead. In hope? Eternally, forever?

Wishing that he'd never said those words, but they'd just come out. He'd thought them, and maybe that would have been enough anyway, but actually saying them: that gave them real traction, real *power*, he now knew. If only he'd been more specific, that was where he'd gone wrong, really, when you got right down to it. That was all it would have taken, he felt sure; a couple of words more. Some specificity, as that character had said in the film about dreams. A hook to hang it on, rather than a generalisation that could have meant anything. Could have killed her, or him, both or *all* of them for that matter.

But that hadn't happened either. Fate, or whatever the hell it was, had seen fit to keep them alive for this long, to play out this bloody pantomime until its conclusion. And beyond, if it carried on after death, as he feared it might.

Regardless of the state he'd been in, Stuart could recall that moment in time, that frozen moment he'd tweak just a little if he was in one of those VR machines or what have you, something from another one of those sodding SF movies he loved so much. Weren't they always popping pills to cure this, that and the other in those films? Kidney problems, sure – here you go, no more dialysis. Brain damage, yeah, here you are, take this with a glass of water and the neural pathways will repair themselves. Something eating away at your body, that's fine. That's just... It was usually at this point he'd start to cry uncontrollably; a condition he'd become used to over the years.

Back to that night, though, and to put it into some context, he'd had to endure all kinds of torture that week – back when Stuart hadn't really known the meaning of the word. Not real torture, not actual pain. Psychological. Ironic, really, as that was what he'd been studying at uni around that time. Around the time he'd first met *her*.

His inspiration, his everything.

His downfall.

She'd been hanging out in halls with friends of friends, like people did when they first got to that place. Homesick, not really knowing what was what. Arse looking a lot like an elbow. Loving the freedom and personal space, but at the same time missing someone to do their laundry or make their meals for them. Huddling together in that shared experience, getting to know folk from all over the place, this country and abroad. Clubbing, getting wasted. Sleeping with complete strangers – experimenting – and making pals who'd be there for life, or you *hoped* would be. That word again.

Stuart had spotted her in the common room, chatting to one of the girls on his course called Heidi. Those two were from the same area, apparently, or just down the road from each other, down south. A million miles away from this place in the industrial north. Where Stuart was from. Anyway, he'd paused in the doorway, dawdling there when he saw her. Didn't even know her name, just spotted her and froze. Another, altogether better moment in time.

She was wearing a tartan dress with thick black tights and trainers, her brown hair whoofed up on the top of her head. Those big, round glasses she used to wear back then only accentuated her equally big hazel eyes. Unlike most of the girls around her, she hadn't caked on the make-up. Her eyebrows were faintly drawn on, and didn't look like someone had been at them with a marker pen; her lipstick subtle instead of bright, glowing red. Stuart couldn't be entirely sure, but he always thought his heart had skipped a beat in that moment. Had assumed crap like this was just for stupid love songs and Valentine's Day cards – a holiday which he'd always hated before, but would revel in if whoever was running the show would just give him that girl over there perched on the arm of the battered sofa.

When Heidi – bubbly, hair dyed blue (this week), Heidi – called him over to introduce them, it seemed like his prayers might just be answered.

"Stu! Hey there, Stu!" Heidi had already been at the vodka that was being passed around. "This is Athena, can you believe that?"

Athena, like the Greek goddess, and he'd certainly worshipped her liked one, even then. Always thought, however, that she should have been named after Aphrodite. Not because she didn't have the intelligence or reasoning of Athena, but simply because he was captivated by her beauty. She'd pulled a face at her introduction, anyway, said she wished (but you can't go back) she'd never told Heidi that. Another casualty of the vodka.

"My parents are kinda ageing hippies, out of their time. Athena's way too wanky." She preferred her second name, Maisie, or just plain May. Which was also beautiful, Stuart reckoned. May, when Spring had already sprung and you were on the verge of summer months. And when May looked at you a certain way, it was like the sun was shining on you in summer. You could feel the heat, the warmth. The love.

May had shaken his hand then, saying she was pleased to meet him – the feeling was definitely mutual – and that had been that. They'd spent the entire evening chatting, sharing likes and dislikes, comparing bands they followed, shows they watched, favourite movies. He'd been surprised when she'd come out and asked, "You like *Blade Runner*? And, bear in mind, I will judge you on this."

Like it? Was she kidding? "When a person is tired of *Blade Runner*, they are tired of life," he quoted, though Stuart couldn't remember who'd said it originally.

May nodded and laughed. She had such a wonderful laugh, like birdsong in the morning. Oh, he *had* got it bad! The more they talked, the more he realised that if he didn't spend the rest of his life with this girl, this woman, then there would be no point to it at all. She could make or break him, that much was clear. It was just one of those things: Stuart had never been so certain about anything, ever. He was destined to be with her, in that George and Lorraine McFly 'density' way – another shared favourite – and if it didn't happen the universe might simply explode, or he'd just fade away into nothing. No such luck, sadly.

They'd had so much in common, so many shared experiences, even though they'd gone to different schools. And from that evening on, the pair of them had been pretty much inseparable – regardless of the fact she was studying Health and Social Care (and an argument could be made that they were both sort of heading in the same directions with their career choices).

When groups of their friends had gone out, they'd inevitably ended up together in some corner, drinking and trying to hear themselves think. Very often they'd bail on whatever club was having a happy hour (more like several hours) and find a quiet pub they could natter away in. Finishing each other's sentences, always knowing what the other one was going to say or ask. Yet it never seemed to progress from there.

"If you're not careful mate," his next-door neighbour in halls, Vikram, said to him, "you'll end up getting friend-zoned."

"I'm just...I just want to take my time, be respectful. May's worth it. I can wait."

"Just don't wait too long, is all I'm saying, before making your move."

Stuart couldn't say he hadn't been warned. All through first year and even into the second, after they'd been apart for the whole summer – which had been dreadful, messaging, phone calls and even visits not really cutting it as far as he was concerned – it had been the same story. "You know I think the world of you, Stuart," she'd tell him, "I'm just not ready for anything like that yet." She'd been hurt by guys in the past; he got it. He'd been hurt by girls. One, especially, he'd thought was pretty bloody special back in the dim and distant past of sixteen, and who'd totally trampled on his feelings. It had made him more than a bit gun-shy too, as he'd explained to her.

But then there'd been that feeling as well, the closeness they shared. It was more than just friendship, surely? Was he imagining that? He thought the world of her too, but was he just projecting what he wanted to happen onto the situation? That ship sailed when she kissed him. Properly, full on, searching for the other person's tonsils with your tongue, kissing.

Okay, she'd had a few too many that night, was feeling particularly melancholy about how things had worked out with her love-life so far. "I mean," she'd pontificated, sitting on another couch in the flat Stu now shared with a couple of other students, "why can't I find a guy like *you*, Stu?" May had tittered then at the rhyme, batting his chest with her hand.

A guy *like* me, he'd thought. Why *not* me? And he'd wished that night for something to happen, only for it to come true. Only for May to suddenly look at him intently over the rims of those spherical glasses, a look that practically caused him to melt. Then she was kissing him, and he was kissing her back. It was fantastic, he'd go as far as to say magical, and he was lost in the moment. Would have lived the entirety of his life in that moment, actually – which would have been better than living the one he had.

Except those kinds of moments don't last forever. They end. And this one didn't end well. May was suddenly pulling away, saying how wrong it was. Mumbling shit like they were going to ruin their friendship and how much it meant to her, that she couldn't bear it if things went wrong.

"But...But it's not going to go wrong," he'd spluttered. Couldn't get her to see that at all. To see it was worth taking a risk, a chance on him and her. They weren't connecting now, were they? Knowing what the other was thinking? Weren't on the same wavelength at all. Then, when she'd got up to leave, he'd grabbed her by the arm. It had been instinctive, a knee-jerk – elbow-jerk? – reaction, just to get her to stay so he could explain, tell her how much he loved her and wanted to be with her. The look she was giving him, though. He'd blown it. Probably blown their friendship as well, even though he hadn't been the one to make that so-called first move. Stuart had been waiting, so long – it really wasn't fair!

"I'll see you, Stuart." Not Stu, and she wanted to just get away from him. Out through the door and away; as far away as possible.

He hadn't helped himself by messaging repeatedly, trying to call her and leaving voicemails. Waiting to see May after she'd done with her classes, and she'd head off in another group. Waiting like some kind of stalker, some sort of creep. When he was so far away from that it—

"Mate, just leave it. Treat 'em mean and keep 'em keen." Vikram again, who had trouble pulling in a room full of singletons. But Stuart figured he was right about leaving it alone. May needed some time and space to work things out, needed to know there was no need to feel embarrassed about what had happened. That they could wipe the slate clean, start again and maybe someday…

Unfortunately, what she did with that time was meet Robert. Rob, as he liked to call himself. A Sports Science student with a six-pack and a smile so white you could set up camp in his mouth and study the polar bears. Fucking Rob! Which, of course, once he'd turned on the charm – the stuff of legend in their year – May started doing. He'd see them arm-in-arm on campus, and he'd see Rob just stop and pull her in for a snog – looked like he was trying to eat her face with those perfect teeth. Grabbing her arse at the same time (*he* had no problems differentiating it from an elbow), saying to everyone around that May was his. His property.

Ironically, she was okay with Stu after that – began talking to him at least, in short bursts anyway. Like he was safe now she had a fella. During an evening out, he'd made the mistake – when Rob was in the loo or wherever (maybe chatting up another girl somewhere) – of asking her what she saw in the guy.

"He's… Rob's just fun. I really like him," she'd stated in all seriousness. They say love alters your brain chemistry, that you can't see anything clearly – and Stu couldn't really talk – that it's like a drug you crave at the beginning, wanting more and more. If so, May's brain was mush and she was so addicted she would have done anything just to have Rob look in her direction. Yeah, he'd really done a number on her.

All charm, all smarm. People thought he was terrific, even his exes didn't have a bad word to say about him. But Stuart could see it on him, the meanness there. The way he treated folk he thought were beneath him; a spoilt brat, only child. Golden boy. Who hadn't even moved that far from home – Stuart had moved further than him! That guy didn't have to worry about washing his own clothes, getting homecooked meals, because he'd pop back to the bosom of his middle-class family, for his mum to wait on him hand and foot and his builder father to bung him money, supplementing his loan. Everything handed to him on a plate.

May, handed to him on a plate.

Why couldn't she see it? That she'd fallen into those same old traps, falling for the same kind of guy as before. That she'd get hurt again, same as ever. Stu had listened to so many stories about that, could relate to some of them from his own perspective.

His suspicions about Rob had been confirmed when the bloke had caught him on his way out of the bar, shoving him against the wall. "Heard you and May used to be close." Used to be. Yep. "Seems like you might be trying to worm your way back in. Well, one word for you: don't."

Stuart had said nothing, done nothing. What could he do, he was no match for Rob. Instead he'd nodded, run off when the thug let him go, his whole body shaking. Sat in his room trying to think of ways he could get the woman he loved so much, who he'd do anything for, away from that walking turd of a man. Came up with nothing. He couldn't fight Rob, and May wouldn't thank him for it anyway. She wouldn't even believe it if he told her the prick had warned him off.

All he could do was watch, and wait – the pain excruciating the more he saw them together. The nights were the worst, imagining them in bed together, doing all sorts. Rob doing all sorts *to* May (willingly, remember?). It was enough to drive a person mad, which, looking back, Stu guessed he was.

Crazy enough to drink himself into a stupor on that one fateful evening, to accept the dope Vikram offered him. Drunk and high, back in his room again, thinking about Rob pawing at May. What they'd definitely be doing on this of all days. On her birthday, and after he'd called in to her house party and seen them together. Stu had already sent a message wishing her a lovely day – risking one kiss: too many, not enough, overthinking it as usual – and that had been seen and ignored. Probably Rob poisoning her against him.

So there he was, after weeks, months of watching this shit. Out of his skull, wanting to do something – anything – that might... Veering between feeling sorry for himself, feeling sorry for May (who apparently gave not a shit), sadness at what might have been, and anger. Hatred. Directed at him, at her, remembering the night things had gone awry. How she'd 'led him on' as he'd said to her once afterwards, which definitely hadn't helped.

He remembered falling off the end of the bed, hurting himself. Tears pouring from his eyes, in just the right frame of mind to think those words (but don't say them!).

No, in the mood to fucking well say them *out loud*! Looking up and shaking a fist theatrically at nothing in particular. "I-I curse their relationship!" Didn't even need to say their names, because whoever, whatever, had heard him had known. Known his heart's desire.

Except it hadn't. What Stuart had meant was he wanted it to end. Wanted the pain, the torture of it all to stop. Wanted May *back*. Even as a friend, a best friend. Fuck, he missed her so, *so* much! Hadn't worked out quite that way, though, had it?

Had Stu been thinking then about the stories his old gran had told him, the nonsense his mother had told her not to fill his head with. "Mum, please…" About the bloodline, the lineage reaching back to the Middle Ages and the Trials. Where he'd come from and what he could do – if he put his mind to it. If he had his heart set on it.

He'd wanted to doom that relationship, and a curse was the way to do it, surely? Put a hex on it, a whammy, or whatever the fuck you wanted to call it!

But it hadn't done a thing, not that he'd been expecting it to. Over the course of the next few weeks, the next few months, he saw May and Rob together all the more. And her contact with Stuart was down to pretty much zero. He'd be lying if he said that hadn't affected his grades going into his third year, but in the end he got his head down and Stu just about managed to scrape a 2:2, rescuing it from the jaws of a 3.

At the graduation, his mum and dad there – the first time that man had worn a suit since he'd buried his own mother, Stu's nan – and proud of their son, the only one in their family to ever get a degree, never mind a middling one, Stu had seen May and Rob again. Him with his arm around her, his possession again. Their own parents hardly mixing, looking as uncomfortable as fuck.

She'd caught his eye at one point during the lengthy ceremony, turning round in her seat and smiling weakly. Stu had smiled back, though it was the last thing in the world he'd felt like doing.

He hadn't bothered with the party afterwards, had headed back home with his family instead; it was one of the last times they all spent together, because his dad passed about a year later from the same thing that was trying to see Stu off. But even as he'd eaten the celebratory roast dinner his mum cooked, watched an old SF movie with his father – who'd actually got him into all that kind of stuff, God bless 'im – Stu's thoughts hadn't wandered too far from May. From Rob and May. His thoughts wouldn't wander too far from them over the next few years, actually.

Life intrudes, however, and time works strangely. Goes by simultaneously in the blink of an eye and takes ages. It was a struggle to get work doing what he was qualified for, mainly because there were applicants *more* qualified than him. So he ended up working some shitty jobs in order to get a certificate in counselling, which was what Stu did till he hit his thirties. Listening to other people's problems to take his mind off his own.

There were women, of course there were (he'd got lonely, as people do; we're not meant to be on our own). Lynda, the smoker, who cared more about her cat than Stu – it was mutual, as it happened. She worked for the trainline, so the discounts came in handy, Stu supposed. When they'd broken up, he felt like it had come as a relief to the both of them, the cat more upset than anyone about losing Stu. Then there was Georgina, George: he'd moved in with her for a little while. George was as close to the real deal as Stu got during that time, with her sweet, caring nature. In the end, though, he'd simply grown bored, the same old story.

"It's not you, it's me." It really was him. But she'd cried and cried, asked if there was anything she could do to make him stay. There wasn't. What a bastard. Should never have...led her on in the first place, when he knew – deep down he knew – that she would never be 'the one'. Only close, but sadly no cigar. Not even one of Lynda's dog-eared ciggies. Enough to fool himself for a while, but in the end he was just going through the motions.

Bev, Carol, Donna, Eve... Same old story. None of them knew – while they were with him – that they weren't the love of his life. Could never be that. Because they could never be:

May.

Stu heard, he couldn't remember where now, as the shock of it caused him to go on a three-day bender, that she'd got engaged to *him*. May had got engaged to Rob. Bloody Robert. It had probably been through an old uni friend, cropping up and chatting about this and that. "Did you hear, so-and-so topped themselves? So-and-so got arrested? Can't say I'm surprised. And so-and-so got engaged, can you imagine?" He could, and the very thought of it made him want to gag. Bad enough they were still a couple, all these years later, that they had presumably gone off and got a place together, were living together. Because if they were engaged, they would be, wouldn't they. Wasn't like the old days when you waited, like he'd waited. But to have pledged herself to him? To be together forever... Although how many marriages lasted in this day and age? What were the statistics again?

Didn't matter, they were still together, the pair of them. She *wasn't* with Stu. And that made him want to just get bladdered. He'd sworn off the drugs a long time ago, but that didn't mean he couldn't get so drunk in the pub he had no clue where he lived – in another flat, but alone, at that time – and almost had to spend the night in a gutter. If it hadn't been for a friendly couple in a car, stopping to see if he was okay and pointing him in the right direction, he might have frozen to death that night. Lucky, eh?

Certainly not the example he should be setting to students if he got the job he was aiming for. Moving on from counselling – because there was only so much he could listen to without feeling suicidal himself, especially when people talked about losing their partners, whether it was a bereavement or to another person – he found himself eventually gravitating back towards the uni again. The same uni, as it happened, which was where he saw her for the first time since attending the place. Not on campus but afterwards, because he was staying in the neighbourhood at a B&B for a couple of nights – just while he had the interview and met other department members on the psychology course.

He'd come away from the interrogation by three senior members of staff – one of which he remembered from his time here – convinced he hadn't got the post. So, Stu had wandered round town, finding a supermarket where he could get cheap booze to drown his sorrows in his room yet again. Turning a corner on one of the aisles, he'd seen her at the other end. Blinking once, twice, because he couldn't believe it – and also because she'd changed, had shorter hair than he'd known it before, smaller glasses, was wearing a plain dress – Stu had stood there gaping until he could figure out whether this was real or not. Some kind of mirage in the frozen section?

No. It was real. *She* was real. And anyway, she hadn't changed *that* much. He'd recognise his May anywhere. Except she wasn't his May, hadn't been for such a long time. Had never really been his, if Stu was being honest with himself. Which was why he should just turn around and walk away, walk off. Convince himself that he hadn't seen what he'd seen, like he'd persuaded himself that the job was forfeit.

Instead of which, she'd turned herself, basket dangling from her arm with an assortment of items in it. She'd done the same thing, gaped down the length of the aisle. They must have looked almost comical, like something from an old Marx Brothers or Laurel and Hardy comedy. Cancelling each other out.

Then she'd mouthed something, head cocked: "Stu?" The lips forming his name, a confused look on her face.

What could he do but nod?

Then suddenly he was walking towards her, like a Jumbo jet on approach for a tricky landing. Taking just as much skill and concentration to get there safely. Stu held up his free hand, the one not holding his own basket. "Hey," he said, but his voice cracked and he was too far away for her to hear him anyway. He repeated the greeting when he was closer.

"Hiya. Oh wow, it's so..." She stepped forwards herself, as if she was going to give him a hug, and he leaned in, but at the last moment they ended up doing the whole awkward handshake thing, mainly because the baskets would have clashed or maybe got stuck together. Lucky baskets. But then she gave him a peck on the cheek as well, hand on his shoulder to steady herself. He noticed, though, that her eyes were darting around, checking who was around her, as if someone might be spying and report back about it. There was nobody else in the aisle.

"How...I mean, it's so..." She didn't finish that the second time, either.

"It... Yeah," said Stu, smiling. And it was.

"How are you?" May looked around again, but this time it was connected to her second question: "What are you doing here?"

"In the supermarket?" asked Stu. He wasn't trying to be funny, he genuinely thought that was what she meant – because he was flustered – but was happy when he saw her laugh at the remark.

"No, silly. *Here*. Back here."

"Oh, yeah, right." He told her about the job at the university, making some kind of joke about it having a hold on him he couldn't escape. Nothing like the hold this woman had on him, though. Not even approaching... "So, yeah, there's that."

"Celebrating or commiserating?" May asked, nodding at the booze in the basket.

"I'm...not entirely sure," he replied. Didn't want to tell her that he thought he'd cocked it up by coming across as too needy, too desperate. Didn't want to do that again here, with her. Put that image of him in her mind again. Stu couldn't help glancing down at what she'd got in her basket: some veg, frozen chips.

"Nothing much changes, does it," she said then.

Oh, it does, he thought. *It* really *does*.

"What are you..." he asked, returning the favour.

"Just grabbing something for dinner tonight. I was looking for—"

"No, I meant..." Stu waved a hand and she laughed; they'd done the same thing. He hadn't meant here in the supermarket, but—

"Oh, right. We live not that far away. It's close enough for Rob's work at the gym, and so he can see his folks more often."

Stu frowned. *What about your folks?* he almost asked her. *When do you see them?* Not very frigging often, would be the reply. Assuming they were still around. Not his business, so instead he asked: "And what are you up to these days?"

May thought about it for a moment, then shrugged. "I was at the hospital for a little while, but the shifts... You know... The house keeps me fairly busy," she said eventually. "How about you, what else do you..."

"Oh, I'm—" He thought quickly and pulled this little gem out of the bag. "I do a bit of writing in my spare time. You remember, I used to talk about writing stories."

May beamed. "Those science fiction ones, yeah, I do! How's *that* going?"

"Had a few published actually." *Ha!* If you can call sticking them up on a site nobody reads published. They weren't very good, anyway; it was probably for the best nobody had ever seen them.

"That's wonderful! You must be so pleased!" May smiled, and it was a smile of genuine delight for him, mixed – he thought – with a bit of pride.

Stu smiled back self-consciously. "Hey, listen. I'm around for a day or two, if you fancy, maybe..." What, a drink? Dinner?

May's smile faded. "I'd love to but, actually, I was looking for the steak. It's steak night tonight, you see, and if Robert doesn't..." She stopped, laughed. "He likes a steak when there's a match on the telly. Oh, there they are!" Stepping to the side, she reached for the pack of steaks in the chiller section, and it was then that Stu saw it. The giant rock of a wedding ring on her finger; marking the territory again. Married; *of course* they were married by now. Couldn't stay engaged forever, right? Living together and married, and it's steak night, so—

"Okay, yeah. No worries at all. Might see you around then, if I...If things work out." They already hadn't, whether he got the job or not.

May smiled again, then looked about her a final time; he got the impression she was used to doing that while she was out. "That would be... Well, it was nice catching up, Stu."

"Yeah," he said, then watched as she put the steaks in the basket and wandered off, glancing back just the once, waving goodbye.

And he just stood there, when he should be going after her. Fate had seen fit to put them together again, it had to be for a reason. But what *could* he do? There was nothing *to* do. He couldn't make her see that all this was wrong, that she should be with him (fucking steak night, seriously?). That he'd take so much more care of her, that she'd have her freedom, could do whatever job she wanted to do, watch sci-fi movies instead of the bloody match if she'd just—

Too late, he rushed after her, rounded the corner that moments earlier he'd seen her turn, only to find she'd gone. Like some kind of magic trick, the disappearing lady. Or teleported? Stu checked every single aisle, raced to the check-outs, but there was no sign of May. His mirage.

So that was that. He'd bought the booze, got wrecked, returned home and found out he'd got the job if he wanted it. Which would mean he might bump into her again, but wasn't that worse? Could he stand to keep seeing her, knowing she was doing the shop for Robert's dinner that evening? Knowing she was returning home to him? Still with him, after all this time?

Stu thanked the uni for the offer, but declined it. Decided to go for another one in another city, somewhere he could try and get on with his life. Because he really needed to. Had to get over this damned obsession he had with a woman he'd met over a decade ago, had only kissed the once, for Christ's sake!

He applied to a few universities, got into one of them, and moved. There had followed a handful of other flings, one with a fellow lecturer and another with a mature ex-student that had threatened to get quite messy, but life had gone on. Stu had job satisfaction, sort of, unless he was marking a particularly terrible assignment, and he actually did start to take his writing more seriously. His tales (all written under a pseudonym) were getting accepted into honest to goodness magazines this time, for honest to goodness cash. Not much, but enough to encourage him to carry on.

Then came the train.

A journey back up to his mum's for Christmas. She'd married again, a decent enough guy called Colin, who treated her well, so Stu couldn't complain. Had even offered to watch a few films with Stu – "What do you say, we could watch that there *Star Wars* with Dr Spock!"; you can imagine how much that had made him cringe – but, as nice as the gesture was, it simply felt disloyal to his late father.

He'd only just made the six o'clock train, having left his shopping till the last minute as usual, so had clambered on board with his bags and was lucky enough to find a seat near the door of the carriage. Stu put his head back, closed his eyes, and let out a slow breath. When he looked again, he took in the rest of the people he was trapped with. An overweight bloke in a suit who looked like he was a Christmas dinner away from a stroke; a mother struggling to keep two kids entertained, screaming at them when that didn't work; a guy wearing a vest in spite of the chilly weather, probably to display his collection of tattoos and piercings, and—

May.

Stu had to look twice again, gawking like the last time he'd seen her back in the supermarket. She'd grown her hair a little more since then, but only a little, wasn't wearing any glasses this time – laser eye treatment? more likely just contacts – and was wrapped up in a warm winter coat. May was staring down sadly at her drink (of tea, coffee, Stu couldn't tell, and probably didn't matter, given the drinks on this service; it was brown, at any rate). The plastic cup was resting on a table which had four seats around it, all occupied. Stu looked, but couldn't see any sign of Robert.

It took a few stops before the woman who'd been sitting opposite May got up to leave the train. Without even thinking about what he was doing, Stu was up and making his way to that seat, lugging his bags. Was almost pipped to the post by a guy who was about to slide in.

"I'm sorry, I know..." Stu nodded to May, who looked up for the first time since he'd got on board. Her mouth fell open in shock, then there was a twitch in the corner of her lips that could have been mistaken for a smile. May snapped out of her reverie, looked from Stu to the other bloke.

"Oh, yes. He's with me," she told him. If only that were true.

The other man backed off and Stu sat down, jamming his bags under his side of the table. "Thanks."

"Stuart," said May. "It's been a while."

"It has," he agreed. If she'd asked, he could have told her down to the minute exactly how long had passed since the supermarket. "How're things?"

"Good," said May, looking down again, avoiding his eyes. "They're...They're good. You?"

"Yeah. Same. Good."

He thought he heard the person on the left of him mumble something like "Get a room", but May didn't catch the remark so Stu left it. "You were after a job at the university back home last time I saw you, right?"

Stu let out a breath. "Didn't work out." Like so many things hadn't.

"That's a shame. I thought I hadn't seen you around."

Had she been looking for him? Stu wondered. "No, I got a gig somewhere else. I climbed on a few stops back. Just heading home for the holidays, to see Mum and her fella."

"Fella?"

Stu's brow furrowed. "Oh, I thought I mentioned it when... Dad passed away."

May looked like she was going to burst into tears. "Oh. Oh, Stu. I'm so sorry. I didn't..." She reached out a hand for his free one – the one not clutching the bags under the table – and he let her take it. Let her give it a squeeze. "I've just been visiting my parents. I don't see them too often these days. They don't get on with..."

Stu nodded, couldn't help giving that hand a squeeze back. "But they're okay, yeah? Still keeping well?"

It was May's turn to nod. "You know, my mum always liked you. Thought we might..." The nod turned into a shake. "Doesn't matter."

It did. It mattered *so* much, and it was the first he was hearing about this. But then he always did have a little chat with May's mum before she put her on the phone, if he was ringing her on the landline. Nice lady.

May shifted the position of her hand then, and he felt the edge of her ring. Her wedding ring. She pulled the fingers free, reached for her drink but didn't have any. "And you, how are things with you? You happy?"

He thought about telling her about the published stories, but held back. Didn't feel the need to boast about stuff like that this time, although now it would simply be about telling her. There was so much he wanted to share with her, however, things that had happened not just since the last time he'd seen her, but before that. Huge chunks of his life she'd missed, and that made him feel like crying, too. Instead, he just nodded as well and avoided her eyes now. "Yeah, happy." Far from chatting about the time that had passed, they sat pretty much in silence until it was almost time for May to get off.

"Look, May. If you ever want to—" Then he stopped, his heart sinking when he saw her rise. Having to dodge the edge of the table because of the swell of her stomach, pushing its way out of the coat. She followed his eyes, staring at the bump, and patted it.

"Not long now, a couple of months or so," she told him.

Stu felt like he'd been punched in his own stomach. It wasn't as if he hadn't known she was sleeping with Robert; had known it for such a long time. But inside there, in May's belly, was the physical evidence of that act and it made Stu sick. May wasn't trying to rub his face in that, although when the train lurched it almost happened for real. Then she smiled, and it was a genuine smile: she was going to have a baby. Didn't matter who the father was (it should have been him, not fucking Rob, that should have been his kid!). "I...congratulations, May."

"Ta. Oh, here we go! See you again sometime, eh Stu?"

He held up a hand. "Yeah, see you soon." Wouldn't happen, Stu realised that. Might never see her again, and his last memory would be of her stepping onto the platform, then as the train pulled away from the station seeing a glimpse of Robert, grabbing her arm and linking them together. His property. Stu did cry then, not just for May, but her little one on the way. Imagine a father like that!

But it was still none of his business. Would never be any of his business.

Or so he thought.

The next time he heard from May it was several years – some grey hair and a stone or so – later, and it was her who got in touch with Stuart.

He'd been surprised to see a message appear on his social media account, the same one he'd had all these years and kept in touch with people like Vikram through (twice divorced, he was looking for lucky lady number three). Hadn't been a secret or anything, May had even been a friend of his on there back in the day, until her account had eventually disappeared. He could never bring himself to look at hers anyway, bad enough to see her and Rob together in person, let alone galleries of photos featuring the happy couple.

"You happy?"

He'd nearly deleted the message because it had come through from an account he didn't recognise – not that he went on there much anyway – called 'Everyday Goddess'. Looking back, why he hadn't got the reference straight away Stu didn't know. It was how May – Athena – had been introduced to him. Then again, the internet was full of people calling themselves all sorts of bollocks – and most of the women who contacted him were 'bots. There was also a photo of an owl, which he found out later on was one of the symbols of the goddess she shared her name with. It all added up to someone trying to keep this account a secret, and the message itself had sounded quite fraught.

"Stu, don't delete this!! It's me, May. I really need to talk to you." Turned out she was also using a computer at a library, because Rob checked her laptop and phone on a regular basis. She wanted to meet up, suggesting the next town along from where she lived (just far enough away, but not too far; somewhere she could make something up about visiting), the third weekend in June if he was free around then.

He was.

Truth be told he'd just split up with a lady called Janine, who he'd moved in with a couple of years earlier. She'd had kids from a previous marriage, and although that hadn't been a problem when they'd first started seeing each other – he'd been Mum's cool new friend Uncle Stu – living with her had been a different kettle of hormones altogether. The two boys, and especially the eldest, who was heading into his teenage years, resented the time Stu spent with her and made his life hell, doing the whole 'who's in charge thing'. Their real dad, who hadn't given a shit about either of them up till this point, was soon back on the scene, which had added another complication. The eldest lad started to emulate him, filling the house with toxic masculinity. They all seemed to think Janine was their personal servant, whether it came to picking things up or cooking or washing up, which apparently also extended to Stu. And in the end it had just seemed easier for everyone concerned if Stu packed his bags and left them to it. Last he'd heard Janine was back with the ex, more fool her.

He often wondered, when this latest attempt at a relationship had gone to shit, if that one hadn't been his subconscious response to the fact May and Rob were breeding. He'd show them, wasn't that right – and here was a ready-made family he could just slot into. When of course he was just gate-crashing someone else's party because he couldn't be arsed to plan one of his own.

All that was beside the point, though, because yes, he was free and May didn't have to know anything about Janine and her clan and the total fuck-up he'd made of things there. (Slot in? Square peg in a round hole, more like.) But when he saw her, Stu realised he wasn't the only one who'd been in a mess lately. Ironically, as bad as it had felt at the time trying to untangle everything with Janine, it was probably easier to get out of than May's situation would be.

"I think Rob might have been seeing other people," May confessed when they'd taken a seat in a nearby coffee shop, after she'd hugged the life out of him on the street. "In fact I'm certain of it. When he's away like he is this weekend, on one of his trips for work."

Everyone knew what that meant, didn't they? Trips for work? Might as well be saying 'shagging anything that moved'. "I-I'm not sure what to say." Actually, he was – cheating fucking bastard, and cheating on May at that! – but Stu wasn't really surprised to hear about it. The only surprise was that May was just waking up to the notion all these many years later. Or was she?

"I mean, it's happened before. I found out about a couple of them, but, well, he promised me all that stuff was over. That after Penny came along, he'd put a stop to it." May looked much older than the last time he'd seen her, but then they were both getting older, weren't they? Closer to forty now than thirty, almost twenty years since they'd first met. Since he'd met and fallen in love with her.

Since he'd said those words. If only he hadn't—

Penny. A little girl, a daddy's girl. She might have been his, but it wasn't to be. "How old is..." He knew exactly how old she was, just hadn't realised she was a she. Penny. Pretty name, like her mother's.

"Almost seven, going on seventy."

"And where..." He looked around to illustrate, as if he thought she might have brought the little girl here and hidden her behind the counter to come out like one of those Long Lost Family shows.

"Oh, she's having a sleepover at one of her friend's. They're going on a treasure hunt, I believe."

"Right," said Stu. "Okay...Look, it's not that I'm not happy to see you, May..."

"You happy?"

"But what's all this got to do with you?" She let out a long sigh. "I...well, nothing. Not really. You don't owe me anything. I guess I just needed to talk to someone about it. A friend."

Owe her... He couldn't help himself, maybe it was the news about Penny, maybe it was the fact that if May had woken up to Rob sooner, then— But she married *him*. She. Fucking. Married. Him! Stu found himself getting a bit annoyed. A friend? They hadn't been friends, not really, for such a long time. She must have seen the look on his face, knew what he was about to ask, because she answered his question in that weird way they had. That bizarre connection.

"I know, I know. I have no right to... But I don't really have any friends of my own, not where I am. I've sort of lost touch with them."

Shocker. You'd lost touch with me too, but you soon got back in *touch when you needed me*, Stu thought. *No. You don't have the right to do that, sit there and complain about your shithead of a husband who once pushed me up against a wall and threatened me. You don't get to—*

"Stu." Tears in her eyes again, as she reached out her hand just like she had on the train. "Stu, I don't know who else to turn to! My mum and dad don't want to know, they'd just say 'we told you so'. And, and..."

He was about to reply when he looked down at the hand that had hold of his. Looked down and spotted the bruises there on May's wrist. "God, did *he* do that to you?" Stu asked, a bit too loudly but was beyond giving a crap right that minute, and all of the anger just faded away. Anger directed at May, that was. Rob he wanted to flat-out murder, felt like it but would never do it because that just wasn't him. But still, Jesus Christ, her *wrist!* Blue and purple from where he must have had hold of her. It made him wonder what else the man had done.

"He was drunk, I shouldn't have said anything."

"May, there's no excuse for this. Not an excuse in the world for—"

She was crying freely, unable to hold back. "I just...I don't know what to do." May was looking at him like he had the answers, like he could save her from this. And he thought then to himself, perhaps this is it: perhaps this was the curse. The thing he'd been waiting for all this time. For it to kick in, for May to come to her senses? It had finally worked, in the most horrendous way possible, yes, but worked nonetheless. There was still time. It would take some untangling, sure, more than his own situation had taken, but it could be done and it would be so, so worth it.

A little voice was crying out at the back of his skull that this was a mistake, that he'd just be inserting himself into another family that wasn't his own, even if Robert fucked off out of it, which he doubted the man would. Let Stu be a father to Penny? Bloody hell, he hadn't even met the girl and he was thinking about—

Not to mention May had come here for a shoulder to cry on, that's all. Her life was complicated enough without him making it more so. Yet this was a start, wasn't it? A way of getting back to how they'd been. It was still there; she wouldn't have got in touch if it wasn't. They wouldn't be here unless—

She hadn't got anyone else. Nobody. Think about it, how you're being used. How much pain this woman's caused you over the years.

How much potentially she still could.

For some reason that didn't matter, all that mattered was listening to May, trying to help her. In the end, once they'd moved on to a quiet pub so she could have a stiff drink and they could carry on talking. Which they'd done, one drink turning into a few. Turning into many. Catching up on the time they'd missed, on what had happened in both their lives. Hers was so much worse than he'd ever imagined. May was expected to be a kind of Stepford Wife, perfect partner and mother, everything monitored and checked up on, which was why she couldn't risk a journey any further afield than this.

"Y-You just need to get out of there," Stu told her, laying the groundwork, his words slurring. "Things will be a lot clearer when you do, I promise."

"But where would I...? I couldn't just—"

"You could stay with me," he said earnestly.

May looked down, then back up again. "I couldn't do that. Not after everything I—" She shook her head emphatically.

It was his turn to take her hand, squeeze it. He'd meant it only as a gesture of friendship, no funny business – same as the offer of somewhere to stay, though there was hardly enough room for him and his stuff let alone three people in the flat he was currently occupying (all that could be sorted out later, he told himself). As she'd done before, back at uni, it had been May who'd turned it into something else. Kissed him for the first time in such a *long* time. A lifetime. "I'm sorry," she said. "About before. I was just scared of losing you."

He wanted to say, to tell her that she'd lost him anyway though, hadn't she? That they'd lost all these years because of that one stupid mistake. But he kept his mouth shut, knew that anything he came out with might just ruin this moment; the same way he didn't say to her "Are you sure?" when she suggested going back to the hotel he'd booked into that night, a much nicer one than the B&B he'd stayed in for the interview.

Didn't say a thing, just went back with her to that place, to his room: drifting, going with the flow. Drunk but not too drunk (he hoped). Was okay when she started to kiss him in the room, passionately, whispering to him: "I need this. Hold me Stuart, I just want to feel like I'm loved."

Stu opened his mouth to tell her that she was definitely that. As much as it was possible to love anyone, he loved this woman. But again he held his tongue, even as she was turning the lights out (no, he wanted to see her, he'd waited so long; but then he thought about those bruises, where she might have more – never the face, they never go for the face, people like Rob). Then it didn't matter, because they found each other in the darkness.

Thinking back now, he only recalled flashes of that night, but remembered it being one of the best of his life. Nothing could take that away from him, could it? What was it Sarah Connor said about spending a lifetime with someone?

Although when he woke the next morning, he wondered whether it had even happened – especially when May wasn't there beside him (where she'd always belonged). Then he heard the sound of her in the shower, actually singing in the shower. Did that mean she was happy?

"You happy?"

He guessed so, Stu had never heard her sing when they were at uni together – not even when she'd got together with Rob, but then why would you? Stu didn't think he'd been any great shakes the previous night, but then had he ever really been? Had some moves, or so he'd been told, but—

When she'd appeared in the doorway, towel around her and hair dripping wet, he'd gaped again – just couldn't help himself. He'd climbed out of the bed and gone over to her, and she'd met him with a kiss. This was Heaven, surely? If Stu had been in Hell before, this was the opposite – like a wish was the opposite of a curse: one positive, one negative – but then he spotted another bruise on her shoulder and she caught him looking, pulled away.

Stu couldn't help himself, opened his mouth and it all came out: about what they needed to do now, how she should get away from Rob. Get Penny and—

It was too much. In the cold light of day, sober, it was just too much. May went very quiet, remained quiet all the while they had breakfast together. Another opposite of the day before when it had poured out of her.

Then he'd seen her off at the taxi rank, she'd paid cash to get here and was going to do the same for the way back; no trace then. May had kissed him on the cheek, promised she'd be in touch about arrangements. To trust her.

So he had, but that voice was back again about her capacity to hurt him. *I hope you know what you're doing,* it said.

Hope.

That's what he'd done next, waited and hoped. Hoped and waited for May to get back to him through her Everyday Goddess account. Or just a goddess to him, nothing everyday about her. Nothing ordinary. A few days went by, and he thought fair enough – give her time to get herself sorted out. Time to talk to Rob, square things away, though Stu would have preferred to be around when she did that in case things got out of hand. Time to talk to Penny ("You're going to have a new daddy!" No. Too soon, *way* too soon).

But then a week went by, another weekend – the memory of the previous one turning bitter-sweet – a fortnight. And Stu started to send messages to her off his own bat, messages wondering how she was. Hoping (that word again) that she was okay. That she wasn't—

Dead. Let's be honest, he thought Rob might have killed her. Stu didn't come right out and say it, but the increasingly worried tone said it for him. Still no response.

Stu began to wonder if he'd made an arse of things again, come on too strong that morning when talking about the future and what *he* thought should happen. The last thing May needed was another controlling dipstick, out of the frying pan and into the fire.

Began to wonder again whether it had even happened at all, flashing right back to the morning when she hadn't been there. Had he imagined the whole thing? No, parts of it had definitely happened. But maybe the night, the sleeping together bit. Had he imagined that? Had he imagined May *wanting* him? Wished for it so hard that he'd made it happen in his own head, when all they'd really done was talk and fall asleep because of the booze?

Finally, just when he was about to go round there – although she'd been careful not to tell him where she, where they *all* lived, hadn't she – May had answered. She was sorry again, but there'd been an accident. Robert had been in an accident, a car crash, and she couldn't think about all this now, leaving or whatever. Because Robert needed her, she couldn't think about abandoning him when he needed her (Stuart needed her too, God did he need her and that twat had had years with May). Would take months for him to recover properly, if at all, so she couldn't... She just *couldn't*. It had been lovely seeing Stu again, but she was going to close down the account now – and if he thought anything of her, he wouldn't try to get in touch again.

Stuart had stared at the screen even as he'd read the words, not really believing them while he was reading. Re-reading them several times, just to let it all sink in. It took him a good while to draft a reply, because he wasn't quite sure what he was going to say that wouldn't be the literary equivalent of grabbing her arm (but not as hard, never as hard as Rob would do and only to stop her leaving when he couldn't really stop her from doing anything). Just as he'd fashioned his reply, was about to copy and paste it into the message thread, the whole thing vanished. Her account vanished, teleported away, not giving him any chance to respond to what she'd said. Another mirage.

He'd sat back again in the chair, frowning. Gazing, frustrated at the screen, his message and the redundant account. Back to square one, worse than square one! He'd have been better off if she'd never contacted him at all!

That one took a bit of getting over. Honestly, he never really did. Wasn't sure he wanted to, or even if he could. Worse than the kiss, than May getting together with Robert in the first place. So much worse than any of the other bullshit, the chance meetings in the supermarket, on the train. Seeing the baby bump. His baby. What should have been Stu's daughter, Penny.

He contemplated hiring someone to track May down, track down their address and just head there to confront Rob – her? – about what had happened. For one thing, though, it wouldn't have done any good; once May had made her mind up about something that was that. For another it might just make things worse for her on a day-to-day (Everyday) basis when she had so much on her plate already, probably waiting on that moron hand and foot. Just like the man's parents, his mother, had once done. Stu knew nothing about Rob's injuries, but found himself questioning whether he might be putting them on, because he'd got wind of what was happening – how, was anyone's guess! Besides, it wouldn't come across well, would it, tackling a cripple? Not his style.

He was left with no choice but to, well, leave it. Nothing he could do but hide away and lick his wounds. Again.

Told you so, that little voice whispered at the back of his mind.

Those next few weeks, few months, few *years* were probably the worst of his life. Stu tried getting back on the dating scene, but he was growing older and he seemed to have lost that ability to connect with the opposite sex, if he'd ever possessed it. Most dates he went on were just more horror stories about past relationships, baggage. Either that or women came with kids in tow and he wasn't falling into that trap again.

He began drinking more, getting back into the recreational drugs, hanging out in some unsavoury places. It was at one of these called 'Mick's' that he met her. Not *the* her, because what would she be doing in a dive like that, but the closest thing Stu had come across in all this time before or since. Looks-wise anyway, not personality. That was okay, because he wasn't paying her to speak.

Trixie, she called herself, though Lord alone knew what her real name was. At first it was just for company, so Stu could pretend. Very often he wanted her to just stay the night with him, stay beside him so he could wake up and see that face. The one which looked a bit like, but really, really wasn't, the love of his—

"You happy?"

It developed into something else then. They'd fuck, and it was here he'd see the difference, because this woman was so skilled in the erotic arts it was hard to conceive of her as May. Then that turned into a bit of an obsession, paying her for weekends on the trot, then wanting her not to see other clients.

It all ended with the police getting involved because he'd frightened the woman in question (who'd always thought he was a bit weird frankly) and Stu losing his post at the university, not that he was doing such a bang-up job of it anyway. Letting his students down when it was the last thing in the world he wanted to do.

A bit of a wake-up call, that car crash. Not a real car crash, or May might have taken more notice of him, eh? More like waking up in a pool of your own vomit, which he did on several occasions, and finally realising you had to do something about your life. Stu went to stay with his mum and Colin for a bit, where he dried out and swore off everything. They were good to him, much better than he deserved after shunning their help for so long; even shouting down the phone at his mother that he didn't need her (he *so* did).

When she'd asked him what he was going to do next, Stu had shrugged. "Haven't got the foggiest, Mum." It had been Colin, bizarrely, who'd given him the idea about trying to make a go of his writing.

"You've done well with those small stories of yours, why don't you try something longer now you have a bit of time on your hands?"

Why *didn't* he? There was nothing stopping him, like an actual job, which paid actual money. But Stuart gave it a go, it was something to do, and he actually found that he enjoyed doing it. In the meantime some of his shorts had come across the desk of an agent, one who'd just branched off to start her own firm and was scouring magazines for talent. Stu was about halfway through his magnum opus when she emailed him asking if he'd ever considered writing a novel. He told her what stage he was at, and she made him promise to let her have a look at it when he was finished – which, in turn, spurred him *on* to finish.

Not only did he do that, but the agent loved it and sold it to a mid-list publisher for an okay amount of dosh. Enough to cover him while he was writing the next one, for him to get a place of his own again – within spitting distance of his mum and Colin – so he could carry on writing. The first book came out and was fairly well received. It was a bit of a Marty McFly's Dad moment when he unpacked his contributor copies and held it for the first time. Not *A Match Made in Space*, but definitely a love story – a doomed one involving time travel and a character's attempts to, as Sam would have said, 'Put right what once went wrong.'

It was the talk of the party when he got there; his gran's 100th birthday party, that was. Good genes, his gran, which she'd passed on to her daughter, she joked. Stu, however, had inherited more of his father's genetic flaws, sadly.

"Going to be on those bestseller lists one day, aren't you, son?" his mum was busy telling all the aunts and uncles, cousins and second cousins. Stu could feel his face burning red. Still, it was better than telling them about him being a pisshead and on drugs, chasing after a prostitute.

"We had hoped we'd see you settled with a nice lady by now, Stuart." That was the other one he got at the party, which just depressed him. He'd thought he might be settled with a nice lady too (not a lady of the night). One lady in particular.

Which had segued into a conversation about it with his gran, about what he'd done. "I mean, I didn't really believe in...so I guess it makes sense. But *you* do. Believe I mean. You always used to say to me that..." He shook his head; those were horror tropes, not SF, and he'd never really liked the former (his genre had the Force, though, didn't it? the Jedi and the Bene Gesserit?). Yet still he asked: "Why didn't it work?"

The wizened old woman had looked at him seriously, staring so hard he wondered if she could see him with all those cataracts. "What exactly did you say, young Stuart?"

So he told her, and she looked more serious than ever then. "But, don't you see? It did work. Your curse worked, Stuart. All too well."

What was she talking about, how could it have worked? May and Robert were still together as far as he knew. He told his gran as much.

"You cursed the relationship. If only you'd had a bit of patience, lad. Waited." But he *had* waited. Waited so long... "She might have just seen sense. Nature has to run its course. You clearly have a link, or you wouldn't keep finding each other. I'd go so far as to say you're right, you probably should have been together. She's your soulmate, but what you did messed all that up. Put a real spoke in the wheels."

Stu still didn't understand, not then. But the more he thought about it afterwards, the more he realised his gran was absolutely right. What he'd done had got in the middle of things he shouldn't have, just like he'd done with Janine. Fucked everything up.

"They're tricky things, curses – which is why you should never use them lightly. They never work in the way you think, or hope, they might." She went on to say more, but Stu was still reeling from those first revelations.

Maybe there was still something he could do about it. "How do I fix this?" he asked his gran, who simply shook her head. "There must be *something* I can do!"

His voice carried and soon relatives came over to see what the shouting was about. Before they arrived and he left, she whispered something to him.

Something that saw him bawling his eyes out, even as he headed home, trying to resist calling into the off-license on the way. Trying to resist just taking a handful of pills and ending it all. Trying to resist making plans to find May and finally showing up on her doorstep. Because none of it would do any good, only make things worse.

Stu's gran died a few months after that conversation, though everyone agreed she'd had a good innings. It was after Stuart's third book came out, and hit the bestseller lists immediately – his loyal fanbase spreading the word of mouth – after he heard there was film interest in his first two books, that Stuart was given the diagnosis. The first one. Life still had a few surprises left, it seemed.

His mum, his doctors, had been all about fighting it – and Stuart had done. Fought it with everything he had while undergoing the treatments. Concentrated everything on trying to get better, which he had done...for a few years anyway.

While he was in the hospital, however, he had a visitor. It was May, who came and sat by his bedside, tears in her eyes. "Oh Stuart," said the woman, taking his hand. There were lines on her face, the years had not been kind to her. But she was still as pretty as ever to him.

"What...?" He struggled to get the words out, but – as always – she knew exactly what he was asking.

"I had to come, when I heard."

Stuart thought about telling May, finally telling her about what he'd done. But he was too ashamed, not that she'd believe him anyway. Would probably think it was the drugs talking. So instead he just apologised.

"Sorry? What have you got to be sorry about? It's me who should be... I've been so..." She started sobbing then, not realising that none of it had been her fault. Not really.

Nature had to run its course.

"You happy?"

She told him about her life, that Penny was getting ready to head off to uni herself soon. That she was still looking after Robert, though most of the time he was confined to an electric chair (not the kind Stu would have preferred), which helped him get up and down so he could shuffle about on his Zimmer. When Stu looked in May's eyes he could see the strain on her, the strain she'd been under all this time because she was a good wife. A loyal partner, which was more than you could ever say for Robert. In his mind's eye, Stu imagined him shouting and growling at May, might still be giving her a back-hander or two if she got close enough; the sheer frustration for an active man would only have made things worse.

Before she left, May told Stuart to fight this and when he was okay, she'd come and see him again. He'd nodded, knowing that she probably wouldn't.

Indeed, Stuart wouldn't see her until he'd been clear of the cancer for a few years, not that it hadn't departed without leaving him with some going away presents. The chronic fatigue, for one. Some were even side-effects of the pills he'd be on for life, however long that was.

Because when it returned it did so with a vengeance, the kind of cancer you didn't get over this time. At least he'd managed to see more of his books published, his creations turned not only into films but TV shows. The sort he'd watched himself as a kid. It was stupid, crazy money, and it helped pay for private treatment in the end. But it was all just about making him comfortable now. And you couldn't take it with you…

Couldn't take it with you, but he could leave it to someone. What he wasn't giving to his old mum, who'd had to bury her second husband only recently. Because, when he put the feelers out, sent for May this time because he knew he needed to at least put some of this right, she'd brought someone along with her.

A young man, in his mid-twenties. Stu had only needed to take a look at him to know, to realise. He was a real mix of May – who walked with a stick now herself, was back to wearing those huge glasses, but with much thicker lenses – and himself. "Lance," she said to the boy after he'd escorted her into the room at the hospice which cost thousands a day, helping her by the arm when she almost stumbled, "this is an old friend of mine, Stuart. I've known him all my life."

"How're you doing?" the young guy asked. *"You happy?"*

Stu waved a hand around at all the tubes running in and out of him, as he sat in his chair by the window, then laughed.

"Listen, would you give us a minute, love," May said to her son. He didn't look too sure, so she added: "It'll be all right."

When he'd gone, she pulled up a chair herself and sat next to Stu. "D-Does he know?" asked Stu in a croaky voice.

May looked him right in the eye and shook her head. "I-I'm sorry, Stuart." They seemed to say that a lot to each other. Had said it so many times over the course of their lives. "That night when we…I convinced myself the baby was Robert's, from before his accident. But, well, look at him. I don't think Robert believes it himself, not really. He's got your eyes, Stu. I see you every time I look into them."

Stuart began to cry, held out his hand for May and she took it. "I have a son," he whispered. This world really hadn't finished with its surprises, had it?

May nodded.

"How...How's Penny?" he asked then. She was doing okay, had graduated as a doctor and gone off to work in some hospital down south. It was where her boyfriend worked, they'd met at university. Stuart couldn't help smiling at that. One kid who should have been his, another he'd never even known about. He'd missed out on both of them growing up, because of his own anger. His own jealousy. Now it was too late, all lost like those tears in the rain from their favourite shared movie.

Fuck.

Not even what he told May about his plans would make up for it.

"You can't, Stuart. It's too much." But it was only what they were owed and he insisted; his people would make all the arrangements. "He writes as well, you know," May told Stu. "He's quite good."

Stuart chuckled again, nodded. Then he started to cough and a nurse came in to usher May out, telling her Stuart was tired.

And when you're tired of Blade Runner...

Telling May she could come again another time if she wanted. But Stu knew that she wouldn't. That he probably wouldn't see her again in this lifetime, though there was always scope for this to continue after he was gone. After they both were.

Because hadn't his gran told him as much, that curses like that are unbreakable. "There's nothing you can do. They last an eternity," she'd whispered, just before he'd left the party.

He thought now, sitting and staring out of the window and feeling the life leaving him, images around him fading like mirages – realised that he should never have said those words. Or, at least, that he should have added those other couple which would have made it all right, less general: "I curse their relationship...to end."

Because in cursing the thing, he'd actually cursed it to last. Cursed them to live inside a damaged relationship that neither one of them could end, which was why May had remained, but also why Robert's affairs had never led anywhere. Why he'd always felt like she was his possession, something to never let go of.

"Nothing to be done. But in cursing them, you also cursed yourself," his gran had told him.

If he didn't spend the rest of his life with this girl, this woman, then there would be no point to it at all...

Could make or break him.

Curses rebound, never work out the way you want them to. Like in the old revenge saying, dig two graves. Or three in this case. He'd cursed them to keep going round in circles, maybe not just in this life, but in countless others to come. It might never end.

Yet still he had to hope, which was why he was wishing. In that last minute of his last hour of his last day. Wished for the last time he hadn't said those words, knowing it wouldn't come true.

Because wishes weren't as powerful as their opposite number, Stuart had come to realise. Were fuelled by hope rather than hatred, and nothing ever tops that one – especially in this world. Because hopes are dashed all the time...

And because he deserved the fate he'd brought upon himself.

GUILTY PLEASURES

There was someone in here with her, someone watching her.

Was that the door? No, just the wind rattling an upstairs window. She peered down the hallway to make sure. Nothing; nobody there. Not her boyfriend back early from the gym, where she should really be – instead of in the kitchen, rifling through the tins in the cupboard to get to her hidden stash of chocolate.

Nobody here. Nobody watching. It was just her imagination playing tricks, her conscience having one last stab at changing her mind.

It didn't work.

She reached in and felt around for the *Mars* bar, her hand like a sniffer dog seeking out dope. Her fingertips recoiled when they touched the wrapper, then caressed the bar, grabbing, pulling it out through the silver barricade of processed peas and soup before closing the door. She fumbled with the plastic-coated sheath, finally ripping it open with her incisors and biting into the delicious gooey sweetness. A thin ribbon of caramel draped itself over her lip and chin; she licked at it with her tongue, not wanting to sacrifice a single morsel. In seconds the bar had been devoured, leaving her with just the black, red and gold remains. She opened the pedal bin with her foot and dropped the wrapper inside, pushing it down below the other garbage, to keep the crumpled fish-and-chip paper company at the bottom. She knew Tim would never find them down there.

But you'll *know they're there, Jodie*, said a voice in her head. *You'll know...and you'll only regret it when you step on those scales.*

"Shut up," Jodie told it.

And telling Tim that you had to work late just so you didn't have to go and exercise. Just so you could secretly binge on chips and chocolate... I hope you're proud of yourself, I really do.

"Shut up, just shut the fuck up!"

You've been doing so well lately, too. Lost a couple of pounds at your last meeting. You do realise you'll have put that back on and more besides.

And so it began. First the pleasure, now the guilt. Jodie bit her lip; if it hadn't been for the pain it caused she might have chomped clean through and swallowed the chunk whole – just like she'd done with the *Mars* bar. It was her nerves, you see, that's what made her—

Quit making excuses. We both know it's got absolutely nothing to do with your nerves. You just like eating: admit it! You love *it. Always have done and always will. Sure, when you first met Tim you hadn't looked too bad, but it's not as easy to hide those rolls now, is it? No wonder he wants to keep the lights off when—*

"Just fucking shut up!" Jodie covered her ears with her hands, as if it would somehow block the voice out. And for a few seconds it did. But it soon returned when she took her hands back down.

If you carry on like this there's no way you'll be able to fit into that bridesmaid's dress for your sister's wedding. It's only a few weeks away, you know, and look how much weight you've put on since you were measured for it!

Jodie ran out of the kitchen, ran down the hallway. From the corner of her eye she spotted the mirror at the bottom of the stairs.

Why don't you take a look? Go on...

"No!"

What are you so frightened of? Go on, take a good look at yourself, Jodie.

Jodie found herself moving towards the mirror, almost as if she was being pushed. Then she was standing in front of it, looking directly at her reflection, scrutinizing every extra bulge, imagined or otherwise. The baggy T-shirt and skirt at least hid some of the damage. Thank God she wasn't naked!

But you can imagine it, can't you? You try your best not to catch a glimpse when you step out of the shower, but you can't help it. You see, you *see…and you can see it now, can't you, Jodie? You've done this to yourself. You've lied and you've let yourself down. It won't be long before Tim sees right through you. Won't be long before he leaves you for somebody less—*

"Stop it, stop it, stop it!" Jodie broke into tears and ran up the stairs, taking them two at a time. There was a slamming of the toilet door.

Another reflection appeared in the mirror now, as the sounds of retching wafted down the staircase. Distorted, blurred almost, it shifted in and out of focus as if it didn't really belong in this reality. Parsley-sauce skin, pock-marked green and stretched taut over a lean frame. Two burning yellow eyes; accusing eyes.

The Guilt Demon smiled with crazy-paving teeth. It would move on in a moment, Its work here done for the time being. The words It had whispered to Jodie would haunt her for a good few days, play on her mind and cultivate the eating disorder she would eventually develop. Then the demon would make her feel guilty about that, too. For spewing up good food when there were people starving in the world. She'd never win. By the time It was finished, Jodie wouldn't know what she was doing.

To eat or not to eat, It said. *That is the question…*

These were interesting times for the Guilt Demon, exciting times. At no other period in history had there been more reasons to feel guilty. Oh, there had always been guilt – ever since the first man and woman stood apart from the animals and realised they were different. Realised they were naked. But so very often in the past the reprehensible acts of this curious species had been blamed on religion, on affinity to a particular group or country. People were burnt at the stake, beheaded and ripped apart with bullets, but this was justified because it was all for the greater good. There were too many constrictions, hardly any room to manoeuvre.

It was all so different now. The inhabitants of this spinning blue and white ball no longer had faith. They no longer followed blindly, they had minds of their own – and that meant they made their own decisions, their own choices. And inevitably those choices turned out to be wrong.

The Guilt Demon didn't interfere, didn't influence these outcomes. Rather, It stepped in after the fact, after the damage had been done. It dealt in remorse, in shame and humiliation. It thrived on lamentation, using hindsight with skill and aplomb. It hadn't forced Jodie to eat the chips or the chocolate...but It would certainly make her wish she hadn't. It would return to taunt her again and again, just as It did with all the others – just as It had for longer than It could remember.

And It revelled in the torment It caused, absolutely *loved* it. The sound of Jodie heaving up her guts as It left her house were like music to Its ears. A concerto in vomit major. She'd had no idea It was there, not really. Jodie put all this down to her *own* guilt, which made the whole thing that much...sweeter.

Desire had a lot to answer for. Greed in Jodie's case, lust in the case of the next two It was visiting.

A little after eight o'clock at night. The Guilt Demon watched for a few seconds at the window, hovering several feet above the ground. It watched the couple in the throes of passion, their coupling frantic. All sweat and moans, sucking and licking. It had never seen the attraction, but was thankful for this ritual's existence. The act was over relatively quickly and the pair lay back on the bed, exhausted. It'd been monitoring their progress for some time and knew that this moment was coming – if you'd pardon the expression. Tonight they'd finally given in to their feelings; the confusing tangle of love and lust proving too much.

Sara's husband, Adrian, was away for the night – his mother had been taken ill. Their daughter, Clare, aged five, was staying at a friend's house. Sara had met Gary at the evening course she'd taken in photography. He made her laugh, made her feel special. Made her feel attractive. Over the ten weeks of the course, Sara found herself looking forward to Tuesday evenings more and more. Couldn't wait to get out of the house and get to the local college. To see Gary. Lovely Gary. He was on her mind all the time and she knew it was the same for him. A group of them had gone out for a drink at the end of term, and that's when they'd kissed for the first time. He'd caught her on the way back from the Ladies, their eyes had met again. She'd tried to resist him but couldn't, and Sara found herself being dragged outside into the pub's yard. The kiss had been electric, the touch of lips on lips, tongue against tongue, neither had been able to deny it.

"I want you so badly," he'd said to her, brushing a strand of nut-brown hair out of her eyes.

"I want you too," she told him. "But not here, not like this.'

So when the opportunity arose, they took it.

Now it was time for the Guilt Demon to go to work.

When Gary finally got up to go to the bathroom, the creature seized Its moment. It crouched down next to Sara on the bed, and as her gaze trailed Gary out of the room It said:

Well that *was stupid! Do you realise what you've done? And for what? For a cheap fumble with a guy you hardly even know.*

"I know enough," Sara replied, her voice low.

Do you? Do you really? You've seen him a couple of hours a week, and most of that time was in class. It's infatuation, that's all. And now you've got it out of your system...

"It's not like that," said Sara. "I—"

You what...? Just couldn't wait for Adrian to get lost so you could do it with him *in the bed you share. Jesus, Sara, don't you have any thought for anyone other than yourself? Do you know what this would do to Adrian if he found out, what it'd do to Clare? I just hope it was 'good for you', that's all. I hope he was worth it.*

"He...I lo—"

You love *him, is that what you're saying to me?* The Guilt Demon pressed Its face up close to hers, spitting as It spoke. *You don't know the meaning of the word. Love isn't about all this, it isn't what you've just been doing. That was sex, Sara. Pure and simple. Sex. Love is when you care so much about someone you're willing to do anything for them, you put them before yourself. Is that what you've done with Adrian tonight? You might not know the meaning of the word, but he does. He worships you, Sara, and you've betrayed him for a bit of fun!*

Sara could hear water running in the bathroom, the splashing as Gary washed his face. Washed his face in the sink Adrian used every morning to shave. Next to the bath they'd once shared together, the room filled with candles on their wedding anniversary.

Don't you feel any shame for what you've done, Sara? Don't you feel any...guilt?

Images flashed in Sara's head now, of a life not yet lived with Gary. Of a messy divorce, of Adrian's face when she told him. Told him? She wouldn't even have to. He'd be able to see it in her eyes, he knew her so well. And this man, Gary, arguing with her because he didn't want to take on another man's kid. Clare growing up resenting her mother for what she'd done, for tearing the family apart all because she didn't have the courage to say no. One simple word: no. Sara put a hand to her mouth, a mouth that still tasted of Gary. She tried to wipe the flavour away, but found that she couldn't. It wouldn't go away, *ever.*

The Guilt Demon found Gary drying his face on a towel, washing away the slick sheen of his labours. It looked the man up and down. Then It began.

So what's the plan of action, Gary? It asked. *You've taken advantage of this woman, so now what? Are you going to walk out of her life, just like you've done with all the rest? Are you going to do that to Sara?*

"No, Sara's different. I-I really like her."

Well, you fucked her, so you must have liked her. But she has no idea about your past, does she? No idea of your track record. You 'really liked' all the others as well, didn't you? You're not going to stick with her for five minutes. You'll be off looking around again before you know it, leaving her to pick up the pieces of a broken marriage. You know she's falling for you. You like her...but do you like her enough? Three wives already, Gary, it's hardly a glowing testament.

"Maybe we could make it work?"

Maybe – and maybe not. There's a first time for everything, I suppose. And maybe you'll win the lottery on Saturday as well! Face it, you're just never going to let anybody into your life like that. You don't like losing control, you'll never tire of the thrill of the chase. And when you've got what you wanted, satisfied your needs, it always ends the same way. Remember what happened with Patsy? Remember how you fucked her, and then really fucked her? You left that woman in such a state.

"No, I didn't mean to."

You never do. Just don't know when to stop, though, do you? Never know where to draw the line.

"Sara's an adult. She knew what she was doing."

That's right, put the blame on her. That's what you always do, try to shift it onto someone else. Try to make it right in your own mind. How many times have you crossed them over, been seeing two at the same time? Never have the decency to drop one first before moving on to the next. Always telling yourself you're protecting the woman you're with by keeping your sordid little affairs a secret. Why didn't you tell Sara about Beth?

Gary sat down on the edge of the bathtub.

Or you make excuses and say that there's something wrong with them. *Well, no, Gary. There isn't* anything *wrong* with *them. But there's something very wrong with* you. *Always has been. You're a user, and you don't care who gets hurt in the process, don't care how many lives you wreck.*

"No...No..."

The phone chose that moment to ring, and Gary started.

The Guilt Demon returned to the bedroom and found Sara holding the receiver to her ear with both hands. It was Adrian, telling her that his mother had had a massive stroke and died tonight, a little after eight o'clock. He was trying to keep his voice even, but it was cracking, and she knew instinctively that he'd been crying.

"I just wish you were here right now, Sara sweetheart. I just want to hold you."

Sara closed her eyes and a tear trickled down her cheek.

"I love you so much," Adrian told her. "You know that, don't you?"

Gary appeared at the door and the tragic scene was complete. There was no need for the Guilt Demon to hang around any longer.

Sated, It moved on to Its next appointment.

*

It's always a mistake to claim you have no conscience. To insist you don't feel guilt. Whenever you tell yourself this you're throwing down the gauntlet, issuing a challenge. And usually when you say it, you've probably got more reason than most to be afraid.

Roy returned to his small flat around eleven. He walked in and locked the door behind him. Then he tossed his bag onto the small bed and peeled off his gloves. He sighed; it had been a long day.

He switched on the TV and flicked around with the remote control. A stupid arts programme on one channel and, on the other, a sitcom so bad it had to be screened when most of the viewing public were fast asleep. He finally found a documentary on shark attacks and let it settle there. Roy cocked his head as he watched a Great White take a lump out of one scuba diver's leg. As it was post-watershed, they showed most of the gory details and Roy found it hard to tear himself away from the screen.

Keeping one eye on the television, Roy went over to the bag and unzipped it. He pulled out the tools of his trade: a selection of knives in various sizes and shapes, from large Bowie to the smaller scalpel-like blade. He'd wiped them at the scene with a cloth, but would still have to clean them properly in the sink to get all the blood off. This he did now, adding the implements to his washing up pile and soaking them in Fairy Liquid, then leaving them on the yellow plastic drainer along with the plates and cups from his dinner earlier.

Next Roy popped the cloth and bag in the washing machine and set the cycle in motion. Easing down into his favourite armchair in front of the TV, he stared intently at the programme – at the bloodletting, the biting, the splashing. He admired the way the sharks crept up on their victims, gliding effortlessly behind them until...

He watched the rest of the documentary, his eyelids heavier by the second. It really had been a long day. But he wanted to watch this; it wasn't very often they put something decent on TV. Besides, he didn't like to sleep...afterwards. Roy's eyes closed, and he quickly snapped them open. Shaking his head to fight off the tiredness.

On the screen another diver was struggling – in the jaws of a Tiger shark this time. Roy leaned forward to get a better view. The diver turned and looked at the underwater camera, his face frozen with shock and fear. No, he was looking right *at* Roy – staring directly at him, as the shark continued its attack. Then the diver pulled off his mask, ripped the oxygen out of his mouth. "What the hell's he doing?" Roy asked himself. He must be panicking, half out of his mind.

Bubbles floated in front of his face, but when they cleared Roy could see him properly.

And he recognised him.

"Why?" gargled the diver, a young boy no more than twenty. "Why, Roy?"

Roy twitched in the chair, opening his mouth. No, it couldn't be...

"Why'd you do it, Roy? Why'd you...kill me?" The shark was really going to town on the lad now, shaking him. Blood was rising with the bubbles, filling the screen, turning it crimson.

Roy jumped up and snapped the TV off. He shook his head. It was late, his mind was playing tricks.

There was a noise from the kitchen.

Roy hesitated, then walked into the room. The washing machine had come to the end of its cycle, that was all. It clattered slightly as the bin inside stopped spinning. Roy let out the breath he'd been holding. Stupid. He was about to move forwards when the door swung open, spilling water onto his kitchen floor. But it wasn't fresh, clean water. It wasn't soapy, detergent-infused either. This was dirty: muddy brown. It reached him where he stood, and it stank. Roy could see green tangles of weed in the spillage.

A body flopped out of the washing machine, covered in the slimy substance. It raised its head, opened its mouth. It was the boy from the shark documentary. Roy gaped at his pleading face, those dead, glassy eyes, those same green weeds clinging to his neck and chin.

"Why, Roy?" he asked again. "Because you enjoy it? Because you love to see them squirm? Because of the feeling of power it gives you? You can decide – do they live, do they die?"

Roy began to back off, but the boy scrambled after him along the wet floor.

There was someone behind him. Roy spun around. There, standing not three feet away, was the figure of a young woman, the flesh missing from one side of her face, bone jutting through the decomposing skin. When she reached up her hand, earth and worms dropped from the appendage. "Why? Why did you kill us, Roy?" she asked bluntly.

"We had our whole lives ahead of us. I was about to start college."

"I was going to be a fire-fighter," spat the boy on the floor, "just like my dad."

"My boyfriend sits alone in our home and cries every night," said a third voice to his left. Roy snapped his head sideways and saw another man, covered in bits of garbage. Maggots crawled over his many knife-wounds.

Now more joined the throng: a woman slit from neck to groin, holding her bowels in her hands; a man with no fingers on his right hand, sliced off one by one; a child sobbing, her neck wide open... So many they filled his small flat: all demanding to know "Why?"

"No, keep back. You're not real, none of this is real!" The sink exploded in a geyser of crimson. The fountain rained down on them all, painting the scene blood red. "This isn't real!" shouted Roy.

Of course it isn't, said one final voice in his ear. *You're fast asleep in that armchair, Roy. You're having a nightmare. But this was the only way I could get to you – the only way I could make you see. Don't like to think about them afterwards, do you? The things you did, the places you left them: dumped in the river, buried in shallow graves, or abandoned on rubbish tips. They're just a means to an end when you're satisfying your cravings. But look, Roy, look at their faces now.*

The Guilt Demon grabbed hold of his head and shoved it in this direction and that, prising open Roy's eyes. *You did this. You did this. But you're so hard and emotionless, aren't you? Such a...cold fish. You could never feel 'cut up' about what you've done. Or could you?*

Roy's victims approached, pressing him against the wall, piling on him. The Guilt Demon was handing out Roy's knives to the crowd and, one by one, they were taking it in turns to slash at him, to have their revenge.

The Guilt Demon stood back from them, smiling with satisfaction as the first screams filled the air.

*

It had many more visits to make in the space of that twenty-four hours. A twelve year-old boy who'd just discovered masturbation, whilst thinking about one of his mother's friends and the low-cut blouse she liked to wear; an ageing headmaster whose unsavoury past at a private school was rapidly catching up with him; an office worker who'd cheated a colleague out of a job promotion and snagged it for herself; a high-ranking politician who'd hired a hit-man to bump off a former lover so she wouldn't jeopardise his marriage or career; the hit-man himself after he'd done the deed; a film star who'd promised his fans and his loved ones he was off drugs, but simply couldn't abide the taste of cold turkey; and a charity worker who was siphoning off money to pay for her very expensive tastes. In every single instance, It goaded and mocked, irritated and argued, until It was content with the results.

But the last stop on this particular guilt trip was a favourite of the demon's. Oh, how It loved this job! It had returned often to this one home, this one woman. Because unlike all the others she was not the architect of her own downfall. No. Instead fate had pointed its finger at her and prodded hard. What had happened wasn't her fault – she'd done nothing wrong – and yet she was still worthy of Its attentions.

The Guilt Demon let Itself in to Kim's semi and looked around. There was nobody home, just a note on the coffee table.

It picked up the paper and scanned the words.

Kim shivered. She watched the sun setting and knew it would be the last time.

The wind buffeted her and she pulled the coat around her tighter. It was an instinctive thing really; in a few moments she'd be colder than she'd ever been before, so what did a little chill matter?

Kim looked down from the top of the multi-storey car park, the most appropriate place she could think of. The view made her feel dizzy. Her eyes were red but no tears came. There were none left.

Night after night, pouring out her sadness until there was nothing left to give.

The parents hadn't blamed her, not even at the funeral. If only they'd kept a closer watch on their son. Their son, Joshua. That name hurt Kim physically. She saw snatches of the accident, everything happening so quickly and yet in achingly slow motion. The parked cars, the small blur dashing out from behind them – rushing across the road to an ice cream van. She'd braked, but he'd bounced over her bonnet and roof like a rubber ball. He only bounced once on the concrete behind her, though.

In her lowest moments, Kim thought she remembered seeing Joshua's eyes, his blue eyes. Thought they'd somehow stared at each other, somehow connected before—

All she could remember after that was the flashing light of the ambulance. The paramedics trying to revive him, then covering him with a blanket.

She hadn't been speeding, hadn't been drinking. Christ, she'd only been to the shops to pick up some milk and eggs. If she'd known what the cost would be, she never would've eaten or drunk again. And although she was cleared by the police, forgiven by Joshua's parents, Kim couldn't even begin to forgive herself.

The voice returned time and again over the months, without fail. *If only you'd seen him sooner, if only you'd reacted more quickly. If only, if only, if only...*

It didn't seem right, didn't seem fair that she should be alive today and he wasn't. So she'd decided, finally, to settle the score. It was time to pay her dues. This wasn't a life she was living, anyway, it was just an existence – and a tormented existence at that. Soon she would silence the voice forever. And hopefully, God willing, she would find peace.

Kim had waited till there was nobody around, waited till she was alone on the top of the building: a building filled with the killing machines she'd been driving that day. And she climbed up onto the ledge, swinging her legs over the barrier railing. Heights had never really bothered her, which was why she'd chosen this particular method of release, but they were bothering her right now. The flat, paved space at the back of the lot loomed up at her and she swallowed dryly.

Could she do it? Could she really do it? Yes, yes, she had to. It was her duty to atone. But still she wavered on the precipice, her legs failing her. For one split second she thought she might even climb back down again, her courage wavering. Then she saw that look in Joshua's eyes once more, and she let herself fall. Over the edge, plummeting to her death.

The Guilt Demon arrived too late to witness the event. It looked down over the side of the multi-storey at the body of Kim, arms and legs at odd angles, a thick puddle seeping out from underneath, the dying sun covering her with its own blanket of darkness.

And It almost felt something.

Look at what you did with your fun and games – you pushed her too far. You know that the accident couldn't have been helped. Just one of those things. And now instead of one wasted life there are two. How can you do what you do each day? How?

It almost felt— No. Stop. That wasn't going to happen. Pulling away from the edge, the creature departed. What was done was done.

Besides, It had exorcised Its own guilt demons so very long ago.

THE ANNIVERSARY

"There now. Isn't that nice?"

"Yes, dear."

Beryl Sutton finished arranging the flowers in their vase. A dozen red roses as a centre-piece. How sweet! Everything was going to be perfect tonight. *Had* to be perfect. After all, it was a very special anniversary.

"You look a little chilly, love. I'll pop a few more cobbles of coal on the fire, shall I?" she said, not waiting for his reply. Beryl did so love to see a roaring fire; very romantic. What was the point of putting the table up in their living room if they couldn't be nice and warm of a winter's evening?

The coal struggled against her metal tongs as it was snatched from the bucket and tossed into a flaming oblivion. Beryl looked at his card on the mantelpiece (*Words cannot express how much you mean...I'll always be there for you*), then across at Trevor, her husband of thirty years. Her sweetheart. He was so handsome, especially in the glow of the fire, lights down low; no need for candles.

"That better?" she asked him.

"Yes. Much better, thanks."

Beryl hung the tongs back on the companion set between the brush and shovel, then rubbed her hands together. She'd been looking forward to this evening for ages. Had planned everything right down to the smallest detail. The food: roast beef, Yorkshire pudding and veg. Trevor's favourite. The music: a lovely Richard Clayderman record on the turntable. Her clothes: a lilac two-piece from the catalogue – buy now, pay later. Even a bottle of the finest red wine from her local supermarket; their own brand, naturally.

Who said you had to go out to some swanky restaurant to enjoy yourself? Much better to stay at home, revel in each other's company. It was something they'd always seen eye to eye on, that. Trevor was a homebody, just like her. And she could tell he appreciated all the effort she'd gone to by the warm smile on his face.

"Can I do anything, love?"

"No, silly. You stay right there while I fetch the dinner." Beryl wandered through into the kitchen, pausing only briefly to examine her reflection in the hall mirror. She patted those curls which the home perm kit had given her; the copper-red tint having also come from the chemists. For sixty she didn't look half bad. Lines around the eyes and neck, but that was only to be expected. God's way of reminding you to enjoy every moment you have left.

"You're only as old as you feel," she murmured to herself, then continued on. And Beryl Sutton felt like a woman in her twenties; exactly how she'd felt when she met Trevor for the first time. Golden memories, they were, and no mistake.

He'd been a new recruit at the bank where she worked – secretarial duties mainly, though she told family members otherwise. A striking example of manhood at twenty-five years old, Trevor. Yes, there was three years difference between them. She often joked even now that he was her toyboy.

Women weren't supposed to do all the running in those days, at least not in the little corner of the world where she lived. However, Beryl was well aware that if she didn't do some sprinting soon it might be too late; twenty-eight wasn't quite on the shelf, but it wasn't sweet sixteen either. After holding out for Mr Right for so long, he'd finally appeared – just as she'd imagined him. And she wasn't about to let him slip away. She made it plain – in all but words – that she was interested in Trevor: dropping her papers when she saw him coming down the corridor in the hopes that he'd stop to help her; walking by his desk several thousand times an hour; making him extra cups of tea… That sort of thing.

Until, at last, the shy young lad of her dreams had asked her out. He later told her that it had been an effort for him to summon up enough courage. But they were both pleased he had. Now, all these years later, they were still together.

Beryl turned off her gas oven and brought out the beef. She'd never been interested in microwaves, no matter how good the adverts said they were. Beryl liked to see exactly how her food was being cooked. She sliced succulent pieces of meat off the side with all the skill of a trained chef. Well, she'd been doing this for some time. Had to, Trevor was simply a hazard in the kitchen. But she didn't mind cooking for him; indeed, she loved it. Beryl laid the beef on round Willow pattern plates, one wedge on top of the other, until she'd created a staggered effect. Next she placed the beef back in the oven and rescued the Yorkshire, which had filled out its square tray adequately – a wave-like quiff rising up at each end. A truly mouth-watering sight. Quickly she divided it up, then turned her attention to the carrots, sprouts and beans, simmering away on the hobs. Beryl spooned equal portions onto each plate. Last, but not least, she poured on the gravy.

A meal fit for a king – and his queen.

Beryl carried these full plates into the front room and deposited them on the table.

"Hmm, smells fabulous," said Trevor.

Beryl beamed from earring to earring. "Oh, the wine! Just hold on a tic." She dashed back to the kitchen and opened the fridge.

She was glad Trevor was happy. That's all she'd ever wanted for him, really. To be happy. With her.

Theirs had been a careful but wondrous courtship. For their first date he'd taken her to see a re-release of *The Odd Couple* at the local Odeon. Walter Matthau and Jack Lemmon had been funny enough, but it wasn't really her cup of tea. Given the choice she would've preferred to have seen something with Paul Newman in it. They'd sat near the back, not quite *at* the back, and Trevor had behaved like a perfect gentleman. Afterwards he walked her back to her parents' home and they kissed on the doorstep. Only a peck, but it made her night. She knew from that moment on he was hers. They belonged together.

The corkscrew slid easily into the top of the wine bottle. She twisted it a few times then jiggled it out. There was a knack to it. Her brother had shown her one time. Dear Harry, she missed him so much... Out it came. No pop. No bang. Just a disappointing hiss as the air was released. The glasses chinked when she lifted them out of the cupboard. A wedding present from the gang at work. A set of eight, out of which only three now remained. It didn't matter. They only needed two.

The bells of St Mary's rang for them on a Saturday in early October. The best day of her entire life. Trevor had looked like a film star and she was on top of the world, with friends and family all telling her the wait had been worth it. That she'd finally hit the jackpot. Beryl couldn't have agreed with them more. Blissful years followed and it wasn't too long before Beryl found herself blessed with a child.

She'd had to leave the bank, obviously, as a baby would mean so much more responsibility at home. But it was what she'd always longed for: a family; a husband; and a gorgeous bundle of joy.

Sadly it wasn't to be, and on 18th February, Thomas Trevor Sutton was delivered stillborn. To this day she couldn't understand it. She'd felt him kicking right up to the last minute. The doctors had told Beryl it would be dangerous for her to conceive again. Next time it might not be just the baby (*just?*). They reeled off some medical nonsense she hadn't understood in the slightest, but she took their word for it; they knew best when all was said and done. He'd be heading towards thirty himself now. She often wondered what he would have become. Whether he would have stayed with her…

Trevor had been mortified, though he maintained the obligatory stiff upper lip, and Beryl had tried not to dwell on what couldn't be changed. There was nothing that could be done. Best to move on, make the most of life. They still had one another. In some strange way she believed it had brought them closer together.

Beryl never had any desire to go back to work. They'd given her job to some teenager anyway, so she devoted herself fully to Trevor. Every day when he came home his dinner was on the table at six o'clock precisely. The house was always spick and span in case anyone visited. Not that they ever did – Beryl had lost touch with most of her friends, and Trevor had never been one for mixing socially; kept himself to himself and his workmates at arm's length. Trevor's parents had passed on before he'd turned nineteen, and now that her own mum and dad had gone to meet their maker – with brother Harry not far behind them; if only he'd stopped smoking – they couldn't even have family get-togethers. Not that they'd had many of those before, either.

Beryl clipped the glasses together between thumb and forefinger, and took the wine by the neck to carry it in. Oh, she was so excited she thought she might actually burst. Yes, anniversaries were such romantic occasions. That wasn't to say Trevor couldn't be just as thoughtful at other times of the year, too, especially on Valentine's Day or birthdays, buying her surprise gifts and the like. Just look at the chest freezer he'd splashed out on a few years back. You could get all your weekly, even monthly, shopping in there and still have room for things like the beef she'd cooked today. All right, not the most personal of gifts, some might say. But Beryl cherished it. Any such offering was a token of his love. You might not be able to wear it on your finger or around your neck; nevertheless, the principle was the same.

She placed the glasses on the table, one at each end, then proceeded to pour the crimson liquid.

"That enough?" Beryl asked Trevor.

"Oh, plenty, dear."

Beryl sat down opposite Trevor and took up her knife and fork. The gravy was still hot, so hot in fact that when she popped a piece of beef into her mouth it seared the surface of her tongue.

"I think you've got the right idea," said Beryl. "Leave it to cool for a minute." She smiled at Trevor. He smiled back. Beryl did adore him so.

Naturally, like any other couple on the planet, they'd had their fair share of bad patches. Arguments at times, the occasional raised voice. Usually Trevor's. Nothing abusive, though, and they'd always kissed and made up afterwards.

Take for instance that incident with the clock. The clock that stood on the three-legged table in the hallway. Trevor had won it by solving a crossword puzzle in a magazine (Trevor and his crosswords!): a china carriage clock with a black and white checked pattern on the side. Quite clever, really. It was a one-off. Unique. And Trevor was so proud he positioned it where anyone who came to the door – Jehovah's

Witnesses, duster salesmen and such – could marvel at his achievement.

But Beryl, stupid, stupid Beryl, had knocked it off when she was cleaning one day. Her hands were quick enough to catch the side of the clock, but not fast enough to prevent the top right-hand corner from striking the floor. The corner broke clean off and left a spider's web crack running down past the clock face.

Panic-stricken, Beryl had tried to glue it back together. But even an idiot could tell.

Trevor had been none too pleased when he came home from work.

"You clumsy— How *could* you?" And so on, well into the night. Beryl had cried. She didn't do it on purpose and had tried her best to fix it. Couldn't he see that? Eventually he had calmed down, forgiven her careless mistake. But for just a while there she had been worried.

Then, of course, there was all that trouble when he'd been made redundant a decade or so ago. Just as he was doing so well; a promotion assured. All those years of working his way up the ladder only for a merger to take place, throwing half the workforce on the scrapheap.

Trevor had moped around for weeks after that. Had not been himself at all. Who could blame him? Having to go through the humiliation of signing on, being turned down for all those other jobs (*too old, sorry*) and looking back on his past triumphs with nostalgia. Thank God she'd managed to set him up with that nice little position working from home, constructing dolls for a company in the Midlands. It was only a few pounds an hour, depending on how many you did, but it *was* work. It kept the wolf from the door, with enough left over for occasional luxuries – saved him from the dole queue, and ensured that Beryl could have him all to herself every day.

Life was good again.

Beryl hadn't even minded...much...when she'd found Trevor's magazines – hidden behind the wardrobe in the spare room, jammed between the wall and the wood where no one would think to look. Why, if she hadn't knocked one of their old records off the top with her feather duster, sending it plunging down the gap, she might never have found them herself.

Imagine her surprise when she saw the pictures inside. Disgusting, ugly images of women doing unspeakable things to themselves, to men, to each other! Beryl had felt physically sick. Surely they could not belong to Trevor, that was her immediate reaction. Perhaps they'd been left there by the previous owners? But how could she ignore such incriminating evidence? The magazines were far too new, and there was writing, Trevor's handwriting, next to some of the adverts: cheap women who would visit your house to give massages. She couldn't believe it!

But she remained silent, hoping it would all go away.

It didn't. It just got worse.

Tuesday was shopping day. Always had been, always would be. 10 till 11:45. But on the Tuesday after she'd found the journals, Beryl returned home early (at 10:50 to be exact). Whether she'd done so consciously or not she didn't know. All she did know was she'd crept into the house through the back door, and silently padded up the stairs.

Beryl heard the noises before she reached the top step. The creaking of the old wooden bed, the grunting of her husband, and the high-pitched cries of someone else; obviously faked. She didn't want to see. She tried to block out the sounds by putting her fists in her ears. It didn't work. Like Lot's wife she had to look, even if it turned her into a pillar of salt the size of a skyscraper.

Through the rails in the banister Beryl had a good view of the bedroom, *their* bedroom, its door ajar, a woman of maybe thirty with long dirty-blonde hair riding her spouse like a jockey on Grand National day. And Trevor's face: screwed up, the sweat streaming from his balding scalp.

Beryl turned and ran, down the stairs and out of the back door. There she sat on the cold stone step, sobbing her heart out. Trevor had said it was okay if they…didn't anymore. It just wasn't right, not after the baby and everything. He'd never complained. If he had, then maybe she—

But now this! How could she ever face him again?

However, face him she did, at 11:45 when she came through the front door, a little less loaded up than usual. Beryl said nothing. She simply kissed Trevor on the cheek. She could forgive him. If that was all he wanted every now and again, well she could turn a blind eye. It was a small price to pay for having him at home with her where he belonged. At least he wasn't having an affair.

Although even that hadn't been the true test of their marriage. This had come a short while later – on the day he announced he was leaving her.

Shocked and stunned, Beryl had stood watching him struggle with his suitcase down the stairs; shirtsleeves and trouser legs sticking out here and there. He never did know how to pack properly.

"I need to get away from here. From this town, this house. From you! Can't you see how I've wasted the last twenty-nine years? How *you've* wasted them?"

Beryl shook her head. No, quite frankly she couldn't. She'd done everything in her power to please Trevor. He wasn't just going to walk out on her like this. How would she cope without him?

Wasted her life? HE WAS HER LIFE!

"No, Trevor, please—"

"This is something I've got to do. It's been on my mind for some time. I'm sorry."

Beryl recalled the scene, one year ago to the day, while she chewed her carrots. She smiled at Trevor. He smiled back. They'd worked through it together. Come out the other side with a greater respect for one another. A greater *understanding*. Although she had to admit he'd scared her quite badly at the time.

Particularly when he'd turned away, heading towards the front door with his case in one hand, his coat gripped in the other. He wouldn't even stop to put it on.

What else was she expected to do? Beryl refused to let him go.

The crossword clock was the first thing that came to hand. It made a wet thudding noise as it connected with the back of Trevor's skull, shattering both the ornament and bone simultaneously.

Trevor had dropped to his knees, the suitcase flung aside as he felt at the wound she'd inflicted on him. His eyes went wide when he turned to face her, as if he couldn't believe what she had done. His mouth a grimace that could almost be mistaken for a smile.

Blood washed down his neck, staining his light blue jumper, turning it the colour of...*red wine.* He fell forward, allowing more of the liquid to seep out, splashing all over her nice clean floor.

Tutting, Beryl had gone through to the kitchen for a cloth.

Trevor, his head pounding, had summoned up enough strength to move. He managed to get his right arm underneath him and push up. His left hand was reaching out for the doorknob. If he could just get out into the street someone would see him and—

But that was when he'd felt something pointed enter his back, rammed in with considerable force. It seemed to take forever for the carving knife to come out the other side, slicing through his flesh and bone, puncturing his heart (*his sweet, sweet heart*) along the way. Even more vital fluid pooled around him. Beryl looked down at Trevor, trying to come to terms with what had happened, to rationalise and justify it. She concluded that he was still here, with her. That was the most important thing.

Then as a 'thank you', she stooped and kissed him on the cheek.

It had taken some cleaning up, that hallway – blood's a swine to get out of your carpet – but somehow Beryl got it all looking shipshape and Bristol fashion again. Alas, there was no salvaging the clock this time. For a while she'd sat Trevor in his favourite armchair. However, some logical sliver of her mind told her that soon he would begin to smell.

That's when she'd struck upon the notion of the freezer. It seemed appropriate. His prophetic gift to her, and now his new quarters. Somewhere he could put his feet up and relax, then come out feeling refreshed and alert. Ready to face the world again.

Although he always stayed at the bottom and the food remained at the top. Couldn't disturb Trevor while he was sleeping.

Because that's all he was doing in there really, sleeping.

Often during the night Beryl would wake up in a cold sweat, believing him to be dead. But how could he be? If he was a corpse, then how come he still talked to her? How was it he'd forgiven her for what she'd done? He'd even told her to take over the doll-making business while he was feeling a bit under the weather. Then they'd have enough to live off each week – the money deposited into their joint account at the bank every Friday.

She actually enjoyed the work, too. It kept her mind active. That and the crossword puzzles. As for any official documents that came, well, she had Trevor's permission to sign his name – she could do this blindfolded after thirty years. That's what marriages were about at the end of the day, sharing the load. *For better or worse, in* sickness *and in health*. In a few years Trevor would be on a pension too, just like her. Then they wouldn't have to worry about a thing. They could both...retire.

Yes, life was just fine at the moment. Couldn't be better. The best it had been for a long time, now she knew Trevor wouldn't leave her.

Beryl looked at Trevor again. He'd hardly touched his food.

"Not hungry, darling?"

Trevor dropped face-first into the dinner, the hole in the rear of his head clearly visible. Beryl pushed him back on the seat and wiped his face clean with a paper napkin.

"Clumsy," she said, giggling. She didn't have long now; the fire was speeding things up. He would have to go back soon.

Beryl took her wineglass in her hand. "I propose a toast. To the anniversary of our marriage. And to the first anniversary of our...*fresh* start together. Here's to the next thirty years!"

Beryl clinked the two glasses together. She smiled at Trevor across the table.

Trevor smiled back.

LADY

Oh, how the mighty can fall.

Aidan Marsh thought this as he examined his surroundings: the streets covered in garbage, the crumbling, graffiti-covered walls of the buildings. And the people, Jesus, the people…

He'd already been propositioned twice since he entered this part of the city – by bus, as he wasn't about to leave the car parked around here – and he didn't even want to think about what was going on down those alleyways. Larry, his friend from *The Gazette*, had only recently mentioned this area when he was doing a spread about national urban decay. Aidan could certainly see why. Even in the daytime, it was the reason he'd brought a screwdriver in his jacket pocket. The reason he was clutching the strap of his shoulder bag so tightly he couldn't feel his fingers. (His digital camera – for a potential photo op – and Dictaphone would be worth a fair bit if anyone was to grab it or look inside.)

But it would all be worth it in the end.

To be honest, he still couldn't quite believe he'd got the call, right out of the blue like that. And to actually get an invite to *his* home.

"This is a wind-up, right?"

"No joke," replied the raspy voice. "I've been following your 'Where are they now?' pieces. I'm impressed."

Aidan nodded. That series had done really well for him, boosting both his rep *and* his bank balance. "Think I might make a good addition?"

A good addition? He'd said it so casually, like the entire Western world *hadn't* been wondering where the hell Trace Edwards vanished to almost twenty-five years ago. Of all the ex-celebs Aidan had covered – pop stars, directors, entertainers – this was definitely the Holy Grail of subjects. Snatching up a pen, Aidan had scribbled down a day, time and address. It was worth checking out on the off-chance this actually was for real, and not some con orchestrated by one of his rivals. It could be the biggest break of his career so far.

He hadn't been able to tell anyone, though – hadn't dared risk it. Not even with Denise. *Especially* not Denise. Reclusive, clingy Denise, who had seemed such a catch at first, but was now starting to really get on his nerves.

It was just another thing he was keeping from her, like the fact Brenda from advertising had recently been coming on to him (probably because of his own dalliances with fame). Breaking down his resistance with skirts so tight he couldn't believe she could walk in them, low-cut tops that treated him to a flash of her ample cleavage. Breaking down his resistance until—

Aidan shook his head. Now was neither the time nor the place to be having erotic thoughts, not when he could get mugged at any moment. So instead, he concentrated on what he was going to say when he finally met the man he'd braved this neighbourhood for. "How have you been keeping?" just didn't seem to cut it somehow. Besides which, Aidan figured the guy hadn't been keeping well *at all* – not if he'd been forced to live in this shithole.

Hardly surprising after what happened. From his research, Aidan knew the stuff that was made public back then, but suspected there was much more to the story than had been reported in the papers and on the news. God, Edwards had gone through the wringer back then, hadn't he? A terrible business, what had happened in that hotel room.

Some might say he'd brought it all on himself, but it was terrible all the same. And as for the accident...

Who could blame him for dropping off the face of the Earth like that?

So why crop back up now? Why did he want to tell his side of things after all this time? Was he hoping for some kind of resurgence? A comeback to beat 'em all? Hardly likely at his age, surely. But possible, still possible. *Anything* was possible.

Aidan checked his piece of paper and found that he'd walked right past the address he'd written down. Flats, with a buzzer at the base. He pressed the button for the right one and waited for a reply.

"Hello," came a croaky voice.

"Er, hi. It's Marsh," Aidan spoke into the speaker, looking over his shoulder in case he'd drawn undue attention to himself.

There was a tinny beep, followed by a click, and he pushed open the main door. Aidan pulled a face when he got inside, his nose wrinkling at the stench. The streets outside had been bad enough, but at least that was in the open air. In here, there was no escape. He called for the lift, but decided against it when the fragrant aroma of piss greeted his nostrils.

Aidan took the stairs to the fifth floor, then walked along the dingy corridor until he got to the room he wanted. He lifted his hand to knock, but found himself hesitating. Why was he so nervous? It wasn't like him; he'd met much bigger names in this biz that was *all* show, and just treated them like they were Joe Bloggs from down the road.

So what was the problem?

Was it because this guy had become a cult figure in his time away from the limelight? A virtual living legend? His films *had* become classics after all, the fact that there weren't that many of them only adding to the allure. Nowadays stars were ten a penny and, thanks to magazines like the one he worked for, there was no mystique about any of them. Maybe that was it. Maybe he was so wired because there was – always had been – a true sense of the mysterious about Trace Edwards. How he'd scaled the heights from extra on a daytime British soap to become the toast of Hollywood was still the subject of much speculation.

Now Aidan was about to find out *exactly* why. And if this went the way he thought it would, it'd also be a fast track to his own widespread acclaim. Hell, there might even be a book in this! He couldn't think of one journo who wouldn't trade their own internal organs to be where he was right now, as much as this corridor reeked of three-week-old takeaways.

So, bloody well get on with it then! he told himself in that tone of voice he always used to get his arse in gear (which sounded more than a little like his deceased father's). *Knock on the door!*

He was just about to, when the door opened anyway. In spite of himself, Aidan jumped. There was a figure holding it back, but he couldn't really make them out in the poor light from the corridor. They seemed to be stooping, though.

"M-Mr Edwards?" Aidan asked.

For a second or two, there was no answer. Then: "Come in. Close the door behind you." Again, the voice had a raspy quality, nothing like the deep, rich tones Aidan was used to from watching Edwards' movies.

The figure limped away into the gloom, leaving Aidan to follow and do as he was told. Again, he paused, but not for very long this time. As much as his nerves had got the better of him, he didn't want to get off on the wrong foot with his most important, and lucrative, interviewee so far.

Aidan ventured inside and closed the door, trailing the figure who was now standing with his back to him in the flat's living room. Actually it was the *only* room that Aidan could see, with attached kitchen – plus a table and two high-backed chairs that obviously served as the dining area. Where Edwards slept was another one of the mysteries surrounding him. The small window across the way only let in a fraction of the potential light available, making the room just as dingy as the hallway outside. Aidan couldn't help letting his eyes wander, taking in the décor – or lack of it. What he noted first were the books, dozens of them, strewn all over the place: some open, some closed. Some new; some very, very old. He would never have pegged Edwards for a great reader. The carpets were brown, though whether this was the original colour or just because of the dirt, Aidan couldn't tell. There was a lone settee against one wall which looked like it had been attacked by a crazed knifeman, haemorrhaging foam in various places.

The walls were plain, and a yellowy pus colour. No posters or even postcards marked the fact that Edwards had once been the focus of so much attention (and possibly could be again?). It was all so different to photos Aidan had seen of Edwards' mansion in LA from the '80s.

A cloud of smoke formed around Edwards' bent head, and now Aidan saw that the man's arms were drawn into his body, protecting the cigarette that he now removed and held by his side. A cough followed that made Edwards' whole body shake. Aidan almost went to him, then thought better of it.

"You...You found the place okay?" Edwards wheezed eventually, still with his back to Aidan – his body half the size it should have been because of the stoop.

"Ah, yes, it wasn't that hard."

Edwards gave a hollow laugh and coughed again. "Do you want a drink or anything, before we get started?"

Straight to the point. Aidan liked that. "No...no, thanks."

"Alright then."

It was now that Edwards turned and faced him. There was still a touch of the theatrical in how he revealed his features to Aidan. Still very much the actor playing a role. But instead of a hero from some action-comedy-romance, which had always been Edwards' forté, what Aidan saw was more like something out of a cheap horror flick.

The once thick head of golden hair was thin, grey and wispy, but that wasn't the most shocking thing – the guy was, after all, a lot older now than when he hit the big time. No, it was the face itself that made Aidan flinch. It looked for all the world like the crazed knifeman, having done all he could to the sofa, had turned his attentions to Edwards. His face was a patchwork of deep scars, including one thick half-moon which started at his hairline and ran across to his left temple. One of his cheekbones was still obviously crushed: the skin there was deflated and floppy, like a tent with no pole to hold it up. He had a sunken right eye which was virtually closed shut, and dents in his nose where there had probably once been gaping holes. But the mouth. Oh Christ, the mouth! Wider than any normal human's should be, lop-sided and drooping on one side like melted wax, it revealed yellowing stumps of teeth that had once been perfect and white. To complete the picture, down the side of his neck and spread across the top of his chest – as far down the open shirt top as Aidan could see – was a web of burns, stretching the skin so taut it looked like it was going to rip open at any moment.

Photo ops would most definitely be out of the question.

For a moment Aidan thought he was going to be sick. Then he breathed in a few times and forced down the bile. These were obviously old wounds, set in place a long time ago, but that didn't make them any easier to stomach.

Edwards grinned, or at least attempted a grin. "Don't worry," he spluttered. "It always has that effect."

Nobody had really seen Trace Edwards after his car crash, apart from the doctors who had treated him – supposedly the best money could buy. It looked more like a team of gorillas had gone at him with surgical instruments. Aidan doubted whether even Edwards' biggest fan would recognise him now. It certainly explained how he was able to keep such a low profile. It also explained why there were no reminders of the man he'd once been on the walls. As Aidan continued to stare, Edwards took another puff of the cigarette and blew out the smoke, a dribble of saliva emerging with it. Edwards coughed again, less harshly than the last time, but with about a pint of phlegm in the back of his throat.

As repulsed as he was, Aidan's mind was ticking over with questions: the most important of which was why the hell didn't he get all this fixed? He'd had the time over the last quarter of a century. He had the money. Or did he? Perhaps that was it, perhaps that was why he'd finally decided to come out of hiding and tell his tale. Nothing had been discussed about payment, Edwards had seemed so keen that Aidan hadn't needed to tempt him with promises of huge amounts of cash.

Didn't mean he wasn't expecting them, of course.

"I know exactly what you're thinking," Edwards said, looking at him sideways out of his one good eye. "And don't think I didn't try. The best plastic surgeons in the world have had a crack at this face, leastwise back when I could afford them."

Yep, definitely about the money.

"None of them could do a damned thing," the former actor continued. "In fact they only made things worse. Every time they operated, infections would set in. It was as though my face *wanted* to stay like this, Marsh. Same goes for my shattered knee." He tapped his leg to illustrate. "Hopeless."

"But...But that was back then. Things have improved with—"

"Trust me, it wouldn't do any good. I accepted that a long time ago." As well as the distinctive rasp, there was more than a hint of defeat in the voice. "Look, it doesn't matter anymore; it's all too late."

"So you don't want the money for surgery?" Aidan couldn't believe he'd just asked that out loud.

Edwards sneered. "Is that what you think?"

Aidan shrugged, it was his only defence. And it was always instinctive.

"No. No, that's not the reason I got in touch with you. Not the reason at all."

"Then, if you don't mind me asking, what *was* the reason, Mr Edwards? Posterity?" All notions about a return to acting were gone now.

"Revenge, Marsh." Edwards paused for dramatic effect. He hadn't lost his touch. "Revenge on the person who did this to me."

*

Aidan set up his Dictaphone on the table, settled down while Edwards sat opposite. The man drew in a sharp breath when he descended, the leg obviously causing him great pain. By now the reporter was somewhat used to Edwards' visage, even if it did cause him a degree of distress to look at it for long.

Edwards nodded for Aidan to start the machine, which he did, and began with a recap of his life. Much of this Aidan already knew, but he let him speak – though he was dying to know who Edwards was so pissed off at. There hadn't been anyone else involved in the crash as far as he knew.

But before getting to the 'good stuff', Edwards talked about his working-class background, his father a bin man (the irony of this didn't escape Aidan, after traipsing the litter-strewn streets where Edwards currently lived) and his mother a dinner lady. He'd endured hard times growing up on that council estate, and the young Trace – then Tony – had been bullied mercilessly for his interest in the arts.

Nevertheless, it hadn't put him off – only making him more determined to get into drama college and pursue his dream. And of course, say 'Fuck you!' to all those twats who beat him up.

Life hadn't been much easier after he left, though, and like most struggling actors he'd had to take the crappiest jobs just to scrape a living. Signing with an extras agency got him tiny parts in ads, and onto TV sets, but didn't really get him noticed – and he tried repeatedly, without success, to secure the services of an agent.

Aidan couldn't help sighing as he checked his Dictaphone, pausing it for a moment.

"What's wrong?" asked Edwards, lighting up again. He coughed as he took a drag.

"Well," said Aidan, "this is all good background and stuff, but it's not exactly anything I didn't know already, Mr Edwards. Who is it you want your revenge on?"

"I'm just coming to that!" grunted the actor. "Do you want your exclusives or not? I was just about to tell you how I got where I did. It's something I've never told anyone before. About the help I got. It's connected with that very same person."

This got Aidan's attention and he started the record once more. "Sorry, please go on."

"Like most tragedies, it revolves around a girl," Edwards announced.

A girl? Which one? thought Aidan. *There had been so many in Edwards' life. If you shut up, moron*, said his dad's voice again, *he's about to tell you.*

"I met her while I was working at a fast-food place. She walked in and...there was just something about her, like she didn't belong there. Like she was too good for the place, y'know?"

Aidan shrugged again.

"I can remember looking at her and just thinking to myself: wow! She was perfect. Now, I was a good-looking bastard in those days," said Edwards, "as you probably know. *I* knew it, too, even then. Usually I didn't have to do much to get a woman into bed. But something about her made me hold back, let fate take its course. Boy meets girl and all that, just like in the movies." He paused to cough, holding a hand up to his mouth – for which Aidan was grateful. Edwards continued: "What happened was just like that, as it goes. Like it was scripted. I tried to give her the free scratchcard that came with her meal, some kind of promotion they were running, but she wouldn't take it. Gave it to me instead, and you know what?"

Another shrug.

"I won £40! That was a lot of money back then, especially to me. Couldn't accept it, of course, as I was an employee. The only way I could get away with it, I told her, was if she let me buy her a meal – a proper meal – with it."

"Clever," admitted Aidan.

"*I* thought so. We agreed to meet at an Italian place down the road. I told her my name, she told me hers: Louise."

Now that really didn't ring any bells. In all the reports on Edwards Aidan had looked at there had been no mention of any woman called Louise. "What happened then?" he prompted.

Edwards sucked in a lungful of smoke and blew it out again. "We ended up talking all night; just talking. It was a new experience for me. I told her all about my acting, about how I was trying to break into TV somehow. She listened, actually listened to me. The first person who'd ever done that." He looked beyond Aidan's shoulder at the small window, lost in thought. A tactful cough from Aidan this time, more to do with the cigarette than to get Edwards moving again, nonetheless did the trick. "We started going out – no funny business at first, that came later, and I respected her for it. By then, of course, all bets were off."

"Bets?"

Edwards looked directly at him. "We were in love. Hook, line, sinker – the whole bloody rod. I've never felt that way about anyone before or since, Marsh, and she said she felt the same way."

"But you split up way before you became famous, right? I mean, there's no mention of her in any—"

"And you won't *find* any mention of her, either," Edwards rasped bitterly. He calmed down a little before adding, "That's how she wanted it; how my new agent wanted it. Gave me more appeal, see? If I was 'single'."

Aidan frowned. "You said this Louise helped you. What was she, some kind of executive? A producer's daughter?"

"I said she helped me get where I got, but not in that way. It's hard to describe but she made me feel like I could truly do it. She gave me confidence, she gave me..." He couldn't finish, then suddenly started up again: "When I was almost at rock bottom, almost ready to give up, she persuaded me to go for the job on *East Crescent*. Said she just wanted to see me happy."

Aidan nodded – this was another part he knew. *The Crescent* (as it was known to its fans) was what gave Edwards his first proper break in England, playing Matt Harding's long-lost brother, Jamie. The character was such a hit that he eclipsed Matt, proving none-too-popular with the 'heartthrob' actor who played him, Dominic Wilde. *Maybe that's who Edwards was talking about*, pondered Aidan, *an old grudge? No, he'd said it had something to do with this Louise. Did Wilde and her have a fling?*

"And the rest is history?" said Aidan, trying hard to keep the cynicism out of his voice.

"Not quite. At least not how you or anyone else knows it." After spending a couple of years on the show, and gaining a huge following, Edwards left for fear he would be typecast. "It was a huge gamble, but again Louise was right there giving me the confidence I needed. Better roles were ahead of me, she said, in TV dramas, even small films over here. And you know what? She was right."

"I know, and I know what comes next," moaned Aidan, beginning to wonder if he was wasting his time here. So far, the only new thing to come out of the interview was that there was yet another chick behind the scenes putting out for the great Trace Edwards.

"I doubt that very much," said Edwards seriously, expelling another cloud of smoke and hacking loudly. "You think she was just one of many, don't you? One of a long string of lays? Would it surprise you to learn that while I was with her, I never slept with another woman? Not back then, at any rate. I can see by that raised eyebrow you don't believe me, but it's the truth. Like I said, I'd never felt that way about anyone before. Oh, don't get me wrong, there was plenty of opportunity – and the press liked to perpetuate the image of me as a ladies' man."

But you were a ladies' man, thought Aidan. *You've admitted as much yourself.*

"It was hard on a relationship, let me tell you," Edwards went on. "Constantly having to reassure Lady that—"

Aidan held up a hand. "Hold on, you've lost me. Who's Lady?" It sounded like the name of a dog to him.

Edwards shook his head. "Sorry. It was a nickname, the pet name I called Louise." (Aidan kept his mouth shut about dogs.) "Came from her two first names, you see? Louise Danielle Boucher. LD. Besides which, it suited her. She *was* a lady."

"I see," said Aidan. "But I'm still confused as to how she fits into all this."

Edwards sighed. "You know where it goes from here, to La-La Land?"

"Yeah." Everybody knew that. Trace Edwards went over to California to make his fortune and the Yanks lapped it up. They loved his good looks, loved his accent. Loved *him*, basically.

"But did you know that the only reason it came about was because my showreel ended up on the wrong producer's desk?"

"No, that's something I *didn't* know. But I don't see what it has to do with—"

"With Louise? No, I didn't either until I started to look back at the bigger picture. That's something you're going to have to do, as well, when you come to write all this up. She refused to go with me to Hollywood, so the only time I saw her was when I flew back to England between projects. She didn't even want to share the spotlight with me at premieres. I told her: I didn't want to be stuck there with some bimbo on my arm, I wanted to be there with *her*. That just made her cry."

"So this would be around the time of *Hearts on Fire*?"

"*Hearts on Fire, The Journeying, Treasure Hunters...*" All number one box office smashes in their time, with the accompanying rock ballads also hitting number one in the charts on both sides of the Atlantic.

"Because didn't people think that something was going on with your co-star on those, Kathryn McBride?"

Edwards was silent.

"So that was true?" Aidan pushed: "Mr Edwards?"

"*No!*" Edwards slammed his fist on the table, so hard the Dictaphone rattled. He coughed again, taking a good few moments to catch his breath. Aidan checked the machine was still working, and when he looked up Edwards was rubbing his scarred face. He caught Aidan watching him. "It never went that far," he said almost inaudibly. "Katy was just a friend. But that didn't stop Lady believing the rumours."

Might've had something to do with a photographer catching you coming out of McBride's place at six in the morning, Aidan said to himself. *Shut up and let the man speak,* his father's voice snapped.

"I did my best to persuade her, and eventually she listened. But I had to stop making movies with Katy."

That did at least clear up one thing, as many had speculated at the time it was because the pair had broken up off-screen. Now it was clear Edwards had done it to appease his secret lover in England instead. "So you went on to do *Forgotten Island* and *Return of the Treasure Hunter* alone?"

"But the rot had already set in by then."

Aidan shifted about in his chair. Was he talking about his relationship, or the fact that those films didn't do nearly as well as the previous three?

"I was getting nothing but grief from Louise, I was drinking way too much. I figured, what the hay: plenty more fish in the sea. Jesus, Marsh, it was all there on a plate for me. What would you have done? What would any red-blooded man have done?"

Aidan did what he did best: he shrugged.

"This time she knew by simply looking me in the eyes. And it was over just like that. 'I loved you,' she said to me the last time I saw her. 'I loved you so, so much.' I let her go. I'd had enough by that point anyway. I wanted to be free of it. Didn't realise till later what a big mistake I'd made." There was that wistful, faraway look again. Aidan had to feel sorry for the man. He'd got what he thought he wanted, only to end up losing the one thing that really meant anything to him. None of this was public knowledge, and it was like gold dust.

"I'm guessing this is when you went on your public binges near the end. Trace the party animal, the gambler?"

"More women, high stakes card games, stronger substances than drink." Edwards looked at the cigarette in his hand, one of many he'd chain-smoked since starting the interview. "But if I could pinpoint exactly when it all went to shit, it was the moment I lost *her* – I felt it, Marsh. I actually felt it, though I told myself I didn't. It was like something breaking inside me."

Your heart? "That's love all right," Aidan reassured him.

"No, something more than love."

"How do you mean?"

Once again, Edwards remained silent.

"Mr Edwards…? Trace?"

Edwards laughed, spluttering: "No-one calls me that anymore. I'm plain old Tony again these days."

"Tony... You were doing all that to try and forget her, weren't you? To try and forget Loui— Lady?"

"That's just the thing," Edwards spluttered, "as soon as she'd gone, packed up her things, left her apartment, I couldn't remember what she even looked like. Just that she'd been there, and now she was gone. I *still* can't remember her."

That wasn't unusual though, was it, blocking out what someone looks like to protect yourself?

"And you never saw her again?"

"Never. Though I looked for her. My God, how I looked. But that was later. After...After..."

"After what happened in the hotel."

Edwards nodded sharply. "I can't for the life of me remember how that girl ended up..." Now he shook his head instead.

Drugs will do that to you.

"I *wasn't* high, regardless of what you've read," Edwards growled, as if reading his thoughts. "I just fell asleep and the next thing I knew—"

"She was dead," Aidan completed for him.

"I was cleared by the courts," argued Edwards.

"But not in the civil action," Aidan reminded him, as if he needed it. The twenty-one-year-old's family had taken Edwards for several million, a massive chunk of his fortune.

"I don't know what to tell you, other than it wasn't my fault."

Aidan leaned forwards on the chair. "And from what you were saying, neither was the crash?"

"No. I lost control of the car somehow. The steering wheel just... Next thing I was waking up in hospital." While it was true Edwards hadn't been drinking the night he flipped his convertible over several times on Mulholland Drive, and no drugs had been found in his system, it was widely believed that the stress of the two legal battles had taken their toll on him both mentally and physically.

Aidan let out a slow breath. "Forgive me if I'm missing something, but I still don't understand what all this has to do with your woman, Louise. Are you suggesting she might have tampered with the car somehow?" *If so, that really* would *make a cracking story.*

Edwards shook his head more slowly and, it seemed to Aidan, somewhat painfully. "Not physically, no."

"I-I still don't understand."

"I hired some of the best private eyes to try and track her down, Marsh. She'd never mentioned any family, said she'd never had any folks, so that was a dead end. For years I spent my time and money hoping to catch up with her. And do you know what I found out: she doesn't bloody exist! There are no records anywhere of a Louise Danielle Boucher."

"People change their names all the time, Mr Edwards," said Aidan, tapping the table. "Especially if they're trying to avoid someone."

"You don't understand. Her letting agents had no record of her, couldn't even remember her. There was even a couple who swore blind they'd been living there for years, had the photos to prove it. I'd *been* in that apartment, Marsh, hundreds of times! We'd fucked in there, for Christ's sake!"

Aidan frowned. It was a good cover job, certainly.

"Do you understand what I'm saying? There was no evidence that she'd lived there *at all*. It was as though she'd never really been here. You can see why I might make it my mission to find out what was going on."

The reporter thought about shrugging, then thought again. He nodded instead.

"And I didn't need the media dogging my tracks. So I vanished myself, paid off a few folk to keep their mouths shut, until eventually people stopping asking questions about me. It was much easier to hide now that I looked like fucking John Merrick."

"But where did you go, what did you do?" This was all vital information if Aidan was to write about 'the wilderness years'.

"I studied *her*. Tried to figure out who she was." Edwards waved his hand to indicate the books in his flat. "In the end I realised the simple, stupid truth. She *has* been here, Marsh, many times."

"Been *here*, what are you talking about?"

"That's probably a bad way of putting it. She's here every day, all around us, though it's very rare for her to take physical form."

"Physical..." Aidan was completely lost now. They were talking about some chick Edwards had been in love with, screwed over, and then left – weren't they?

Edwards got that faraway look in his good eye again, as if somewhere else. "Who knows, you might even have come across her yourself and not known it. You can feel her most strongly in casinos, in betting shops, places like that. That's why I started gambling. Win or lose, win or lose. If you close your eyes you can–"

"Mr Edwards! I still don't know what you're trying to say."

Edwards ground what teeth he had together, then croaked, "It took me a while to see it, the pattern of what had happened. But you're an intelligent man, Marsh. I've read your stuff. You're good at putting two and two together."

"Sometimes I make five," Aidan warned him.

"She kick-started my career, made me successful, because she loved me. Then she took it all away from me." Edwards let the words hang in the air like the smoke he was so fond of blowing from his mouth.

"Look, Mr Edwards, I'm not entirely sure what you want from me. What you want from this piece. But it was *never* about 'where is he now?' was it? You tell me you want revenge, then say that the person you want revenge on doesn't really exist."

Edwards rose off his chair, stubbing out his freshest cigarette and leaning on the table, looming down on Aidan. "I want to *expose* her, Marsh, publicly. Tell the world about her so the next unsuspecting mug she latches on to won't make the same mistakes I did." There was hurt in his voice, hurt that comes from the loss of true love. That turns it into hatred. "And I want to do it before it's too late."

"You...You said that before. Too late, what are you talking about?"

Edwards hesitated before answering: "She's dealt her final hand. I've only got a few months to live. My lungs..."

Aidan couldn't say he was surprised. He'd only been with the bloke a short while and he'd probably inhaled a lifetime of second-hand smoke. But it did make him feel more sorry for Edwards.

Of course, that didn't mean he had to humour the guy. "I can see the makings of a good story here," Aidan told him. "*If* we drop the bullshit with Louise."

"With Lady," Edwards reminded him. It was even there in her name, wasn't it? His obsession, a way of justifying the crap choices he'd made.

"If we drop that," Aidan continued unabated, "and concentrate on the lost love angle. The *real* reason for your..." Fall, Aidan wanted to say, but couldn't finish the sentence.

Edwards banged his fist on the table again. "No, I..." He began to cough, huge spasming coughs this time that caused Aidan to feel sick again. The man was practically bent double with them. Aidan rose and helped him to the ruined couch, sitting him down.

"Listen," he told the actor, "I'll get back to you, see what we can work out. Maybe arrange another session." He gathered up the Dictaphone, turning it off and hastily shoving it into his bag.

Edwards was reaching out a hand to him. "Promise me..."

Aidan was already halfway to the door when he realised Edwards wasn't reaching out to him at all: he was reaching for one of the books, open on a certain page. On one side was an illustration of a woman carved in some kind of stone, ancient and beguiling. On the other, a black and white photograph of a bomber from the war with a woman painted on its side, sitting in a horseshoe. "Marsh, promise me you'll tell my...*Her* story."

Aidan turned away from the man, left the room, left the flat without saying another word – Edwards' painful coughs trailing him.

He ran up the corridor, down the stairs, and out into the street. The light was fading fast – he'd been inside much longer than he thought – and soon it would be dark. Ordinarily he would be worried, but...

Aidan walked through the streets as if in a daze. Everything Edwards had told him could be explained away. The good, the bad – and the ugly. Yet there had been such conviction in the man's voice, such certainty.

"It took me a while to see it, the pattern. But you're an intelligent man, Marsh. I've read your stuff.

You're good at putting two and two together. Who knows, you might even have come across her yourself and not known it."

Why was he running away? Was it because he thought Edwards was dangerous? A lunatic? No, it was more than that.

Aidan thought about the moment his own life had turned around, when he'd first been assigned the run of articles that were rapidly making his name – after years of slaving away copyediting.

Thought about the moment he'd first met Denise in that queue at the newsagents – he'd always remembered it because she was buying a copy of his magazine. And hadn't there been a fuss when that guy came in, the bloke who'd won some money on the lottery?

Plus the way she'd looked. Classy. Too good for him, he'd thought. Something about the way she held herself...and that smile...which made him start chatting to her.

Hold on to that. *Hold on to it and don't you dare forget her face!* screamed his father's voice in his head.

Panicking, Aidan thought about Denise, about how she'd once told him on a date that she hated her first name, so she didn't use it anymore. Now what was it? Think, Aidan, think! Denise, Denise, Denise, Denise...

Laura.

God, that was it! Laura. Denise. Howard. No family, no parents, no background that he really knew about. Not that he'd cared.

A coincidence? What, that you'd get a potential big break like Edwards out of the blue like that? Coincidence, or just plain good I—

There was a noise off to his right. Something down one of those alleyways he'd been so frightened of before.

Aidan thought about Brenda, about her skirt and cleavage, and began to sweat. Did Denise know? Could she see it in *his* eyes the last time they spoke? About how far it had really gone.

"I loved *you, Aidan.* Loved *you so, so much."*

Oh, how the mighty can fall!

Win or lose, win or lose…

Anything *was possible.*

He increased his pace, footsteps quickening. Because Aidan knew that at the moment Luck was on his side.

Though for how much longer was anyone's guess.

BAGGAGE

He was just carrying around too much baggage, that was the problem.

It was worrying Nicholas, even right now. If this one worked out the way he thought, he'd give up completely on finding any kind of happiness. Resolve himself to a life of being alone.

That was what had motivated him to start looking in the first place; the fear he'd probably end his days sad and lonely. No wife, no kids. Nothing. If he could only make some kind of a relationship work, then—

It wasn't so easy, though, was it? Nicholas couldn't help feeling bitter about his previous failures – especially those in his youth. It wasn't as if he was hideous or anything, in fact he'd been told he was quite attractive. He was just incredibly shy, and liked to treat girls with respect. Inevitably, that had led to them either taking him for what little money he had, or taking him for granted.

Even those he'd thought were nice had stabbed him in the back. Take Julie, for instance, back when he was twenty-one – and still a virgin, though he did his best to hide it. They'd worked together at the coffee shop, and he'd been sweet on her for so long. She'd kept him dangling, saying they should just be friends. On the rebound, however, she'd dragged him out to buy her drinks one night, then dragged him back to her place. He hadn't been able to hide his inexperience then; couldn't conceal that he was terrified. And when he asked her if she was *really* sure, that she'd always said they should just be mates, she'd taken it as an insult and told him to get out. The next day, he was the butt of all the jokes at work, while Julie had already moved on to her next conquest.

He'd learned from this mistake, but it hadn't been any better once he'd finally popped his cherry. Nicholas treated all the women he'd dated well, and what had he got in return? "You're just too...nice," they told him. "Too clingy. I need my space." At the same time, they accepted all the nights out he paid for, all the gifts. It drove him to spend years not bothering with the opposite sex for fear of getting hurt.

But man wasn't meant to live by himself, so every now and again he'd get drawn back into the fray. It was easier than ever now the internet was around. He'd found himself surfing the dating sites in his spare time, signing up for free and checking out who might be a suitable match. The first time he'd found what he thought was a nice woman – liked to spend cosy nights in, watching movies – he'd bucked up the courage to mail her, then hadn't even received a response. Despondent, he'd kept away from the site for a fortnight, before finally receiving an email to say he'd had a reply.

Valerie had been away on holiday when he mailed, and yes of course she'd like to talk more. She'd seemed ideal, but when they actually came to meet it had been a disaster. Not on his part – it never was – but because she wasn't what she'd said at all. Turned out she liked nightclubs and picking up blokes by the dozen. She hadn't been on holiday either, she'd been in contact with several men on that same site (and Lord knows how many others on different ones).

Reluctantly, and in desperation, he'd tried a few more profiles, each one more disastrous than the last. GSOH? You'd need one to cope with all the catastrophes: most didn't know what they wanted from a man (or from life in general), others were just straight up crazy. Some had lasted a few days, others a few weeks, but inevitably he got the same response he had out there in the real world. Towards the end, and now seeing forty approaching like the edge of a cliff, he'd also been getting a new brush off: "You're just carrying too much baggage." He'd ask them what they meant, and they'd tell him they could see it on him – like he was dragging around the weight of all those romantic fiascos. You get to a certain age, it's only natural for a person to have some history. Right?

Not as much as him, apparently.

In a strop, he'd given up. Closed all his accounts and walked away from the whole scene. Then another one of those damned emails had arrived in his inbox. From *Date-a-Match*, the one site he must have overlooked – perhaps one of the first he ever signed up to, way back when. 'Gina' had read his profile and wanted to chat. She was new to the area and it seemed like they might have things in common. Nicholas' finger had hovered over the delete button, but something made him click 'open' instead. To his amazement, he then found himself clicking on the link to her profile.

No picture, but his eyes scanned the words: 'Honest and loyal' (yeah, he'd heard that before), 'looking for that special someone' (doesn't exist) and 'have been hurt in the past' (hasn't everyone?). In spite of the fact that last line rang warning bells, said she might be on the rebound just like Julie, Nicholas mailed her back and they struck up a conversation. Like him, she was giving it one last try. Fresh city, fresh start and all that. Nicholas found himself warming to her. They actually did seem quite compatible, and eventually she gave him her mobile number. He rang it and they ended up chatting for three hours, about everything and anything. Forgetting himself, Nicholas found a huge grin appearing on his face as they revealed more and more of themselves, the guards slowly dropping. What he was hearing in Gina was a kindred spirit. Someone who appeared to have suffered just as badly as him on the dating scene.

"I can't explain it," she told him. "None of this makes any sense to me." It could have been him talking.

Now they'd arranged to meet, at a local wine bar one Saturday afternoon. Gina was late and Nicholas feared the worst. That was what set him thinking about the 'baggage' problem. Whether Gina would see it, just like the others – realise he was a bad long-term investment and just walk back out through the door. He hadn't even thought about how she might look yet. She'd seen his picture on his profile, but he hadn't seen one of her.

Thankfully, when she arrived, apologising for being late – she'd been doing some more unpacking and lost track of time – she was exactly how he'd imagined her.

Her beam when she sat down at the table lit up the whole room, and when she kissed Nicholas on the cheek he felt tingly all over. Again, they sat and talked, and the afternoon fell away. Nicholas found himself opening up to her about his previous attempts at dating, even laughing at some of the most painful memories.

"Sometimes I worry," Gina said, playing with her long, chestnut hair and taking a sip of the Chardonnay he'd bought her, "that nothing will ever work out all right. Don't you?"

Nicholas nodded, having a drink of his lager. Then he looked at her, concerned he was putting out those vibes again: that she'd see he was carrying too much baggage; that he was damaged goods. But she said it first: "I'm always being told I hold on to too much from my past. You know, from the guys who hurt me."

And that was it. That was the moment he knew Gina was the woman for him. A female *version* of him, to be frank.

That was when he began to fall for her.

Before they knew it, the barman was calling last orders and Gina looked at him, a little the worse for wear after her wines. "I don't usually... I'm quite a cautious person, but, well, my place isn't too far away if you want to come back for a coffee...maybe?" She smiled again, but it was a nervous one.

Don't do it, he thought to himself. *Don't ruin things by asking if she's sure.* He remembered Julie, and although it had probably been a good thing in the long run he still thought to himself 'what if?' But he was a different person now, why shouldn't he go back with Gina?

"Look, it doesn't matter," she said, smile fading.

"Yes," he replied, a bit too quickly. "That would be lovely."

The beaming smile returned.

So they got a cab back to her home, a rented two bedroom that was slightly further away than she'd implied. "Ignore the mess, won't you? I'm still getting straight," she said, leading the way inside. He would have said "What mess?" but it *was* pretty cluttered. Gina had been right when she said she was still in the middle of unpacking stuff. There were boxes and bags everywhere.

She told him to wait in the living room, while she fixed that coffee. He hadn't expected an actual drink, but was glad when she went off to the kitchen. It gave him time to calm down a little. He knew things were going way too fast, but for once in his life he was willing to take that chance.

For Gina, only for her.

When she sat next to him on the sofa, the tentative kiss that followed felt natural. Like something that was meant to happen. "Hmm, that was nice," he said. Then Nicholas suddenly realised he desperately needed to pee; the coffee mixed with lager had gone right through him. "Hold that thought," he told her, excusing himself with another kiss. Gina nodded, relaxing back on the sofa.

Looking for the bathroom, he made a wrong turn, stumbling into another small room instead. He'd flicked the light on before he realised, noting more bags and crates. The spare room obviously, where Gina had dumped the worst of the detritus from the move. He was about to flick the light off again when Nicholas caught sight of something. One of the holdalls closest to him was open a fraction. Maybe it was his imagination, or the drink, but he thought he saw a finger sticking out.

Nicholas frowned, moving forwards. Wanting to reassure himself that it couldn't be, then needing to see more when he discovered he was right. His own fingers shook as he reached out for the zip, but before he could pull it down he looked past the bag to another one beyond. There was the tip of a foot emerging from that one, toes clearly visible. Next to that was a closed suitcase, but there were tufts of hair trapped where it had been closed.

He didn't need to open that first zip now, because he knew what was inside. The sickly-sweet smell of air freshener alone, which Nicholas was suddenly aware of, gave it away. Masking another smell entirely. It made him cough. Now he knew why Gina was usually such a cautious person.

"I told you to *ignore* the mess," he heard from behind. "What a terrible shame."

Whirling around, he saw Gina with a kitchen knife in her hand. Then suddenly she was plunging it into his chest. He looked down, mouth open. All he could think was, at least it wasn't in his back.

"I knew it was too good to be true, that sooner or later you'd find out *how much* baggage I was carrying from my past. It's probably just as well, Nicholas; they all end in disasters, my relationships. Better to strike first, before *I* get all the heartache. Too bad. I was beginning to like living here, as well."

Nicholas shook his head as he stumbled backwards and fell. It could have been different for them. Might have worked out.

Christ, what was he saying?

"I'm sorry," she said, blood dripping from her knife. There were genuine tears in her eyes, but no trace of that smile. "I really, really am. I honestly thought— No, it doesn't matter."

Nicholas' eyes, conversely, were bone dry. From the floor where he lay, staring up at her, one thought was nagging at him: still he was wondering what might have been.

If he could find anything positive about the fact that he was dying, it was this: Gina, it seemed, was fated to live with all of her previous encounters. Couldn't part with them, no matter what. And he would soon add to her burden, his body crammed into a bag, suitcase or crate. Ironically, it would probably be the longest relationship he'd ever had or would have with a woman, especially now.

Gina had so much baggage, but she'd actually done him a favour.

Because now, as the darkness took him, Nicholas realised he had finally, at last, been freed from his own.

Forever.

SIN

When the box arrived, it was treated as suspicious from the start.

For one thing, it was left on the steps of the police station – rather than being brought with the rest of the post. Nothing was signed for, and it was delivered very early; it was still quite dark outside. The parcel was simply left, and reported by some of the early morning shift heading in to work. One young officer called Wells even made a joke about it, effecting Brad Pitt's gravelly tones as he asked: "What's in the box? What's in the goddamn box?"

Not particularly funny, given that the whole station was being evacuated at the time and the bomb squad was called in to make sure the package was safe. From a distance, they all watched as men dressed in heavily-padded clothing approached the oblong and went about their business, finally signalling that it wasn't an explosive device; not that anyone had ever targeted their small station, in their small town (which had only recently been granted city status; some argued prematurely). He'd never thought it was. Somehow he'd known this was connected with the case, his detective's intuition or 'Spider-sense' he'd always relied on – that and the size and shape of the container.

Because, when the people who had opened it reported back on the contents, they confirmed that not only wasn't it about to go off and take out half the street, that this wasn't in fact Gwyneth Paltrow's head either, they conveyed instead that it was what looked like a foot. A human foot, severed at the ankle.

The killer had finally given one back.

As DI Patrick Hammond approached the – now unwrapped and open – box to peer inside, he felt his stomach rolling. Not because of the colour of the foot, grey almost white, nor the fact that from his angle he could see right down inside to the crimson meat packed around the bone, bits of ragged flesh skirting the edges where the foot had been sawn off. It was more because he knew whose foot this was, even before he spotted the star tattoo just below the ankle bone, standing out more than ever now against the starkness of the dead skin.

Knew it belonged to *her*, the woman he loved.

Wouldn't take the pathologist Dr Foxborough to verify that the foot had been attached to one of the most recent...no, *the* most recent victim. Wouldn't take matching this against any of the corpses that had been stacking up these past few months in the morgue: all missing one foot; the left or the right, it didn't seem to matter which. This one particular foot they wouldn't be able to match against a corpse they had back there, because she was still missing – an abductee.

And now amputee, his mind provided; sometimes it just didn't know when to shut up. Hammond fought to hold back the tears at this, fought to control the memories that were coming back to him, of kissing that foot, of kissing the toes covered in ruby red nail polish – and which were still that same colour, if more than a little faded and chipped now. It helped with his composure that his boss, DCI Eddie Balfour – a man who bore more than a passing resemblance to Homer Simpson, right down to the yellow tinge of his skin which was due to a liver complaint – was now standing beside him.

"Fuck," the balding man whispered, which simultaneously said nothing and everything. It was a good job the press were being held back behind a cordon, otherwise they might have taken that as an official statement – and it was as good as any, Hammond supposed. Probably more than he could muster himself. Then Balfour asked his DI: "What do you make of it?"

Hammond opened his mouth, and closed it again just as quickly. Shook his head. It was better not to speak at that moment, better to say nothing than let it all spill out.

"Looks like a job for Sherlock Holmes to me," said a voice from behind them, that same wet behind the ears tosser Wells who'd been doing the Pitt impressions earlier on.

"Come again?" asked Balfour.

"Well, y'know, the game is a foot," the officer clarified, then sniggered. Hammond looked at the ground, gritted his teeth, the clenching of his jaw causing a muscle in his cheek to twitch. He felt like lunging for the man, pounding his head into the pavement – but gallows humour was part and parcel (very poor choice of words) of their job. How many crime scenes had he visited and made jokes at, because he didn't know the vics, because if you didn't you'd go stark, staring mad. Poor unfortunates who'd had their hands bound behind their backs and hung, only to be met with gags like, "He'll be tied up for a while…"; people stabbed, only for some smart arse to state they "Got the point…"; electrocutions that were "Just shocking", and if it had been delivered by this pillock, then no doubt the Connery accent would have been wheeled out. Different, though, when it was someone you knew, wasn't it? Someone you cared more about than anyone – anything – in this whole world. Loved so much, but couldn't show that you did. A secret love that—

"You get it?" prompted the young lad. "That's what he used to say, Sherlock Hol—"

Release valve or no release valve, Hammond was seconds away from having this joker.

"Yes, yes," said Balfour, waving the officer away like the nuisance he was. Like a fly buzzing round that didn't know how close it had come to getting swatted. "Very good. You'll be live at the Apollo doing stand-up in no time... If you're not careful."

The officer got the hint about his job and sauntered off. "Twat," Hammond couldn't help muttering.

When he looked up again, he saw that Balfour was watching him, studying him. He had to be careful with that kind of shit – not because he was ashamed or anything, but because he would get taken off the case. He'd be no use to anyone then, especially *her*. "This one's really getting to you, isn't it?"

Hammond gave a half-shrug that was perhaps a little too exaggerated. "Shouldn't have got this far. We should have had the bastard by now. Before..." He nodded at the box, but couldn't bring himself to look at it again.

Balfour placed a hand on his shoulder. "Don't beat yourself up about it." What he actually meant, and what had been coming across since this investigation began, particularly in certain narrow-minded quarters was: "What's the big deal? They're only prostitutes." The papers had said pretty much the same thing, after sensationalising those first few disappearances; letters columns especially, commenting that these women knew the risks, that they kept putting themselves out there amongst all these perverts – what did they expect to happen? Wasn't as simple as that, wasn't as clear cut. Yes, there might have been a time of day when Hammond would have agreed, but he knew so much about that world now – so much about the brave women who inhabited it. Knew one intimately. To him, it *was* a big deal – not least because these were people, living breathing people (or had been), some of them with families. Hell, some only did this *because* they had families to support. But maybe he'd been underestimating Balfour, because when he continued the man said: "We have a lead now, at any rate. Our biggest clue yet."

Or maybe he was just keen to get this one sorted, get it off the books because it was making them all look bad. If the press got hold of this new turn of events, it would like as not send them into another feeding frenzy. Either way, it was time to take a step back now and let Foxborough and the SOCOs do their work.

Take a step back? If only he could.

She certainly wouldn't be able to now, would she? his mind said, at it again – reminding him of what she'd lost. Maybe even her life? It explained why he'd not been able to get hold of her in days, all that worry hadn't been wasted after all. Every morning Hammond would wake up expecting there to be another body; expecting it to be hers. Though not expecting this, never expecting this.

Hadn't he begged her not to keep going out there? Indeed, the last time they'd seen each other they'd argued about it, and he regretted that massively. She'd seen it as him telling her what to do, when that was the last thing he wanted – nobody could ever tell her what to do, she was much too strong for that. No, he just wanted her to be safe and – be honest – he was getting to the point where the thought of all those hands on her, what those men she went with did to her, was driving him crazy.

Should have said something, should have told her how you really *feel.*

That he wanted to spend the rest of his life with her, take her away to the coast like she'd talked about that time, wash away all this dirt and grime and filth. Live the life he...they'd always wanted, that she'd been trying to save up for all these years and failing. That although he couldn't promise her the world, he could at least give her his heart, his devotion. But he hadn't said any of those things, had he? Didn't seem the time or place when they were having a slanging match, and suddenly things were coming out of his mouth that he really didn't mean:

"If that's how you want it, then fuck off and get yourself killed."

Be careful what you wish for. Hammond was wishing for something else entirely now, though, wasn't he? Something he'd asked Foxborough when they visited him later.

"Is the vic...is she still alive, Doctor?"

Foxborough had looked up at him from his position over the metal table, those bulging eyes rotating in his direction like gun turrets ready to fire. Mouth open and poised to shoot him with information that could wound or kill as effectively as any bullet. "She was when the foot was severed, anyway, that I *can* tell you."

Hammond closed his own eyes, rubbed his face. Not quite the answer he was looking for, but it would do. It gave him hope. Wasn't a dead body, just a dead right foot: there on the table, staring up at him as accusingly as Foxborough.

"Of course, chances of re-attachment now are slim – it's way past the six-to-twelve-hour window, and that's if it had been packed in ice."

So, that perfect body was mutilated for life. She'd never be whole again, and it was all his fault. If only he'd got to the bottom of this earlier. If only—

"There were no clues as to the identity of the person who did this from the foot, the wrapping or box. No prints, DNA. Nothing," Foxborough told them, as if he thought he was being helpful.

"But we do know who the victim is, thanks to Inspector Hammond," Balfour had said from his position beside him again. Hammond had told them he'd spoken to a few of the contacts he'd cultivated on this case, asked who hadn't been seen in a while – it wasn't a lie, he had made sure she hadn't been around lately on her usual patch. Said it like he hadn't known immediately who the foot's owner was; said it as if he hadn't really known the vic at all and wasn't biting back the yelp that almost followed when he spoke her name.

"And we have a lead on who left the package," Balfour added. "CCTV outside the station picked up the license plate of the delivery van – driven by one Mr Gerry Millard. We're confident he had nothing to do with it, seeing as he didn't make any attempt to disguise himself as he left *that* on the steps. He was just doing his job, basically."

"He didn't think it strange that he had instructions to leave it there?" asked Foxborough, poking at the foot again with one of his instruments.

Balfour shrugged. "Christ knows. To be honest, after speaking with him I'm not sure the man's all there." He tapped the side of his head. "If you know what I mean?"

"Your average delivery man, then," said Foxborough without any hint of humour this time; Foxborough didn't really do jokes, and if he did they were so deadpan they weren't really recognised as such.

"Anyway, he checks out – mainly because we have more CCTV from the depot where the delivery was arranged, of the actual person who paid for it." A solidly built man, wearing a padded coat, jeans and hoodie, which was up; who kept his head turned or tilted away from the camera – had probably scoped the place out beforehand a few times – and paid in cash so there was no card to trace. The woman who'd dealt with him couldn't remember much more than they'd seen themselves, because they dealt with so many people in a day. Nevertheless, the grainy picture was being circulated around the troops and through the media – the only time they actually were of use. Nothing as of yet.

Hammond had spent a long time staring at that image, staring at his enemy. The person who had done this to her. To so many others before her. He recalled the first of them now, left in a skip down an alleyway like so much trash; some would argue that's what she was, where she belonged. But Maggie Graham hadn't deserved that end – *nobody* deserved that. Not even animals deserved to be treated so poorly; and some of those same people would put their pets above the human lives in question here.

Maggie, staring up, glassy-eyed, with her tongue lolling out black – a thin red line around her neck where she'd been garrotted. Staring up from her final resting place amongst the crisp packets, beer bottles and half-empty cartons of junk food – her frizzy hair actually containing bits of that food. They hadn't noticed the missing left foot until some of that rubbish had been cleared away, each bit taken to be painstakingly examined – the skip itself scrutinised for prints and anything else that might have given the killer away, though they'd yielded the same results as this most recent find. It had been removed quite clumsily, really; torn away from the ankle when the saw had nearly finished its job, like a lumberjack hacking impatiently at branches. They had no idea why, until the next body had been found washed up out of the local canal.

Phoebe James was missing that same appendage, except it was the right not the left. Where Maggie still had some of her clothes on, half of Phoebe's were torn or missing, though whether that was to do with being in the water for so long was debatable. She was younger than Maggie's thirty-eight, but strangely looked older – and that definitely had nothing to do with the canal's attentions, because Hammond had seen photos of her when she was still alive. Drugs and alcohol abuse were to blame, something he suspected she did to take her mind off her job and which had become a vicious circle; the only way she could pay for her cravings. Phoebe had been garrotted as well, the same MO. That was when they knew they had a multiple murderer on their hands. When they found victims three and four – Willow Clark and Vera Humphreys (the oldest of the bunch at forty-five), one in a car park and the other in woods not that far away – they knew they definitely had a serial killer on their hands.

To begin with, certain resources had been at their disposal, in spite of the fact that recent budget cuts had meant even beat patrols had become a luxury of late. Stake-outs to watch these 'ladies of the night' – as someone poetically called them; it was the politest term Hammond had heard during all this time – even an undercover officer posted on a few street corners for a week or two. WPC Charlotte (Charlie) Grant, the subject of many a male fantasy at their station, even before they saw her done up in that plastered on make-up, wearing a leather mini-skirt and vest-top. Hammond had winced at the dirty language she had to put up with as she walked through corridors on her way to do her duty – the wolf whistles and propositions, from single and married officers alike. To her credit, she'd given back as good as she got – she'd learned to do that very quickly when she joined the force, rather than running off to report it as so many of her colleagues had done and come up against brick walls. But that still didn't make it right.

Keeping an eye on her those evenings in his unmarked car, Hammond had been given a first-hand taster of the life of those women who risked everything out here. Seeing the trouble she'd gotten into a few times, though again Charlie had handled herself well, only having to pull her badge a couple of times. They'd been false alarms, of course; not the guy they were looking for. He never showed on those evenings, or at least he never had a crack at Charlie.

And Hammond couldn't help thinking, as he watched her putting her own life on the line for a different reason altogether, that as good looking as Charlie was, she still wasn't a patch on his girl. On *her*.

On his Ella.

Only that wasn't what she called herself, wasn't even what she wanted him to call her, not at first anyway. That name had slipped out when she hadn't been focussed one night, when she'd had a bit too much to drink. He'd tried to find out more, but she'd clamped up on that occasion. If she'd been with anyone else but him, they might have forced her to tell – forced her to do a lot more besides. But he didn't; he respected her privacy. Respected *her*, actually.

A surprise, really, given how they'd met. It had been a private bash thrown by a local 'businessman' a year or more ago, to get both members of the criminal underworld and a corrupt police force on side. Hammond couldn't say that he was entirely comfortable with those fraternities rubbing shoulders at the shin-dig, but was well aware of how it all worked in this town – corrupt politicians mediating between them more often than not. Backs were scratched on a regular basis, the odd blind eye turned; checks and balances, was how it had been explained to him. The alcohol had flowed – and probably much harder stuff out of sight – and as part of the evening's entertainment, 'escorts' had been laid on (though it was clear to anyone with half a brain that these girls hadn't come from any kind of established escort company). A string of them had been paraded in front of Hammond, and he'd been asked to pick which one he wanted: black; oriental; Indian… "Whatever floats your boat," he'd been told, by the fellow who'd brought them in. A snivelling little weasel who seemed to live to please.

Back in the day, back before Ella, he probably wouldn't have hesitated – just like the married Balfour, pointing out a thin, athletic girl, the exact opposite of himself. They'd then disappeared upstairs in the hotel where the party was being held. If he was being honest, Hammond was about to refuse the offer…when he saw *her*. She looked stunning, with that golden hair taken up and in that blue off the shoulder dress which clung to every curve of her; a choker at the neck completing the outfit (he genuinely hoped now that hadn't been an omen of things to come).

But he wasn't looking at her body – not really. It was those equally blue eyes he spotted first, being fanned by huge black eyelashes; that cute button nose and lips which looked naturally red, though he could have been wrong. Her expression, aided by the fair eyebrows that were slightly raised, was one of innocence – at odds with the profession he knew even then she was in. It didn't so much make him want to *have* her, as protect her – not that she needed it, as he later discovered. No, Ella was tough – and she'd been through so much.

While he was standing there, gaping, probably even had his mouth wide open, one of the other men in the room came over and approached her. Hammond recognised him as a lowlife called Nichols, involved in hardcore fetish webcam sites and not averse to knocking his performers about if the rumours were correct. "Hi there, beautiful," he said, practically drooling over Ella. He rubbed a finger down her cheek and across her chin, which made Hammond's stomach flip; particularly when he saw those blue eyes of hers brush the floor.

He couldn't help himself – before he knew it, he was cutting in, grabbing Nichols' arm and lowering it. "I think you'll find she's spoken for," Hammond insisted, as if he was some half-arsed knight of old.

"That so?" replied the man, snatching his arm away.

Hammond didn't want any trouble, not here, so he looked over to the guy who'd told him he could pick whichever girl he wanted. A guy who also knew he was a copper. "Gentlemen, gentlemen, I'm sure we can work something out," he'd said in those same sycophantic tones.

"I'm sure we can," said Hammond, eyes narrowing – a threat he couldn't really carry out implied; to look a bit more carefully into Nichols' affairs, perhaps?

"Hey, hey. Plenty more to choose from," said the intermediary, his voice practically begging Nichols to let it go. There was a moment or so, when the criminal looked from Ella, to Hammond, to the toadying man – a moment when it could have gone either way – then thankfully he backed off, hands raised. No harm, no foul. The sycophant led him over to the other girls and he seemed happy enough to go with a brunette that had a chest which looked like it had been inflated with a bicycle pump. Leaving Hammond with Ella. Except he hadn't known she was Ella back then. Back then, she'd introduced herself as:

"Sindy."

"With a 'C'?" he'd asked her, like *that* mattered.

She'd shaken her head.

Like the doll, then? he'd thought to himself, but didn't say it. *A plaything – from her childhood?*

"I'm Hammond. Patrick."

Already, she was gesturing for them to leave, to head upstairs. Hammond went with her, more because he wanted to get away from everyone else than anything, but found himself tongue-tied as they headed for the lift. She pressed the button and stepped inside, and he followed – would have followed her anywhere, he realised at that moment. As they ascended, he caught her looking across at him, and she smiled, said: "I'm glad."

"Sorry?" Hammond replied, eventually finding his voice.

"Glad it was you," she explained. "And not him."

"Oh," he said.

When they got to the room, one of those allocated for use by 'guests' at the party, she'd entered first again and he'd trailed her inside. She'd told him to make himself comfortable, while she poured a glass of champagne from a bottle provided. He took off his jacket, loosened his tie, and sat on the bed, accepting the glass gratefully from Sindy. But when she suddenly stepped back and reached around, pulling down the zipper on the back of her dress, he stood up again. "No, no, wait... Don't."

She'd looked puzzled then, and he felt terrible – didn't want her to think he didn't find her attractive. It wasn't that; dear God, it *so* wasn't that. He just didn't want to spoil things – the sight of her in that dress, the illusion of her, the...perfectness of her. "Oh, no. I don't mean... I just..."

Then a look of realisation washed over her face. "You want me to keep my clothes on? I get it."

He shook his head and the bewildered expression returned. "Can we just... I mean, is it okay if we just spend some time together?"

The concept was clearly alien to her. She was probably used to men grabbing and tearing at her, not being able to wait to get her out of her clothes and into bed. "O-kay," she replied, unsure.

Hammond wasn't quite certain what he was doing, either.

He nodded for Sindy to sit down on the bed with him and they sat in silence for a while, until one of them – he could never remember which – broke it with some nonsense. Chit-chat about nothing really, what they'd seen on TV recently, at the cinema, what kind of food they liked. Awkward at first, but then flowing more easily. And the rest was just a blur, his mouth working, words coming out, but concentrating, fixated on her face – those eyes!

Right up until the moment she noticed the clock. "Is that the time – listen, I've really got to go."

"But it's only..." Hammond followed her gaze to the bedside clock and realised it was almost midnight; not late, but not really early, either.

"They only paid us until twelve," she explained.

"Then maybe we could..." he began, but she was already standing, already walking towards the door. "No, wait!" he called after her. "*I'll* pay you."

Sindy turned the handle, shaking her head. "No. I really should be going. I enjoyed meeting you, though, Pat. I honestly did."

And suddenly she was gone, as quickly as she'd appeared in the first place. Dipping in and out of his life. Hammond raced to the door, but the lift was already descending. He stabbed at the buttons, but it didn't stop. He raced to the stairs, raced down them, though by the time he reached the foyer, there was no sign of Sindy. Hardly anyone around at all from the party.

He'd spoken to the people who'd organised it, however, asked about her – and it was as he'd thought, Sindy hadn't been hired via any kind of agency, but through recommendations. "I'm not surprised you want to see her again, the things she can do," one guy he'd spoken to had said and Hammond's lip curled.

It took him a while to track her down, a week or so and on his own time, but it was what he did – as a detective (*can't track her down now, though, can you? as much as you'd like to*). She'd been in an area of town notorious for that kind of activity when he spotted her, leaning back against a wall and having a drag on a cigarette. Her hair was down over her shoulders this time, clothing much less classy than it had been the night of the party; the coat with the fake fur collar looked positively shabby by comparison. Not that any of it mattered to Hammond, not even a little bit. To him, she looked Heaven-sent in the glow from the street-lamp.

He'd crawled up to the curb, risking all kinds of trouble – risking his career, but not caring. And she'd kicked back off the wall, gone to engage her next client only to find Hammond leaning across as the passenger side window came down. "Patrick?" she'd said, looking left and right – probably wondering if she was about to get arrested, knowing as she did what line of work he was in. "W-What are *you* doing here?"

He found that he couldn't really answer that, now he'd been asked. So he just said, "I was wondering...if maybe you'd like a coffee or something?"

"A coffee?" She glanced about her again, nervous. "I'm working. You...you really shouldn't be here."

"Then tell me to go away."

She opened her mouth to speak and he swore his heart missed a few beats until the words came out, fearful that Sindy was just going to tell him to get lost. "Please," she said then. "I can't."

He was bringing out his wallet, opening it up – really putting himself in the frame if he got caught.

There was a time and a place, and out in public wasn't it. "If it's money then—"

"Put that away, Patrick." She climbed into the car with him and he drove off, taking her for that coffee. It had been the start of his seeing her on a semi-regular basis; whenever he could, and wherever. He'd taken her for coffees, drinks, meals, even out to see films a couple of times – but hadn't wanted to rush anything else. Sindy had always refused any offer of cash, which only fed into his delusions that he was, what, dating her? He'd often ask himself just what the hell he thought he was doing. If he got caught, a copper seeing a prossie – and not in the usual way – it would be the end of him, even in this town. But then he'd think of that face again and all would be right with his world.

He was keenly aware of the age difference as well, Hammond being a good few years older than Sindy, but she never made an issue of it – then again, why would she? Sindy was used to dealing with men of all ages and making them feel good about themselves. No, it wasn't that – *couldn't* be that! There was something more between them, he could feel it. Could sense it with that same detective's intuition which told him when things weren't right, when people – even expert liars – were hiding the truth.

Expert liars like a woman who could be anyone for anybody? Could play any part, from a dominatrix to a schoolgirl? Hammond always shook away the thoughts before they could take hold – it would only ruin how he thought of her, his Sindy. His Ella.

And they'd slept together eventually, of course they had – at his flat, never hers – though the first couple of times they'd come close, he hadn't been able to bring himself to. "It's okay," she'd told him. "Happens to everyone sometimes." He'd nodded, not able to explain it was the sight of Sindy in all her glory that had done it, the reality even more breathtaking than he could have possibly imagined; the thought that all he could offer her was his lacking body, past its prime but every molecule of it hers if she wanted. Then it had happened, and it was like nothing he'd ever experienced before. All the others in the past, including Karen who he'd almost married, were like shadows – pale imitations of the real thing.

Real emotions, real feelings. Real...love.

The subject had come up more than a few times after that, about their respective occupations. He'd even felt brave enough, after talking about his own history – growing up in a family where you either landed on one side of the law or the other, and sometimes straddled both – to ask her how she'd gotten into this game, if you'd pardon the expression. He thought she wasn't going to answer him at first – it took so much for her to let her guard down, to properly trust. But then he found out why. She'd spoken in vagaries about a dead father, and about how things had changed after that; about a step-mother she hadn't seen eye-to-eye with and had her own kids anyway; about running away, living rough from the age of sixteen – about a woman called Ruth who'd taken her under her wing for a little while and shown her the ropes of that particular world, before moving on to bigger and better things. Last she'd heard of the woman, she'd married rich, taken on a daughter of her own.

It had been a start, however, and this job was a way for her to earn a bit of money, not be reliant on anyone. Be self-sufficient. But oh, those dreams of the coast, of being by the sea. She'd always loved the sea.

Not the time nor the place to talk about her jacking it all in, just being with him – even if it meant moving to somewhere else entirely. And the more Hammond left it, the harder it became; the more he felt it would look like trying to strong-arm her, that he was attempting to take over her life, tell her what to do. That hadn't happened until the murders began...

Then he'd started, subtly at first with the warnings – that it wasn't safe out there. "Patrick, it never *has* been," she would tell him.

Finally, in the end, he'd argued with her about it; hadn't been able to get her to see reason. To see the danger. He'd even offered her the money if she'd stay off the streets, which she'd taken quite badly. That had led to the row, and those words he wanted to take back so much. That he couldn't now she was gone; now that bits of her were being sent to them. The first time their killer had kept the body (no, they didn't *know* she was dead) and just sent the foot. A reversal of all the other times – but why?

The cutting off of the feet had led them to conclude they might be dealing with a fetishist, which in turn had led to them trawling sites where those kinds of people hung out. Sites like the ones Nichols ran (he'd actually been a suspect for all of five minutes). Or more specifically a young DC called Crabtree, who was an IT specialist, had been trawling them. He'd come up with some interesting finds as well, but nothing that ever amounted to anything concrete. This one threw everything into confusion, though; why would their perp give the foot away instead of keeping it as a trophy, like he must have done with the others.

Why. Keep. Sindy (Ella)?

Hammond had spent a couple of very sleepless nights – on top of the ones where he'd been worrying about her – trying to figure it out, but drawing a blank. Of course, it's always when you're trying of think of an answer that something else hits you. Something, which turned out this time to be just as important.

"It's been fucking staring us in the face, don't you see?" he'd said to Balfour. The man's expression told him that he clearly hadn't. "The box. The box that the foot was delivered in."

"What about it?" asked Balfour, still looking confused.

"It was a *shoe* box," Hammond stated.

"So what? Probably just because it was the right size and shape for a foot."

Hammond shook his head. "He could have used *any* kind of box. Didn't Crabtree say that a lot of the weirdos on those sites were into shoes as well?"

"And you're suggesting we arrest everyone who bought a pair of shoes in the last, what, ten years?" Balfour laughed.

"I'm saying what if our guy used that box because he had it to hand. What if he's around this kind of shit all the time? Works in a shoe shop, or a factory that—"

"Hammond, you're reaching. Whoever this is wouldn't be that stupid, not after covering themselves like they have."

"Didn't one of those knobs from the local college who came in to talk to us about psychology say that deep down all these creeps *want* to get caught?"

Balfour sighed. "We don't have the manpower to go talking to everyone in shoe factories all over the land, on the off-chance your flights of fancy are right."

"Just give me a few people. Look," he said as she wandered past, causing the woman to pause, "give me Charlie Grant – she's not assigned to anything at the moment. She knows the case."

Reluctantly, Balfour agreed: Charlie, plus a couple of other PCs, until the weekend – that's all he could spare. So they headed off to talk to those who had any kind of connection with the trade. There was a mall not that far outside of town, so they started there, Hammond and Charlie. Two large stores, but staffed with tweenies who barely had a brain cell to share amongst them. Certainly nobody who could have engineered half the things they'd seen, or would have wanted to. He'd caught Charlie examining the items on offer more than once and just rolled his eyes at her. "What?" she'd said in return. "Women and shoes..."

But it was as they'd grabbed a quick lunch of Mega-Burgers and fries there in the 'Oasis' that she'd said to him: "This is personal for you, isn't it?"

Wasn't just shoes women were known for, Hammond thought to himself, it was also their intuition; more powerful than anything he could muster. "How do you mean?"

Charlie took a sip of her Coke before answering. "I've seen you with this, like a dog with a bone. You care about those girls, don't you?"

"Of course," Hammond said, but didn't clarify that he cared about one more than any of the others.

"I like that," said Charlie, smiling at him and taking a bite of her burger. "You're a nice guy, Pat, you know that?"

He offered a smile back, but said nothing in return. A few years ago, before he'd met Ella, he would have been in there like a rat up a drainpipe. Would never have worked out, obviously, but that wouldn't have stopped him with a woman like Charlie; shit, he'd have been getting down on his hands and knees and kissing the ground that she might be interested. But there was no-one else for him now, never would be. That's what made it personal, and that's why he could never tell anyone about it.

They checked out a couple more places that afternoon, but it wasn't until the following day that there was a development. Nothing was reported by the other officers, and it was the last store on their list – a mom and pop place as the Americans might have called it, name of Watterson's – that bore fruit. It was run by an elderly man who had owned the shop since the 1960s and also offered shoe repairs, as well as selling new ones. They'd talked to him, looked around a bit, chatted to the assistants, and come up empty; no odd feelings that anything was wrong, nothing. It was only as they were leaving and Hammond happened to look up – his 'Spider-sense' swiftly and forcefully kicking in – that he saw the curtains twitch in the flat above the store. Could have been anything, just someone being nosy, but Hammond insisted on going back inside and asking about it. About who exactly lived *above* the store.

"Well, I do," said Mr Watterson. "Why?"

"Alone?" demanded Hammond.

The white-haired man had scratched his head. "Since my wife passed away. There's my son, of course. But he's only been back a few—"

Hammond wasn't listening anymore, had already clocked someone through the open side door – heading down the stairs, sloping away towards the back of the building. He pushed Mr Watterson aside, probably a little too roughly but then he wasn't thinking clearly; he was thinking only of Ella. Then Hammond was out through the back door himself and in pursuit, the man ahead of him running down the alley – and though it was only from behind, Hammond could see that he might well be a match for the person on that CCTV footage. That he might well be their guy.

"Stop!" he shouted, even though in all his years on the force that tactic had never, ever worked. In spite of his size, the man was fast and it had been a while since Hammond had set foot inside a gym, let alone used any of the equipment. He was lucky, though, in that there was a fence at the far end of the alley. The man leapt at it, scrambling to get over the top, but Hammond had his legs before he could reach that height. "Oh no you don't," he grunted, holding on to the writhing figure. Watterson's kid kicked out, catching Hammond in the cheek and pitching him backwards. Seconds later, he was up and over, leaving the inspector behind.

It took Hammond a bit longer to clamber over the fence, but he made it – and still had the man in sight: just. He was running towards the road now, not stopping even for the traffic. Hammond ran as fast as he could after him, halting cars coming from the left and right, one clipping him as it braked. "Bastard!" he growled, not even sure himself if he meant the driver or the man he was chasing.

There was a park ahead, and Hammond knew if the guy reached that he'd be lost. He put on a spurt, but had no chance of catching him before he reached the gates. Then, out of nowhere, Charlie entered stage left and flew at the figure – tackling him and bringing him to the ground. Hammond couldn't help grinning. She was already cuffing the bloke as Hammond joined them, winded and trying to catch his breath. "Thought I'd skirt around," she told him. "You did a good job of distracting him, though."

Hammond nodded his thanks to the woman and she nodded back – still having no idea what this actually meant to him.

*

The suspect had spoken not a word on the drive back in the car, and continued to remain silent in the interview room – even after a grilling from both Balfour and Hammond.

"You sure this is our guy?" his boss had asked when they'd taken a break.

"Why else would he have bolted?" argued Hammond.

"If I saw your ugly mug coming, I'd probably do a runner as well," replied Balfour, but he conceded his officer had a point. Why would the man have fled if he didn't have *something* to hide.

Turned out he did – not in the shop itself, which was scoured inch by inch, but in a shed on the allotment Toby Watterson's father owned but didn't really use any more. Toby had made use of it, though, as they'd soon discovered when they searched it and found all the missing – all the severed – feet inside, plus the handsaw that had been used to detach them. Not to mention what else they'd seen when a black light had been flashed around the place.

"The sick fuck," Balfour had whispered after he'd been told.

When Hammond confronted the man with photos from the scene, he'd looked up at the inspector and smirked; the grin threatening to split his fleshy face in two. Then that grin had turned into a giggle, before evolving into a full-blown guffaw.

"You think this is *funny*?" Hammond had snarled, rising and banging his fist down on the photos.

"Easy," Balfour cautioned, placing a hand on Hammond's arm – nodding over at the camera to remind him that the interview was being recorded for posterity.

Hammond nodded and took his seat again. The last thing they wanted was for Toby to get off because of a cry of police brutality – although right at that moment all Hammond wanted to do was ram his fist into that face. Ram it so hard it exploded out the back of the man's skull. But there was something he needed to know first.

"So you kept the feet, dumped the rest of their bodies."

"Only bit I needed," admitted Watterson, who'd become more talkative once he knew they had their evidence; even confessed to using thick bootlaces he'd then disposed of as his murder weapon of choice. He'd grown up around shoes, around feet – helped out in the shop sometimes, though he'd had to stop because the temptation was too much. The temptation to kiss the feet of female customers, to lick them (and Hammond again had to switch off the memories of doing the same with Ella). Inside that shed he'd been able to do whatever he liked with them, though, whenever he liked. It didn't bear thinking about.

"But why change it up? Why send us the foot this time?" Balfour enquired.

"And," Hammond asked yet again, "where is the rest of her? Is she even still alive?"

Toby Watterson merely shook his head, the remains of that smirk lingering. Hammond grimaced, his hand still balled into a fist.

"Answer me, *damn you!*"

"Patrick," Balfour warned again.

"Tell me!" Hammond said, getting up once more and rounding the table. Grabbing Watterson and screaming into his face, removing all traces of that smile. "Tell me you little shit, or so help me I'll—"

Balfour was there in a flash, pulling Hammond away. "*Inspector!*" But it took a couple more PCs to actually wrestle him out of the room. "What the hell has gotten into you?" asked the DCI when they were outside.

"What's the matter, did he put his foot in it?" said the smart-arse Wells; just passing by, wrong time, wrong place.

Definitely the wrong thing to say.

Hammond lashed out before anyone could stop him, striking the man with a fist that was still searching for a target. He backed off, backed away – looking around at startled faces, then down at the ground, at the copper rubbing his jaw. Then his eyes found Charlie in the corridor; she'd seen what had happened and they exchanged a look. Her lip was trembling and Hammond thought he saw her eyes watering – because she knew for sure now. Knew what she'd only suspected previously.

He got out of there before anyone had a chance to say anything, left the station and got into his old Nissan, driving away at speed. Hammond got about a mile from there before he had to pull over. Before he started slamming the steering wheel.

Before he started crying himself. Crying, and thinking that he might never, ever stop.

*

In light of what had happened, both inside the interview room and just outside it, Hammond was taken off the case and suspended.

The comedian Wells decided not to press charges, especially after Balfour explained that it was in his best career interests not to. It was all put down to the stress of such a high-profile investigation, although Charlie had called, left messages to say that if he needed to talk she was a good listener. Hammond didn't need to talk, he needed to know what had happened to Ella.

Had Watterson garrotted her, like the rest? Would she be found in some skip or washed up on the banks of the canal? It seemed less likely, the more time that passed, that they'd ever get the answer – and particularly when Hammond wasn't allowed access to the prisoner. And seemingly all but impossible once Watterson took his own life whilst in custody. He'd bitten into his wrists to open up the veins after being visited by a distraught father who'd essentially disowned him. Those family ties having more impact than any screaming policemen. You could take away belts and laces, but if someone was determined they could still find a way to end it and take their mysteries with them.

Mysteries like Ella.

Hammond would dream about her, when he could get to sleep, that was – often with the aid of large amounts of vodka. In those dreams she would be running towards him on a beach, like in all those god-awful romance movies. It was usually the thing that tipped him off he was dreaming in the first place, the running; but he would try to push that to the back of his mind and enjoy the fact he was with her again, even if he knew it wasn't real. He could look into those blue eyes, stroke that golden hair and kiss those lips. Then he'd wake abruptly, be wrenched away from her all over again and end up reaching for the vodka.

At some point he decided that he should visit her home. Not the one she had in town, that dingy bed-sit she'd tried to keep hidden but he'd followed her to one night anyway, just to be able to picture where she was when she wasn't with him (and not have to think about her with all those other guys). That had also given Hammond her second name, Tyrell, which was on the lease.

No, the place she'd come from. The place she'd told him about – if nothing else, her mother…her step-mother had a right to know exactly what had happened to her daughter, face-to-face rather than being told about it impersonally on the phone. If he couldn't have any part in Ella's future, then perhaps he could connect with her past. Sure, they hadn't got on (which family ever really did?), but they *were* still family – and family was all important. Family ties…

So, he'd got the address and set off – locating the property in a nice little corner of the suburbs.

Looking at all those houses, it was hard to imagine why Ella had left in the first place; he certainly wouldn't have done. Cushy, very cushy. Her mother was one Hester Tyrell, who was at Number 24, Langley Avenue: a white, two storey property with a 4x4 parked outside on the driveway that made the Nissan he was parking up look like a horse and cart by comparison. This family had money then, maybe not fortunes but they were doing all right. Again, he wondered what kind of argument could have led to Ella storming off and never coming back.

"If that's how you want it, then fuck off and get yourself killed."

He closed his eyes, breathing slowly in and out. Had to keep it together, at least long enough to get through this. Hammond climbed out and walked up the driveway, admiring the pretty arrangements of flowers in the front garden, the tiny tree in the middle of the lawn. When he reached the front door – ringing the bell as he did so – Hammond was surprised to see it open almost immediately. Standing there was a woman with dark grey hair, streaked through with lighter shades of the same colour. She was wearing a maroon dress that covered every inch of her, right up to the neck, and over the top of that a shawl – the effect of which was to make her look much older than she probably was. "Yes?" she asked eventually, her voice tinged with more than a hint of suspicion.

"Er...hell-hello. My name's Patrick Hammond, I hope you don't mind me dropping by but—"

"If you're selling something, then..."

He held up a hand. "No, no. Nothing like that. I know, well, I knew your daughter."

She looked at him sideways then, her suspicion deepening. "Which one?"

It was his turn to pause, then he remembered this woman had kids of her own. "Your step-daughter, Ella."

Hester Tyrell's face soured at the name.

"I was part of the investigation leading up to what happened," Hammond clarified.

"A policeman?" Hammond nodded. "Then I suppose you'd better come inside."

He was shown into and through a hallway with a set of stairs ahead, then right into a living room. The décor did little to dispel the old-fashioned air, tasteful but stuck somewhere in the mid-1930s. Hester Tyrell bid him to take a seat on the sofa, which had elaborately-carved wooden arms and was just as hard as it looked. "I-I expect you were told what happened," Hammond began. "About Ella's…disappearance."

The woman took a seat opposite him, but didn't lean back – instead keeping her posture very straight. Hammond had to wonder whether she'd ever really relaxed in her life. The fact she answered the door so quickly meant that she must have seen him pull up outside through those net curtains, the bay window affording her a view of the entire street from this angle. "I was informed, yes. Terrible business. But then, that was the kind of world she lived in, wasn't it."

A statement, not a question; Hammond ignored it. "I was wondering if you might be able to shed some light on her background at all? About her time living with you?"

Hester Tyrell let out a long breath. "She was a wilful child, right from the start. I should probably have thought twice about taking her on, but then I did so love her father."

"Mr Tyrell?"

She nodded. "He sadly passed away when she – when Ella was still only a little girl, really. Ten, eleven. She was the apple of that man's eye. And, between us, he was much too lenient with her. I did my best but, well, it explains a lot about where she ended up. A streetwalker! I ask you, how in God's name..." The woman shook her head in despair. "The shame of it. I'm glad we never had anything to do with each other after she left."

It was Hammond's turn to sigh. This wasn't exactly how he'd pictured the conversation going. "And you never re-married? No boyfriends or anything? No man of the house?"

"Mr Hammond," she said seriously, inching forwards but still keeping her back rigid, "I have loved only two men in my entire life, and I married them both. There have certainly never been any 'boyfriends', as you call them. Only suitors. Two of them, who courted me. The first, my sweet Kenneth, blessed me with my girls – but only after we were wed."

Suitors? Fucking hell, thought Hammond. The décor wasn't the only thing stuck in the past.

"Anything else would have been a sin, as you can probably appreciate."

"Oh, definitely," he replied, then straight away regretted the sarcasm in his voice. He needn't have worried, it wasn't even noticed as the woman continued her sermon:

"It's values such as these I have tried to instil in my daughters now that they're older," she stated, matter of factly. "I keep telling them, when it's the right one, you just know – don't you think?"

Now *that* Hammond did agree with. It's how he had felt the first time he clapped eyes on Ella.

As if reading his mind, she now asked: "And how did *you* know my step-daughter, exactly, Mr Hammond? Just through the case?"

"We were...I'm...I was her friend," he figured would be the safest answer.

She stared at him. "I see. And the man who did all this, he came to a bad end, I understand."

"He did."

"His guilt finally catching up with him. Agent of the Devil," Mrs Tyrell told Hammond, giving a sharp nod. "Oh, would you look at me," she suddenly said after a pause, "where are my manners? I haven't even offered you a drink. Tea, coffee?"

"Coffee, please," he said, "if you have it."

"Of course, just bear with me." He rose when she did, out of politeness. But when she disappeared into the kitchen – through an open doorway inside the living room – he couldn't help wandering around and looking at some of the pictures on the wall, hanging over the fireplace: photos of Hester's daughters when they were small wearing knitted cardigans, and with their hair cut short. There were no photos of Ella on display, however. Various religious mantras covered another wall, including one that caught his eye, footprints on a beach: *During your times of trial and suffering, when you see only one set of footprints*, the text said, *it was when I carried you.*

"Do you take milk, sugar?" a voice wafted in from the other room.

"Oh, er, black please," Hammond answered. It was then that he heard the creaking from upstairs, floorboards above him. Could have been the house settling, but it sounded a lot like a person. "Mrs Tyrell, are we alone in the house?" he called.

"Oh yes, quite alone," came the reply. "Apart from the cat, of course – he's probably hiding, doesn't like strangers you see."

Could be a cat, he supposed, but Hammond's Spider-sense was tingling like mad. He made his way across the room to the door Hester Tyrell had disappeared through. "So there's just you and—" He stopped, the kitchen was empty. No sign of Hester

Tyrell. What he did see, when he looked across the way, was a coat hanging from the back door, which was swinging open. A coat he recognised: the padded coat from that CCTV footage he'd studied so long and so hard.

No man of the house, my foo— Hammond thought, then was suddenly aware of someone behind him, someone swinging something, which connected with his left arm as he turned and sent it numb. He was shoved backwards, back into a small kitchen table by the large figure that had struck him; the large figure who must have been upstairs all this time. Hammond just about had the chance to move sideways before what he could now see was a cricket bat came crashing down onto the table beside him.

As he rolled off and onto the floor he took in the sight of the sturdy guy in front, a hoodie pulled up over his head. The bat was drawn back again, ready to take another swipe at Hammond, but he was ready this time. Barrelling into his attacker, he shoved him against the wall, causing all the air to explode out of the man's body. Hammond brought up the back of his skull, catching the guy under the chin and whipping his head back. Hammond retreated a step or two, tried moving his left arm, but found he couldn't; it was definitely broken. He didn't have much time to think about this, though, because the man was coming at him again, swiping the bat from side to side. He lunged and Hammond ducked, the bat striking one of the cupboards and smashing the wood to pieces, smashing some of the crockery inside as well.

Hammond punched the bloke in the face with his good hand, felt the satisfying splinter of bone as the nose exploded with redness. The man dropped the bat, hands going to his face, before Hammond followed this up with a knee to the stomach. The big man doubled over, as Hammond scooped up the bat and brought that down on the back of his head. His attacker fell forward and sideways, unconscious or dead – it didn't matter to Hammond.

"Thanks for this," he muttered as he carried the bat out through the back door and into the garden. Hammond quickly spotted where Mrs Tyrell must have gone, one door still open on what looked like a coal bunker. He should be calling for back-up, waiting until it arrived before going after the woman, but he had only one thing on his mind: Ella. This woman, her stepmother, was – as insane as it sounded – somehow responsible for what had happened to her, and he was going to get to the bottom of it no matter what.

Hammond reached the bunker, looked down at the steps which descended into the darkness. That wasn't completely true, there was a flickering light down there – breaking up the black. "Mrs Tyrell? I'm coming down there now, and just to warn you, I'm armed." It wasn't a lie, and though he would have preferred to have an armed response unit with him, or even a pistol himself, the weight of the bat was quite comforting as he made his way down those steps.

There were several of them, taking him what must have been deep under the garden – perhaps the property had come with this place originally? In any event, Hammond found the bottom step at last, looking around for the source of the light, which appeared to be some kind of lamp fitted to the wall. There was indeed coal still down here, for the fire inside the house, he assumed, but there was also something else. And, as his eyes adjusted to the dimness, he finally saw what it was.

Chained to the back of the bunker, slumped forward with matted hair over its face, was a body. Naked and filthy, Hammond could see this was a woman, a stripped woman, and it was a testament to the state of her that he didn't recognise Ella until his eyes dropped to take in the stump at the end of her right leg; the wound cauterised but still angry-looking.

"My...My God," he finally breathed out, taking a step towards her. Ella wasn't moving; and like the person who'd attacked him in the kitchen, it was unclear whether she was alive or dead.

"Your *God*?" came a voice off to the side of him, unmistakably Mrs Tyrell's. "Do you even have a God, Mr Hammond, liar and fornicator that you are?"

He was having trouble even processing any of this, didn't know how to answer. Hammond just wanted to go to Ella, to get her down from there. Mrs Tyrell stepped between them, casting a look backwards at her step-daughter. "She's where she belongs, your whore, in the filth and the dirt. Always wild, she was. Always unruly. I tried my best, tried to get her to follow the right path – but nothing ever worked, not even when I was forced to...correct her. Forced to punish her by locking her down here. Imagine how horrified I was when I finally discovered where she'd gone when she ran away, what she'd been up to. There was only one way I could see to help her, to *stop* her."

A streetwalker! Not any more.

"The others," Hammond managed. "You used what was happening to do this?"

Hester Tyrell let out a shrill laugh. "Of course not. Of course I didn't use it. I *initiated* it!"

Hammond's face screwed up. "You did what?"

"That agent of the Devil... He wasn't hard to find, on one of those perverted sites you must have looked into yourself. Wasn't hard to manipulate – he was halfway there already. An agent of the Devil to destroy the Devil's work. So much sin...so much..."

"Sin? Jesus. What do you call murder?"

"Do not blaspheme!" Mrs Tyrell shrieked. "And I did not kill *anyone*!"

"No, not you personally. But you sent the box, didn't you? You led us to him," spat Hammond.

"I knew someone would put it all together, you're *detectives*, after all. Doing good deeds. Well, some of the time. And it was an offering. An atonement of sorts, her road back to a righteous path."

"What was to stop him from turning you in? Watterson?"

"Oh, Heavens." She touched her chest. "I never even met the maggot."

"No, you had help. Your friend back there in the kitchen."

"My...my friend?"

"Or whatever you want to call him, your fucking suitor – whatever. Look, just get out of the way."

"My...? I don't understand."

"It doesn't matter, don't you get it? He's in a pool of blood back there. Now get the fuck out of the—"

The scream that followed didn't come from Mrs Tyrell; it came from behind him. Hammond wasn't expecting it, wasn't prepared for it – for the notion that Mrs Tyrell might have had more than one helper. Yet another guy, and for someone who thought all that was a sin she sure put it about. He whirled and began bringing the bat up, but it was knocked out of his hand by something else: a coal shovel, wielded by this newcomer. A shovel they then swung, missing Hammond only by inches – their intention to open him up.

"Shit!" he said, stumbling backwards and losing his footing because of a rogue piece of coal on the ground. Hammond landed awkwardly, banging his injured arm – the pain was incredible.

The scream turned into a voice: "What did you do to her?"

In spite of the agony he was in, Hammond couldn't help thinking: *who?*

"Anna...Mum, what did he do to Anna?" The man looked over towards Mrs Tyrell, before stepping forward so Hammond could see his...*her* face, framed by that same haircut he'd seen in those photos.

"I don't know, Diana," answered Mrs Tyrell.

Fuck! thought Hammond – it hadn't been a man at all, not in the CCTV footage at the post depot, not in the kitchen with the bat; probably not even in contact with Watterson on those sites! These were Tyrell's children, hers and Kenneth's girls – though easily mistaken for men at first glance, built as they were. Ella's damned step-sisters! Diana moved forwards, holding the shovel high like the Sword of Damocles over Hammond. "He can't be allowed to live," she stated.

"An eye for an eye?" said Hester Tyrell, like it was the most reasonable thing in the world.

"How about," said Hammond, getting his breath back, "turning the other fucking cheek!" He threw the piece of coal he'd tripped on, striking Diana in the face – hard. Causing her to drop the shovel. Giving Hammond time enough to get to his feet, to kick out at the woman. She went backwards, striking the bunker wall, which shook and rained coal dust on her. Biting down the pain, Hammond snatched up the shovel and ran into her with it, this time like a jousting knight. The blade rammed into her stomach, and she hawked up blood.

Now it was her mother's turn to scream, running at Hammond and drawing a carving knife she'd had behind her back. He turned to face her and was slashed across the chest for his trouble. "You crazy bitch!" he shouted, headbutting the woman.

Hester Tyrell staggered backwards, a cut opening on her brow. She snarled, then came at him again with the knife, holding it out in front of her. Hammond sidestepped the woman, then stuck his leg out, which sent her flying. He looked around for the only weapon left, snatching up the bat and hitting Mrs Tyrell as she was starting to pick herself up off the floor. Hammond's breath was coming in short bursts, slowing up finally. He looked over at the other body, slumped and held by chains.

Family ties...

"Ella," he said, dropping the bat and shambling across to her. Even after all this, she wasn't moving. Not even a twitch.

"*I did not kill* anyone!*"*

Hammond hoped against hope Tyrell had been telling the truth. Of course, one of those equally deranged daughters might have done the honours. He reached out, fingers trembling, and repeated her name. "Ella? Ella, it's Patrick."

Her skin was cold as he lifted her head up, but then she'd been in this place probably for weeks. "Ella, *please!*"

He couldn't see her eyes, because the hair was still hanging over them – couldn't see whether they were open or closed. But then there was a breath, a whisper, and he could see her smile beneath the dirt. "I-I knew you'd come," she managed. "I...I made a wish."

Hammond moved forward, letting her head rest on his shoulder, and now he cried simple tears of joy.

*

It was warm in the sun.

Warm on the beach as they walked along it. Ella wouldn't be running anytime soon, but the prosthetic he'd helped her with that morning, as she sat on the bed and he'd attached it to her stump, enabled her to make her way along the sand – arm in arm with Hammond. She got him to stop for a minute, and he thought it might be because she was sore, but it was only so she could look out over the sea. He'd found out why she loved it so much, the coast – it was where she'd lived growing up with her parents, her real parents. And then her and her dad – before he met Hester, before he'd died.

The things that woman, that *family* had put Ella through afterwards. Hammond didn't wonder any more about why she'd left, about what had placed her on the road to where she'd ended up. She'd finally let him in – trusted him with everything.

"You okay?" he asked her, brushing a strand of that golden hair out of her face now he was able to. Using the hand that was only recently free of its cast, up to above the elbow.

"Yeah," she answered, and smiled. She knew how much he loved her – should do, because he told her a million times a day. In fact, they told each other. Knew that the foot thing didn't bother him in the slightest, that she was still perfect in his eyes. He'd even drawn on that star in marker pen, to replace the tattoo, to make her feel better.

"It was never a star," she said as he did it, taking the pen from him and adding a stick underneath. "A wand. A magic wand, like the kind your fairy godmother uses."

"My fairy what?" he'd asked.

"Never mind," Ella had replied with a laugh.

As she watched the ocean, he watched her. He'd never let anything happen to her again, and she never wanted him to. They'd agreed to both leave their former lives behind and start afresh, out here. It had been the best thing either of them had ever done. Of course, the past has a way of coming back to haunt you – and news had reached them that week of the trial coming up.

"You sure you're okay?" he asked her again.

"Oh, yeah." She looked at him with those blue eyes. "I am. Just thinking about, well, y'know."

"I do," he told her.

"What do you think will happen to them?"

"If there's any justice, the judge will lock 'em up and throw away the key," Hammond answered. Incredibly, all three of the Tyrells had survived what happened, though with extensive injuries. Diana would never walk again, he'd been told, and there was a certain kind of justice in that alone. He just wished it was all three of them. Hammond put his arm around her shoulder. "I'll make sure of it," he promised her, knowing that with both their testimonies it should be enough to see the trio put away for life.

Then they could get on with their own lives. Maybe marry, have kids someday? They were subjects he hadn't dared broach, but he would, when the time was right; he wouldn't put things off this time. Ella had enough on her mind for the time being, though, enough on her plate. She'd get through it, of course, she was strong, tough. Actually, they'd both get through it as a couple.

"Come on," she said, starting to walk again and he fell in step at the side of her. "You can buy me an ice cream."

He chuckled. "With pleasure." And as they walked, he took one last look over his shoulder. Two sets of footprints, side-by-side. But if Ella happened to get tired, or her leg was aching, Hammond would pick her up and carry her in his arms. Then there would be only one pair.

Because then, as always from this point on, after all the trials and suffering were behind them, they would still be together.

They would be one.

THE CAVE OF LOST SOULS

The unforgiving wind whipped past as the flaming sun lost its grip on the sky. Chris Thompson pulled his coat tight around him and took another step towards the edge of the cliff.

Below, a lone seagull flew past, squawking at the stranger on its patch. *Oh God, to be so ignorant.*

"Chris? Chris!" a concerned voice behind him called. "Come away, it's not safe up here."

"It's not safe anywhere, didn't you know?" Chris murmured.

The soil was loose beneath his feet. One step and it would be over. But wasn't that what he wanted? To end it all, right here and now?

"Go away, Terry. I'm okay."

"Looks like it. Come back to the chalet, we can talk about—"

Chris moved closer to the drop.

Crumbling limestone broke away from the pinnacle and Terry grabbed him under the arms just in time. Denied the oblivion he sought, Chris broke down.

"It wasn't your fault. When are you going to realise that? Sandra knows it, wherever she is." Terry held him as sobs wracked his body.

"I-I should have been driving, not her. If I hadn't had that last drink..." His words dug deep into Terry's shoulder, buried forever.

The angry water crashed onto the shore, covering the tiny blanket of sand down there. Through soaking eyes Chris saw a dim light in the cove. It was coming from the very water's edge, where the waves pounded the cliff without mercy.

"I'm here for you, Christopher. That's what brothers are for."

Chris looked at Terry, then back at the cove. The light had gone.

"Let's get indoors," said his brother.

*

The sun was already high in the clouds as Chris made his way down the steep gravel path. His trainers were woefully inadequate for this terrain, but he didn't care.

Big brother (in more ways than one) had sat up with him most of the night – like he had so often recently – and was consequently still sleeping. Dead to the world in the chalet they'd hired for the weekend. It had been Terry's idea to get away from the city, if only for a few brief days. There were too many reminders of Sandra at home. Too many people around offering their condolences. *"I know how you must be feeling."* No, no they really didn't. How could they? He'd lost the only thing that mattered to him. Life was pointless. If only they'd gone together, that would have been something, at least. But to survive with hardly a scratch. Well, it just didn't seem— What, fair? Since when was life ever fair?

Chris stared at the bay he'd almost thrown himself into last night. It would all have been over if Terry hadn't come along.

Sea-air filled his lungs and he paused a moment to catch his breath. It was a long trek down to the beach, flanked on either side by cliff-faces. However, he felt drawn to this place in a way he couldn't explain.

The picture-postcard view was lovely, but he had other things on his mind. In contrast to the previous evening, the sea was calm; beautiful, even. Chris thought how much Sandra would have loved this.

He clambered over chalky stones worn smooth by the water. Every now and again he'd pick up a pebble and throw it at the blue expanse. Each time, he inclined his head as the stone plopped into the liquid, envying its decent into darkness.

"Dangerous on them rocks, son. Could slip and break yer neck!"

The warning came out of nowhere and Chris nearly toppled over. A coarse hand clasped his shoulder to steady him.

Chris looked round to see a bulky man with the arms of a wrestler standing beside him. His face was suntanned leather, and the wispy beard covering his chin, a light shade of grey.

"Jesus! You scared me to death."

"Didn't mean to frighten ye. Come for the fishing, see?"

Chris noticed the man was dragging a battered old dinghy. A sudden thought struck him.

"Hey, you weren't out here last night, were you? With a torch?"

"Me? Naw. Too rough to fish at night, lad."

"Only I thought I saw someone, something, down here."

The man pondered this for a second then replied, "Might have been smugglers."

Chris examined his deadpan expression and was relieved when the man eventually cracked a smile.

"Very funny."

"So what brings ye here, then?"

"I'm not really sure." Chris searched around in his pocket and produced a packet of cigarettes. He offered one to the fisherman, who shook his head violently.

"Those'll kill ye, lad."

Chris shrugged at the admonition and lit up his

weed. The smoke started off thick and grey but was soon taken by a gentle breeze that was building up, disappearing into nothing.

"Ah, ye can't fool me. I bet you've come to look at the Cave. That's what most tourists want. Bit late in the year, though."

The young man frowned and scratched his stubbled cheek. "What Cave?"

His weathered acquaintance raised an eyebrow and said plainly: "The Cave of Lost Souls, 'course. The place where restless spirits come."

Chris looked for the smile, but it never materialised. "You're serious, aren't you?"

"Can't live here and not believe in the Cave. It's been around forever."

He pointed over to the edge of the cliffs – the general area where Chris had seen the light. There was indeed a gap in the cliff-face.

The fisherman sighed. "Anyway, can't stand about here all day long natterin'. Too much work to do. Now ye mind what I said about them rocks."

Chris continued to gaze in the direction of the mythical Cave. The Cave of Lost Souls... He remembered what the light had looked like last night, faint and soft. Chris took hardly any notice of the seadog dragging his 'vessel' out to the ocean. When he turned to ask the man more, the dinghy was already in the water. Chris thought about calling out to him, but what was the point? Before he knew it, the man was just a shape in the distance.

Chris stood looking out at the sea a while longer, but his eyes found their way back to the Cave. The words of the fisherman had piqued his curiosity, and once again he felt drawn by a compulsion to explore.

He crushed the cigarette beneath his trainer and began across the plane of stones.

*

The entranceway wasn't particularly high, but it was exceptionally wide. It looked for all the world like the hand of God had punched a hole into that rock. The only thing Chris could see was blackness and more blackness.

Inside, the wall had an interesting texture and was warm to the touch. Chris kept to the sides to avoid a flood of seawater flowing down the middle. He lit a match and ventured further in.

He walked for what seemed like ages, striking one light after another and trying to discern what lay ahead of him. *Surely the cliff wasn't this broad?* he thought. Maybe the makeshift tunnel hooked up with another somewhere down the line. There was no way of telling whether he'd already made a turn or not. As the walls led him on and on, he became increasingly disorientated.

Suddenly it was icy cold. The match he was holding flickered once, twice: then blew out. A wind brushed his face and he shivered.

In the murky womb he couldn't tell which way he was facing, and the entrance wasn't visible at all.

Chris was just about to mentally chastise himself for travelling so far, when he heard a sound.

The noise was coming from somewhere deep in the Cave. The echoes made it difficult to locate, but it was growing louder, getting closer and closer. The very thought of something in there with him – a bat, perhaps, or a rodent; big and ugly with sharp teeth – was enough to get Chris moving.

He attempted to retreat, but slipped on the slimy rock and tippled forwards. Chris caught his forehead on the low ceiling, a protruding dagger of stone slicing into the skin and forcing it apart. He felt something trickle down his face and realised it was blood. There was a splash, and he was up to his knees in freezing water. He'd fallen into the channel that ran down the middle of the Cave. Chris cursed his foolishness.

Arms out in front, he felt around for something to latch on to. Then he found he couldn't shift. His left foot was trapped under the water.

The noise was getting louder and he felt the chill again. It gushed over him and streamed down his back. Once more he shivered.

In front of him a luminescence appeared. It lit up the cave, allowing Chris a glimpse of the horrors surrounding him.

"Wha—" The words dried up instantly in his throat.

The walls were covered with faces: men's, women's and children's, etched into the fleshy stone. They were in torment, groans issuing from their gaping mouths. All had their eyes wide open, focused on him.

A deathly wail filled the cavern and Chris clapped his hands to his ears. It did no good.

Into the light stepped a figure. Cobalt in colour, it glided effortlessly across the water. A veil was draped over its face, and as it moved nearer Chris could see it wore a wedding dress, tattered and riddled with holes.

The lace was pulled back to reveal a familiar visage.

"Sandra!" he shouted, though he couldn't hear his own voice.

Her head was at an inhuman angle, resting on her shoulder. Two emerald eyes shone out of an ashen face. Streaks of crimson ran from a gaping hole in her cranium.

It was how she'd looked after the accident.

"Oh my God, *no!*" Chris screamed. In his terrified state, he didn't notice the water level rising in the Cave.

She was mouthing something and he could barely make out the words. "I called to you, be with me."

Tears mingled with the blood on his face. "Not like this, I—"

"Blame...your fault..." She raised an arm, spikes of glass clinging to the torn flesh.

"No... No it *wasn't!*"

"Already one of us, a lost soul."

The water was up to his chin now and inching higher. It had appeared out of nowhere, just like the vision of his lost love.

The more he struggled to free his leg, the tighter the grip became. He tore his gaze away from Sandra for a moment, expecting to see his ankle jammed in a crack, or wedged between two rocks.

But there were hands down below, waxen and lifeless, holding his feet, clutching at him. Chris saw more eyes in the watery grave beneath him.

Salty fluid entered his mouth and his chest became tight.

"I want to live," he tried to say, but liquid gushed in faster, taking away the cherished air that had once resided in his lungs.

The light glowed through the water. Chris could just make out Sandra's form – submerged as she was – except now she was beautiful; the scars and abrasions gone.

She smiled sweetly. Chris blinked and the salt stung his eyes. His last memory was of Sandra gently kissing him.

Then there was only oblivion.

*

The first thing he was aware of was a pressure on his lips, but there was little tenderness about it.

The second thing he felt was a rush of hot seawater in his throat. Rising bile that begged to be coughed up.

"Ye all right?"

That voice, Chris thought, *I'm still alive!*

Slowly, he opened his bloodshot eyes. Hovering above him was the fisherman, an expression of sheer relief on his face.

"I-I want...I want to live," spluttered Chris.

"Don't ye worry, you'll live right enough. Though I dread t'think what would've happened if I hadn't found ye in the water."

"The light—"

"Got a nasty bump on your head, an' a broken ankle too, probably. Just take it easy and we'll get ye to a doctor. I said them rocks were dangerous, son."

Chris felt himself being hoisted up by the arms.

"My brother...let him know...I'm all right," he gasped.

"First things first," his saviour said, grinning.

Through a clouded mind Chris relived the encounter in the Cave. Had the bang on the head caused him to see all those sights? His rational side would have said yes, how could such things exist? And yet...

Chris recalled what Sandra had done, but now he understood why. He'd known all along he wasn't to blame; you couldn't cheat fate, or death. As usual, his wife had found a way to make him see that.

It wasn't their time to be together again, but perhaps one day. Until then he had to go on without her – only then could she rest. Life was too precious a gift to just throw away, he understood that now.

Already the sun was in its descent, but the sea was much calmer than the day before. And as they progressed up the incline, Chris leaning heavily on the fisherman, he thought he heard a voice on the gently slapping waves.

"Goodbye, my love," it whispered.

Chris answered silently in his head, then passed out again, safe in the knowledge that both their lost souls had found peace that day.

REMOTE

The office building looks much the same as any other: an amalgam of glass and metal and concrete existing in the same space.

But it hides dark, dark secrets.

Every weekday for the last ten years he has trod its drab corridors, used its lifts and sat in its offices to do his job. Ten years – ever since they found out about him. He is walking to his office right now, following the directions, though he'd know the way blindfolded. First thing Monday morning and his observers will be waiting for him, ready to give him his brief, to run down the company's mission statement. The man takes in very little of his surroundings, as little as possible, in fact. They're meant to be drab, after all: no pictures on the walls or fancy patterns here. No distractions.

At last, he comes to his own office. The title on its varnished wooden door reads: G786. It is not the room number; this is his name. Not the name he was christened with, you understand, but the one they gave to him. The one he is known by at work. The one he has begun to think of as his true moniker. He has no idea what the letter or the numbers mean. It's quite possible that his superiors have no idea either, but it is *his*. It belongs to him.

Grasping the smooth metal knob, he opens the door. Inside is a fair-sized rectangular table, around which his observers are seated. There are three of them, and never the same ones twice: a stocky man with bad teeth and a crown of grey-white hair; a very tall light-ginger man with circular glasses who has the annoying habit of jamming his tongue firmly into his cheek; and a middle-aged woman with a kindly face. As is evidenced by the building itself, though, looks can be very deceptive.

The closest to him, tall ginger, rises first. He doesn't say anything, he just points to a manila file at the head of the table. G786 nods and sits down in front of the file, opening it up to glance inside.

The first thing he sees is a colour photograph of a man dressed in military garb, peaked cap and sunglasses. There's a name at the bottom, and a short bio. G786 doesn't take any of this in; there's really no need. He doesn't care a great deal anymore. One guerrilla leader is much the same as another, and he doesn't need to know the ins and outs, the justifications – if indeed there are any. All he needs to know is the country, a vague idea of the whereabouts. He flips through the other papers and finds a map of the area, fairly detailed. Though not as detailed as the satellite pictures that come next, pinpointing buildings, guards, watch-towers.

The place where this target is located is like a fortress. It would take an expert in security and special operations to infiltrate its defences, and even then a successful strike could not be guaranteed – plus a highly trained operative would almost certainly be lost. No, it is much better this way. Much more convenient. Much easier…for them. As for what it is doing to him, well that doesn't really enter into the equation.

Last, but not least, there's a scrap of material pinned to the back of the file. This was very difficult to acquire, cut from one of the target's old uniforms. G786's fingers hover over the square of khaki, but then they withdraw, as if almost touching a flame. Not yet, not yet…

They allow G786 a further ten minutes or so to look through the reports again. He doesn't really read them, just shuffles through for the sake of appearances. It is expected of him, so he obliges. He has no choice.

"When you're ready," prompts the stocky man.

Ready? He is never ready.

G786 nods, and thin ginger walks over to the window to close the blinds. The slats slice into the bright morning sunlight for a moment, striping the grey walls white and yellow temporarily. Then all the brightness goes away.

Tall ginger finally takes his seat again as G786 passes his hands over the papers, his fingers now seeking out the scrap of material at the back. He closes his eyes, and allows the sensations to develop; stops fighting what is supposed to come so 'naturally'. It always starts off with a tunnel, a rolling spiral of colours: of reds, golds, blues, greens, twisting round and around. He accesses this without any problems at all, letting the conduit take him away, lead him in the direction his mind needs to travel. At certain points there are crossroads and intersections, but he instinctively knows which ones to avoid and which to take. The feel of the cloth acts like scent to a hunting dog, linking him to his target, allowing him to cut across great distances in the blink of an eye.

The arrival is always slightly more disorienting. It's instantaneous and he's thrown back into the world without warning. Or at least a piece of him is. He sees the base now, the one from the photograph. He slips past alarms and guards without being seen, because there isn't really that much of him *to* be seen, and he carries on following his senses. He begins to rub the fabric between thumb and forefinger now, centring in on the man from the photograph. Passing through walls, through locked doors, without a second thought.

Then here he is. In a room not much bigger than his office. G786 recognises the target immediately; he is sat talking to another man in a language G786 doesn't understand. It doesn't matter really what they are saying. All that matters is that a sighting has been confirmed. G786 knows what has to come next, even though he dreads it. In his present form it is simplicity itself to enter the target's body. The method has been left entirely up to him, it can be slow and painful – such as an internal bleed – or fast and merciful, like the popping of a brain cell here or there. But whichever course of action is taken, one thing is for certain: he must exit the body before it is over or risk being trapped inside forever.

It must be done, however. No matter how much he wavers, G786 knows this. He wants to get it over with as quickly as possible and so goes for the swifter option. G786 ingratiates himself into the target's head, yet still he hesitates before doing the deed. Even after all this time, there's a part of him that— He mentally shrugs this off. No room for a conscience, for emotions, he continues with the operation. A tweak here, a tweak there. Then he gets out.

The other man in the room is quite surprised by what happens next. His superior suddenly clutches his forehead, eyes clicking backwards in their sockets, and he falls out of his chair onto the floor. There is an effort made to save him, naturally, and physicians are even called in to help. But none of it will do any good. G786 hangs around just long enough to make sure his mission has been completed successfully, as if there was ever any doubt, and then departs – searches out the tunnel once more for the return journey.

Back in the office his eyes snap open. "It's done," he tells them.

That day he is assigned two more cases, with long breaks between each one, before being allowed to clock out. The first is a senior politician who has risen in the ranks far too quickly and is becoming too idealistic for their liking; the second is an intelligence operative who has defected to the other side – whatever the other side is supposed to be these days.

Now it is time to leave.

G786 walks to his maroon car in the lot and climbs inside. He pulls out into traffic on the main road, then begins the half-hour drive to the place he calls home, although the significance of the word has long since shrivelled away into nothing. Once, long ago, it had actually meant something. But that was before he had been forced into the programme, ironically by their threats to tear his homelife apart. Before his talents had been detected by a routine screening, and before they had enhanced his basic abilities with a daily cocktail of drugs. At first it had been just spying missions, the usual stuff for national security; finding out plans and schemes before they could be used. Locating 'enemy' safe houses and monitoring the movement of certain key individuals. It hadn't been hard work; indeed, he'd almost found himself enjoying it. Not many people could do what he did and at least he was putting it to use, for the good of his country. He was also being compensated adequately for his trouble. Looked after.

But then they started to talk about pushing him further. To see what else he was capable of. To train him in other methods and techniques – the kind that weren't so palatable or easy to excuse. To send him on jobs that took a little piece of him away every time he returned, that left him feeling cold and numb afterwards: a shadow of a man.

His car journey mirrors the ones he has taken invisibly that day, except instead of a tunnel there is a road – still, the junctions and turn-offs are the same. One of these brings him to his house, a pretty white abode with net curtains in the windows and hanging baskets over the front door. G786 opens the garage door with the remote control on his keyring, and parks the car inside. He can get to the house proper through a side-door, which opens out into the kitchen.

On the hob is a boiling pan, steam rising in spirals to touch the ceiling. His wife is cooking spaghetti again, as always on a Monday. He hears singing – sweet singing that should touch his heart – coming from the hallway, and suddenly she is at the kitchen door. Even dressed in jeans and an old sweatshirt, she looks so beautiful. Her long, dark hair cascading onto her shoulders like a waterfall. She blinks with those wide eyes and tries to smile. It is not the smile of yesteryear, the smile that first attracted him to her, that he fell in love with so long ago. This is a smile worn away by heartache and pain.

"Hello, Simon." That's G786's real name. It feels as alien to him now as the house he's in, the woman standing in front of him. She walks across to the hob, turns it down a fraction, then continues across to him.

"Hello, Amy," he says eventually. Even her name is pretty, but you'd hardly think so the way it comes out of *his* mouth. She rises to kiss him on that mouth now, applying pressure but receiving none in return. He doesn't even put his arms around her, doesn't hold her the way he used to.

She pulls away and returns to the cooker. "Dinner won't be much longer. Why don't you sit down?"

G786 takes a seat at the kitchen table and listens as Amy makes small talk about her day, about the friends she's seen and the things she's done.

None of it really interests him. Then, as she's serving up dinner, Amy asks him how his own day has been – after all this time she still thinks he works for a finance company. He mumbles the usual "Fine," but doesn't go into any details. And while they eat she keeps looking at him, trying to find an answer, uncover some clues. She used to be able to tell what he was thinking by just gazing at him, looking into his eyes. Now she sees only a miniature reflection looking back. As usual, she wonders why he has gradually grown so distant, how the man she married could have become the person sitting there now. Had it been something she'd done? Had he gone off her? The fact that she couldn't bear him a child? Or maybe his love had just dwindled away, eroded over time.

That evening they watch the television; he has no preference. Doesn't laugh at the sitcoms anymore, doesn't cheer at the football or get passionate about the news reports. He just lets it all wash over him, and they sit there together on the couch like strangers, Amy trying to snuggle up to him and getting nowhere. It's the same in bed. They undress, climb inside. She makes the first move, hoping against hope, but he presents his cold back to her. *Why doesn't he care anymore?* she wonders. If only he'd care. If only he'd...love her. Instead he sleeps, a mechanical action – a robot recharging. Amy herself lies awake for hours, worrying about what has happened to her marriage, and what might happen in the future.

One thing is for sure, they cannot carry on like this forever.

*

In fact they only have to carry on like this for another two weeks.

G786 reports to the office on a Thursday morning this time. He is assigned one mission – the assassination of a scientist about to uncover a secret that might mean the end of civilisation as we know it…being as it's such a civilised world to begin with – before the alarms go off.

There are only two observers in his office today for a change, a puffy-faced man with triangular shoulders and a slender woman with long, blonde hair, and they both rush out into the corridor. G786 follows, but more slowly. They all believe there has been some sort of attack on the building; that some intelligence somewhere has discovered its true nature and detonated a bomb. As it transpires the wailing throb of the siren is simply an ordinary fire alarm. A soon-to-be *very* ex-employee has thrown a cigarette into a wastepaper bin in one of the downstairs offices without checking whether it was properly out. The offices are meant to be a non-smoking environment anyway, so this was his first mistake. The cigarette set fire to the rubbish inside, which in turn set fire to a desk beside it and the carpet on which it rests.

After the local smoke alarm went off, somebody smashed the glass on a larger one on the wall and it is this that's causing the panic. The sprinklers come on eventually. The standard procedure in any emergency is to get out and ask questions later, so this is what occurs. G786 and his supervisors do not risk the lifts. Instead, they join a group of other workers making their way down the stairs. None of G786's fellow numbers are panicking as such – only their observers.

They make it outside safely and stand around in the car park, unsure of what to do next. It takes twenty minutes for the cause of the accident to be discovered and dealt with by internal security. There is no way the proper authorities can be alerted: who knows what they might see inside? The culprit is identified not long afterwards and detained, but the powers that be decide that all other staff might as well take the rest of the day off and return in the morning fresh. This will give security time to make doubly sure the building is safe and fit for the 'workers'.

This is how G786 comes to be driving home at such an early hour on a Thursday afternoon. He takes the same route as always, and makes very good time because there isn't much traffic. He uses the remote and parks his car in the garage, then enters his house through the kitchen door again. The kitchen is empty this time. He walks through into the hall and then checks the living room. Amy is not there. G786 doesn't call out; he simply goes upstairs to use the toilet. While he's up there he checks to see if his wife is around. She isn't in either of the bedrooms or the study. He uses the toilet and flushes.

G786 knows that Amy sometimes goes out in the day. He doesn't know where, because he doesn't really listen when she tells him things. To a friend's house, probably, or shopping, he doesn't care. Or at least he shouldn't. Except it's strange to return home and not find her here. Every day since they've been married she's been there to greet him when he walks through that kitchen door. Back when they'd first started living together, he used to sweep her up in his arms and kiss every available inch of her face. Why is he thinking about that now? He doesn't usually. He shouldn't. Could it be that...that he misses her being here? That emotions he thought he'd suppressed, that he thought had been driven out of him by months and months of doing what he now does, are actually still there? And have been all along...?

He shakes his head. You can't afford to think, to feel. To care. Not when you end people's lives for a living. Not when you are a number rather than a name. A tool rather than a man.

A weapon.

On his way back to the stairs he finds himself pausing outside the bedroom they share. He enters this again. What, is he tired? Does he need to lie down? No. G786 walks around the bed, as if he's never seen it before. It is a bed they sleep in together, inches apart and yet it might as well be miles. The miles he travels to take out a—

On the bedside table, on Amy's side: a photograph he hasn't looked at in a long time; he's tried not to. Their wedding day. G786 and Amy smiling, laughing, as the crowd throws confetti on them. He knows that he was there that day, but it seems like another man's memory. Actually, it *is* another man's memory, isn't it: Simon's. G786 goes over to the picture, touches the frame with his fingers, touches the glass. Hopes that just as he can travel distances, he might somehow also be able to travel through time. Back to that day, to experience it all over again, just to remember what it felt like to—

Why? Why bother? What is the point? What would it achieve? It certainly wouldn't alter his reality.

But it is too late. He needs to see Amy now, if only for his own sake. *She'll be back soon*, he tells himself. Then he can see her all he wants. That's not the same, though; she'll be here with him. It was never the same when she was here. G786 just needs to look upon her face without her knowing. It is a bizarre thing to admit, but true. He can't explain it, either, nor why he is now going to the window to close the curtains, going over to the wardrobe to get something out. A piece of her clothing; a dress, a skirt, a blouse…a jumper. One of her favourite fluffy jumpers. She wears this all the time when the cold weather bites. G786 grabs hold of it and sits back down on the bed.

He concentrates, rubbing the material between his thumb and fingers. G786 closes his eyes and enters the rainbow tunnel, the bright multi-coloured conduit. He zips up 'roads', turns off 'junctions', but doesn't have to go that far this time. His wife is not in another country or on the other side of the world. She is in the next town. He arrives outside a building, tall and brown; doesn't really recognise the place but knows she is inside. He senses her. It's strange, but G786 thinks little of this. He just enters via the nearest wall, passing through bricks and mortar like a ghost. And enters a wide-open space with a counter on one side and a set of stairs on the other.

Ignoring the rest of it, he travels up these stairs without ever having to touch one of them. He flies, up through level after level, up and down corridor after corridor. Until at last he comes to a door. It's one of many, but it's the only one he sees. There is a number on the outside, very much like the one on his office door at work – except this one says 505. This time it's a room rather than a person's number.

G786 passes through it.

Once inside, he sees his wife. But wishes to God – if there is a God – that he couldn't. She is in a room, in a bed. And she is not alone. A man, G786 doesn't recognise him, is on top of her. The sheets that cover the bottom half of his body are rising with him. Slowly, gently, tenderly. Amy's hands are clutching his back, stroking the skin, digging her nails in as he speeds up. Now he is kissing her as he works, his lips brushing neck, and cheeks. Amy's head flops to one side and G786 can see her face.

What's the matter? You wanted *to see her face, didn't you? Only not like this. Not like this.*

Amy is in the throes of ecstasy, and G786 feels almost sick. A whirlwind of buried emotions is churning up inside him. Where before there was nothing – or almost nothing – he now feels love, jealously, anger, betrayal, hatred, and above all envy. Yes, envy. He, G786, Simon, wants to be in that bed with Amy, as he once was, as he could have been all those many, many nights when he'd turned her away, ignored her, forced her to seek comfort in the arms of another. Forced her to find someone whom she *could* love and who would love her. Who'd give her what Simon could not. Warmth, humanity even.

It is too much for him to bear. No sooner has he thought about it than he is there: inside the body of this stranger screwing his wife. Simon can feel the beating of the man's heart, faster and faster. How easy it would be to just squeeze that muscle until it burst. But he isn't going to do that. He has other things in mind.

Amy looks up at the slick, rugged face above her. She's never felt so alive in her life; well, not since she and Simon used to— But suddenly something is wrong with the picture. Will – for that is the name of the man she finally gave herself to after months of resisting – is grimacing. Not because he is about to finish, but because of something else. His sweet, handsome face is swelling up. Forehead bloating, eyes bulging. And now his body is following suit. Shoulders inflating and skin stretching taut.

He rolls away and gets up off the bed. She watches as he staggers about there, clutching his head, his chest, his whole torso, in fact; not knowing where to put his hands first, or what help they could possibly be when they got there. A trickle of blood is running from the corner of his mouth, then another down his nose. He begins to convulse, crying out in agony as spasms plague his now unrecognisable body.

It is only after Will explodes that Amy starts to scream. Bits of him adorn the walls, the furniture, and her. Free of the stranger, Simon looks down at his wife. The woman he loved, splattered in redness and screaming. *He* has done that, and he will do more besides. For he is not really a person at all, is he? He is a number, a tool, a weapon.

And this is what he does...

*

Monday morning. G786 called in sick for the last day of the previous week, but he is back at work now. He drives to the offices in his car and parks it in the car park. He takes the lift and walks down the corridor to his office.

Inside, there are three people waiting. A small man with curly hair, a bearded man with enormous ears, and a woman with a long, pointed nose. They are his observers for the day. The man with large ears rises and points to the file at the front.

G786 sits down and examines the pictures inside. He doesn't really look at them, doesn't need to. Just needs a vague idea of the location – that and the piece of material at the back.

They give him time to look anyway, then the small man closes the blinds.

"When you're ready," says curly hair.

And he *is* ready now. Oh, so ready!

They wait as G786 shuts his eyes and rubs the material. They wait for him to join them back in the real world again, for him to open his eyes, tell them the mission was a success. But all he says when he eventually returns is:

"It is done. It is done."

PLEASURES OF THE FLESH

This was where they all came to satisfy their needs.

The police knew it existed, but chose to ignore that fact most of the time. Only every so often would they run in a suspect, or do a drive-by, just to keep their superiors happy. Mostly though, they understood the advantages of such a place. Rapes were down in this area, as was domestic violence. Trimberly was a sort of release valve; somewhere people of *that kind* (in other words anybody and everybody, from all walks of life) could get their kicks. And the men, women and children – yes, sweet Jesus, children! – who plied their trade here, running a risk that the rest of the population thought unacceptable, well they were happy enough. After a fashion. They were born to this, even enjoyed it. Must do, so the more cynical would say, otherwise they'd go out and get a proper job like everyone else. It helped them sleep at night to think this way.

Into this den of inequity drove Dustin, headlights dipped, body hunched over the steering wheel. He turned the corner into Riley Street. The bridge was only a stone's throw away now, and up and down this tract of dull concrete the businessmen and women walked. Some in groups, most on their own.

Every time a car came into view they would stroll to the curbs, trying to attract the driver's attention, hoping (*though not deep down*) that they would be chosen next. Mortgages or rent had to be paid, food had to be bought, families provided for. All that took money.

Dustin drove slowly, looking from side to side. He bit the skin around his thumbnail, a nasty habit he'd picked up. It wasn't that he was nervous, well maybe just a little. He had paid for it before, when he couldn't find it easily in the clubs and bars – one-night stands, never anything more. Dustin hadn't been involved seriously with anyone since his first girlfriend, Linda. It just wasn't worth the waiting, the wooing, the courtship rituals. He knew what he needed and the sooner the better as far as he was concerned. It didn't worry him in the slightest. What he was doing was only what came naturally.

Looks were not important to Dustin, though. He could see the beauty in most people. And he didn't mind what shape his partner was either: big, small, fat, thin. He couldn't care less, even about the gender. As long as he had a good time, as long as they both had a good time getting it together; that last bit was important to him. Okay, so these men and women had slept with half the city's population, but he still prided himself on his technique.

One solitary girl was leaning against the side of a building, shoulders pressed up to the brick. She looked promising. Dressed in a red leather skirt and jacket, she stood with her arms folded, scanning the road. When she saw Dustin she forced a smile, her painted lips curving upwards. With a certain reluctance, she swayed over to the crawling car, her high heels clacking on the concrete. Dustin was enthralled at the sight of her, a young face (eighteen, twenty at the outside) with shoulder-length brunette hair, medium height, and with legs a model would kill for; here encased in what looked to be fishnet stockings from this distance. She didn't seem very experienced, but that didn't matter to Dustin.

He pressed on the brake until he was parallel to her, then flipped down the passenger window. The girl put one elbow on the top of the car and bent over. The skin from her neck to her black satin top was exposed. Dustin gazed at it, eyes travelling down to her cleavage.

"See anything you like?" she asked him.

"Oh yes," said Dustin.

"I can be anything you want me to be," she told him, running a hand over her hip. "You only have to ask."

Pretend to be anything: nurse, schoolgirl, nun… He didn't want any of that. "Just be yourself," he told her.

They negotiated, getting the business side of it out of the way first. The woman looked trustworthy, so he gave her the money in advance. She stared at it in amazement; clients never paid in advance, always afterwards. What was to stop her from running off with it right this second? Nothing, except that now she would have a good feeling about this man. Like she should go with him or might miss out on something.

"Climb in," he said in that gentle voice.

And she did just that.

"My name's Dustin," he told her, holding out his hand. The woman slid her own inside his and he kissed the knuckles. A proper gentleman. His lips tingled as they brushed against her skin.

"I'm Amber." Neither green nor red, but could turn either at any time.

Eventually he took her hand away from his mouth and said, "Very pleased to meet you, Amber." The car pulled away from the curb, leaving Riley Street behind.

There was very little conversation after this. Amber preferred it that way, she told him. The less personal the better. However, when Dustin quizzed her about how long she'd been doing this, he saw her frown then answer. Not only that, but answer truthfully.

"Eight months," she informed him. "I'm trying to put myself through college." She shook her head, knew she shouldn't be saying all that. Never reveal anything about yourself, that's what she would've been taught by the older girls on Riley Street.

Dustin picked up on her nerves. "Don't worry, I'm not an axe-wielding lunatic or anything like that." It was true, he wasn't. He didn't want to hurt her.

"Glad to hear it," said Amber, a hitch still in her voice. "Although if you were, I doubt whether you'd tell me."

Dustin laughed. "No, I suppose not." He felt the desire now, inside. Was growing impatient, needed her.

"Where are we going?" Amber asked him, as if all of a sudden realising she didn't know. "Hotel?"

"No, back to my place. I have a house."

"You aren't married, then?" Not that it should make any difference, but for some strange reason it did.

"No. I'm not the marrying kind."

The car sped on, first one turning, then another. Amber shifted around uncomfortably so he tried to put her at her ease. "I'll drive you back, of course," he said. Amber nodded; she believed him.

"Almost there." Dustin pulled into a side road and then into a driveway. Amber twisted round so she could see the house. He knew what she was thinking: *Not bad*. If the payment in advance hadn't signalled it, now she knew he had money. Who knows, might even become a regular? But she was also probably wondering what he needed her services for. Dustin was quite good looking in a Latin-American kind of way; even his five o'clock shadow was appealing, he'd been told. He had a nice car and home. Surely he could find women in the normal way? Unless, of course, he *wasn't* normal. Was she going to get inside only to find vast arrays of S&M

equipment, or maybe he'd want to lick her feet for half an hour? He couldn't help chuckling at that thought.

"What?" she asked.

"Nothing," answered Dustin and she frowned again.

He got out, went round and opened the door for her. Again, such a gentleman. Then he guided her to the front door. The house was fairly secluded, willowy trees blocking off the view left and right, so he wouldn't have to worry about anyone seeing him come in. That was handy.

"Have...Have you done this kind of thing before?" she ventured.

He opened his mouth to reply, then closed it again. But the truth was: yes, he had. Probably more times than her, if he was being honest.

Dustin fiddled with the key and stepped inside.

With the lights on she could now see that it was tastefully decorated, too. Modern, without being too sterile. Amber smiled, clearly liking what she saw. She was starting to like him, too, which Dustin understood was a definite 'no go' in her line of work. Would have been one of the first things she learned: don't get involved, too messy.

But surely if the right man came along, someone with money, someone handsome. It had been known to happen...

"Would you like a drink?" Dustin asked her. "Tea, coffee? Something stronger?"

"I don't usually, but..." She nodded. Didn't usually drink on the job, because it would affect her reasoning, make her more vulnerable. Though how much more vulnerable could she be than she was right now? "I'll have a Bacardi if you've got any."

"Sure, just give me a second. Oh, make yourself at home, won't you."

Dustin disappeared into the kitchen, while Amber made herself comfortable on the couch, a cream-coloured leather one.

As he returned, she was running a hand down the arm, clearly enjoying the feel of it.

"Here you go." Dustin gave her the glass of Bacardi.

Amber shrugged off her red coat and accepted the drink, taking a sip straight away.

"Do you mind if I ask you something, Amber?" Dustin sat on the sofa, not too close, but not miles away, either.

"I guess," she said, voice trembling.

"Are you happy with what you do? How your life's turned out?"

Another frown. It was a strange question, he realised. She'd probably been expecting something along the lines of: "Would you mind if I brought out the whips now?"

"Sure. I mean, well it's not perfect, but then again whose is? College is going okay, kind of. And this is..." Amber paused. "I don't mind it too much."

"But have you ever wondered if there was something more? True happiness."

"I suppose so. But I don't really—"

He could no longer resist, the anticipation, the build-up too much. Dustin knew all he needed to know. *He* would make her happy tonight, truly happy. "Drink up," he said. "It's time."

"What, here?"

"To start with." Dustin watched as she gulped a little more of the Bacardi, before setting it down on the coffee table. Then he moved closer, taking control; he could see her trembling. Amber was scared. But scared and excited at the same time, he could sense it. No client would ever have had this effect on her, not even the first (*especially* not the first). It was almost like she was a virgin waiting for the big night.

Dustin took her arm, her bare arm up to the shoulder, and started to kiss it. Softly, tenderly. Amber shivered. The brush of his lips alone was enough to arouse her. She probably knew that every part of a woman's body became an erogenous zone when they were excited, but the forearm? The elbow? Ridiculous! Yet it was happening. She closed her eyes, losing herself to the experience as his kisses reached higher and higher, savouring every inch of her arm. Until he came to the strap of her silky top.

"Why don't you take this off?" Dustin told her, and Amber was more than willing. Ready for whatever came next.

She stood in front of him and pulled the top over her head, casting it to one side. Then she undid the zip on her leather skirt and eased it over her hips. It dropped to the floor, resting alongside the top. Underneath she wore a black bra, panties and hold-up fish-nets.

Amber was just about to join him on the couch again when he said, "No, take it *all* off."

She cocked her head. "Most of them like me to keep this stuff on."

"I don't. Please, Amber."

Amber shrugged and reached round to undo the clasp on her bra. She pulled the straps down her arms and dropped it to the floor. Dustin gazed at her exposed breasts. They were perfect. Not too large, not too small, with dark, pert nipples already rising up. The stockings came off next, followed by the panties. These she slid provocatively down her long legs, obviously taking pleasure in Dustin's face.

"Now the jewellery," Dustin said.

Amber was once more puzzled by his request, but the punter was always right. Besides, she looked more than eager to see what else he could do with those lips of his. Quickly, she took off her earrings, her pearl necklace and the few rings she had on.

Now she was completely naked.

Dustin was captivated by the sight of her, his breathing erratic, his eyes wide. This gave Amber pleasure, too. She *wanted* him to find her attractive. She needed it badly.

The girl sat back down on the couch again and waited for it to begin.

Most of her clients would only be interested in their own gratification, with no thought for hers. Why should they be when they were paying? She may as well have been a blow-up doll for all they cared. Dustin was different. He would take his time, and the idea of foreplay was no stranger to him.

With his hands and lips he explored her now. Not just her arms, hands, but the whole of her upper half. When Dustin reached her neck, licking the skin there with his darting tongue, Amber cried out with joy. His hands played over her breasts at the same time, which were now ultra-sensitive, responding eagerly to his touch. He tweaked a nipple, only softly, but it was enough to make her cry out again.

There would be all kinds of thoughts rushing through her mind, all kinds of questions: how was he doing this to her, how was it possible to feel so much pleasure, wave upon wave? Dustin was confident it would be nothing she'd ever experienced before, not even with those she had professed to love.

He purposefully steered clear of below the waist. For now. Dustin didn't need to go *down there*. Not when he could enflame Amber by just stroking her shoulders, trailing his nails across her belly, nibbling the flesh behind her ear.

The first racking spasm took Amber completely by surprise, in spite of everything leading up to it. But not him. He'd seen it before. She tipped back her head, breath coming through clenched teeth, and held on to Dustin as his lengthy, energetic tongue did the work.

Sometime between the first of these explosions of pure delight and the next, Dustin carried her up to the bedroom. Amber hardly noticed she was moving, such was the intensity of her bliss. The next thing she was aware of, vaguely at best, was being laid down on a large bed.

Dustin's bed.

Amber was still reeling, but she watched with admiration as he stripped off his own clothes. Opening the wardrobe door, he hung the garments up on hangers. There was a flash of light as the mirror on the inside reflected his face, then he closed the door. When he turned, Dustin saw the uncertainty in her eyes. That moment's respite would have given her pause to think, to wonder whether he'd slipped something into her Bacardi. Surely no one could do the things he'd done to her, not that way, at least.

Then it was gone again. She wanted more.

He could see she took almost as much pleasure in the sight of him as the feel of his skin on hers. His body was well-muscled and perfectly-proportioned. Her eyes were driven downwards, and she was far from disappointed. He could feel her own impatience now, Amber wanting him to hurry, to come across to her right that second, to continue pleasuring her as he had downstairs, but she could barely speak.

Then he appeared above her, smiling.

Amber smiled back.

Dustin began to kiss her once more, lips brushing her neck, her shoulders, licking once again; tongue leaving a trail of saliva like a slug. The tingling returned and he knew Amber could feel it too. His mouth found one of her nipples, which was already erect. Covering it, Dustin began to alternate between sucking on it and flicking it back and forth with his tongue. She let out a wail of delight, hands finding his own shoulders and holding him, nails digging in.

She paused for a second, suddenly realising what she'd done. Hurt the client when he hadn't asked for that – for the rough stuff. She just hadn't been able to help herself, Dustin knew that. He pulled his head back. "It's okay," he told her. "Just let yourself go. Let yourself enjoy every single moment of this. The happiness, the pure joy."

Amber nodded, still a little uncertain. That was meant to be her line, surely. She was meant to be showing him the time of his life, not the other way around. Then it didn't matter because he was sucking on the other nipple, teasing it and playing with it until she let out another loud moan.

When he felt like she couldn't take any more, Dustin went down and down, kissing and licking her toned stomach muscles until she bucked beneath him. But that was as nothing compared with when his tongue found her sex. Already slick from her first orgasms, he lapped at her juices greedily like he wanted to drain them all, dry her out. Fortunately, they just kept on coming, the more he worked – and Amber yelled out once again as she climaxed.

But Dustin was only really getting started. And now, to give her time to recover, he began slickening her thighs, her knees, her calves – all the way down to her feet, where he paid special attention to her ankles and toes, nibbling each one in turn, much to Amber's obvious glee.

Bending to take in his face at the bottom of the bed, she said to him: "I want you. I want you inside me." Didn't care about protection, about diseases or anything else. Just needed him, *right now*.

Dustin grinned. He was more than happy to oblige; it was time anyway, he'd only been prolonging the moment. So he pulled himself back up the duvet like he was swimming, then suddenly dove. Hitting the target first time, shoving himself in up to the root and causing Amber to draw in breath sharply.

As he began to build up a rhythm, Dustin didn't ignore the rest of Amber – returned to old haunts like the breasts and nipples, the shoulders, the neck. He knew they could both feel the tingling sensations mounting, Amber shivering with ecstasy beneath him was evidence of that. The pleasures of the flesh, something that most people thought they had experienced but were so, so wrong. Tip of the iceberg stuff, nothing like the pair of them were going through right at that moment. The dizzying heights of rapture.

Dustin pushed in and pulled out, making sure he stimulated her most sensitive area – not that every single fibre of her wasn't currently sensitive. Wasn't responsive to his touch. She was putty in his hands, in fact, but willingly so. Desperate for him to make her even happier, to deliver more complete bliss, which was what he wanted, too, after all. The smile on her face, eyes closed, head back, told him how much she was relishing all of this, heading for yet another orgasm which he would try to double or triple by angling himself so that he could reach her G-spot inside, rubbing against that as well, delaying his own release.

Amber snaked her legs around his back, locking him in position, urging him on, her cries louder and louder with each fresh movement he made. Her hands were under his arms, cupping his back now as she met his thrusts. The fingernails were digging in once more, drawing blood Dustin knew – the wetness running down as she raked the flesh there. He didn't care, it was getting towards the end now; once Amber had come for the final time, it would be his turn and then all this would be over.

Then there it was, finally – having taken so long and yet no time at all. Amber's whole body was shaking with the powerful sensations she was feeling, but Dustin was determined to finish what he had started, even back there on the street. To have his own climax, unable to do anything except let go.

But instead of what would normally happen, his seed pumping out into her, it was quite the reverse. A suction was being created down there that made his efforts with her nipples earlier seem tame by comparison. A pumping, certainly, but of Amber *into* him. He was inside her, but he was starting to draw her back inside himself.

And next, the look – the realisation that something was very wrong indeed. That this wasn't normal. Amber's body was still tingling, Dustin knew, still wet with a combination of sweat and his spit. Changing her, making her more malleable, just as her mind had been earlier; no match for his from the start.

"What...What's...?"

Amber tried to move, to wrestle herself free, but she couldn't – mainly because her fingers, her whole hands were sinking into Dustin's back like it was made of hot tar. Her legs and feet were doing the same, melting into him. She was aware of what was happening, but it shouldn't be possible.

His own hands, where they met her skin, were doing the same as his organ inside her, sucking her up like a vacuum cleaner. Amber let out a scream, not of satisfaction this time but of absolute terror.

Dustin hated this part, hated that he had to do it. He didn't *want* to hurt her, but he must. It was necessary. That's why he had to make sure that her last moments were pleasurable, so he didn't feel quite as guilty. He'd given something to them, now they had to give something back.

Amber's face was slack, skin there stretched like some kind of weird mask. Eyes dribbling out of their sockets as she was pulled into him. Where they met at the chest it was almost like they were melding together, two people literally becoming one; forget the old song by that girl group years ago, this was the real thing.

The screams were petering out because Amber's mouth was being pulled downwards, and her lungs were already halfway inside Dustin. He brushed his own mouth against her, then his cheek, then his whole face, rubbing her flesh until it was absorbed like a sponge mopping up a spillage on a wet kitchen floor.

He shivered himself as the last of her bled into his pores, sinking onto the duvet where Amber had been only seconds before, enjoying the most magical and intense evening of her short life. Gone now, wiped away like she had never existed at all. Dustin let out his own satisfied cry.

Then, and only then, did he say: "I'm sorry. I'm really sorry." He had the good grace to acknowledge that at least. That he'd taken Amber's life – well, her body at any rate – in order to feed. That she was no more now, because two beings couldn't possibly exist in the same space.

Or could they?

Dustin jerked. Twitched. He frowned, as Amber had done so often while he was coaxing her back to his home. Then came the pain, and he knew the look of terror she'd sported back there was being mirrored on his own face.

Something was wrong, terribly wrong.

Dustin got onto all fours on the bed, felt like he was going to throw up. Christ, in all these years, after all those meals, he'd never felt like this before.

Maybe it was like when you ate something bad? Food poisoning? Stood to reason that it could happen whatever way you digested something, didn't it? Or...or an allergic reaction? Amber like poison to him and he didn't even know it?

He staggered off the bed, half-collapsing off it actually, to crawl across the bedroom floor. Heading for the bathroom, heading for the toilet where he fully expected to be violently ill.

Dustin was shivering again, but there was no pleasure in it this time; no satisfaction. Using the door, he managed to get to his feet and caught a glimpse of himself in the bathroom mirror. White as a sheet, but that wasn't all. His flesh was undulating in a way he hadn't seen outside of when he fed. Like it was losing coherence.

"*Fuck!*" he shouted, hands going to his face – where they almost sank in, if he hadn't pulled them back in time. "What's...What's happening...to me?" Wasn't as if he could just ring an ambulance either, he couldn't let the outside world see this. See what he really was. He'd end up in some facility somewhere being experimented on. Dissected.

But it was definitely tempting, especially as he bent double again, the sheer agony amazing. The tingling was back as well, and when he looked down at his legs he saw they were rippling too, like the surface of a lake someone had thrown a rock into. Jerking, kicking out...

Getting his kicks.

His arms followed suit, then the rest of him: altering, changing, taking on another shape.

A more female shape.

Gone was his impressive manhood, which had retreated back up inside him – never to be seen again. And as he slowly rose, he could feel the weight of the swelling at his chest. Two breasts emerging, pushing outwards to his disgust. The dark nipples of each sprang out, like they were being released from captivity, standing to attention. Pert.

The hair was disappearing from his arms, his torso, but conversely that on his head was darkening and growing. Brunette, shoulder length. When he looked in the mirror this time, he knew what he would see. The full red lips, the eyes of a young girl, eighteen, twenty at the outside.

Was aware of what was happening, though it shouldn't be possible.

It was his final thought before losing his grip on himself, Dustin's features, his body wiped away so completely it was like he had never existed at all.

*

Amber righted herself, looked in the mirror. Looked down at herself.

She seemed fine, nothing out of place. Which was a miracle considering what she'd just been through. Poor Dustin. No, not poor Dustin. Fuck him! He'd been trying to make a meal out of her. Assuming she was like the rest of the populace, when she was just pretending, like him. Could be anything she wanted to be.

Still, it was a shame. In all her time doing this, living this kind of life, in a place that would give her a greater choice of victim, men, women and children – yes, sweet Jesus, children! – she'd never come across another one like her. A person of *that kind*. Who was born to this, even enjoyed it. After a fashion.

Had often wondered, but never thought... She'd known what was happening as soon as it started of course, the tingling intensifying. The release valve, then the absorption. And she'd been scared, *of course* she'd been scared. Didn't have a bloody clue what would follow once it began, but couldn't back out. Scared – but excited at the same time.

In the end, though, it had come down to who was the strongest. She might be young, but Amber was feisty, regardless of the vibes she was giving off. Amber, who could turn green or red at a moment's notice. And you really didn't want to be around when she was on green!

What had also helped, she realised, was to let Dustin think he had won. Let him think she was like all the others, and let him believe she was gone. Then it was just a simple matter of taking control. Taking his body, or her body *back* more accurately.

She should go soon, gather her things and take off – not that she was expecting there to be anyone else who lived here, not with Dustin the way he was. Maybe she'd have more Bacardi first. That would make her happy.

Was she really happy with her life? Dustin had asked.

College was okay, she was paying her way through that to give her some sort of decent job. The kind Dustin must have had to afford this kind of place. But this, doing this. Well, it was necessary. She didn't want to hurt anyone, but must – she'd realised that quite early on.

It was the only way to satisfy her needs.

KINDRED SPIRITS

The ghost returned to the bridge at noon, and found that he was not alone today.

Of course, he was never truly alone. The world carried on turning around him; it was just that he couldn't be a part of it anymore. The people who dashed to and fro, rushing to work or meeting with loved ones (*don't dwell on this*) couldn't see him, couldn't feel him – apart from the odd shiver when they walked right through his 'body'. They were totally oblivious to his presence. He sometimes tried speaking to them, joining in with their conversations, but it wasn't the same. For one thing he didn't know these folk from Adam, had no connection with their friends and family. Inevitably it only left him missing the company of those who were once close to him even more, something he'd sacrificed a long time ago.

However, this was different. As he approached the bridge, its worn brown brickwork arcing high across a torrid river below, the figure hunched over the side looked up. It was a girl, about his age – that is the age he'd been when he died. Maybe slightly younger, but definitely in that area. She was dressed in a T-shirt and jeans, had long, dark-blonde hair and deep green eyes. They were so sad, those eyes, regarding him with a mixture of bewilderment and morbid curiosity. It amazed him how she could even regard him at all. Perhaps she was a psychic. He remembered seeing a film once when he was alive about a medium who could see ghosts, and even talk to them. It was an enticing thought, but he didn't get his hopes up quite yet.

She continued to watch him as he strolled up and parked himself beside her.

"Hello," said the ghost, testing the waters.

The girl didn't reply at first. She just stood there staring at him, her brow creased. Then she said: "You can *see* me?"

The ghost was puzzled, too, by this remark. Of course he could see her, he could see everyone. He wasn't blind. Okay, so technically he didn't have eyes any longer, but the principle was the same. "I was just about to ask you the same question," he said.

"Oh, thank God! All morning I've been standing here trying to attract someone's attention, but everybody just keeps ignoring me. It's like I've ceased to exist or something."

A switch seemed to mentally click inside what passed for the ghost's head, turning on an invisible light bulb. And he suddenly understood what she'd *become*. The problem was he'd never seen – never been allowed to see? – another ghost before. Not in the flesh, so to speak. And she certainly looked like she was in the flesh – no glowing white translucent ghost, her. Did she see him in the same way? He hadn't even seen *himself* since he'd died. The ghost didn't appear in any reflective surfaces, unfortunately – he'd tried looking in car wing mirrors and in shop windows, but all he could see was a strange sort of pale outline. He'd often wondered why he hadn't encountered any of his brethren, especially at the bridge itself. Surely it must have been used before for such purposes; he hadn't been the only one.

Well, no. This proved he hadn't. The girl looking at him and cocking her head sideways had definitely used the bridge. It must have been some time after he left yesterday evening; and the ghost had taken his time walking back to the bridge that morning. Only to find *her* there, waiting. Another one like him.

"Ah..." he began. "I don't know quite how to put this, but I think you *have* ceased to exist. At least as far as everyone around here is concerned." He waved his hand to indicate the various people round and about.

"What do you mean?" she said. Her voice was shaky, but it had a beautiful lilt to it. Such confusion wasn't uncommon. When he'd first died, he had no idea what was going on. The ghost had done exactly the same thing, shouting, screaming at the crowds to acknowledge him. Running out into the middle of the road, playing chicken with the traffic and flapping his arms about. None of it had done any good. In the end he was forced to admit that something terrible had happened, and then when the memories came flooding back to him of his demise, he knew *why* it had happened as well.

"Do you remember anything about yesterday? About last night?" asked the ghost.

"I..." She shook her head. "There are vague images, but— The bridge, I remember the bridge!" She smiled, as if this tiny scrap of information was highly significant. The ghost had already worked that out for himself; it was why she was here in the first place. The bridge was her central location. Her base of operations, the place she would feel compelled to return to if she ever wandered too far – say, in search of her past. It was where...where she had crossed over.

"Right, that's good."

"What's your name?" she enquired.

He'd been so thrown by this whole encounter the ghost had completely forgotten his manners. "I'm sorry. My name's Darryl." And without thinking, he held out his hand.

She took it in her own and shook it gently. Her touch overwhelmed him. Darryl could actually feel her 'skin', the softness of her hand, as smooth as silken sheets. It had been a long, long time since he'd felt anything at all – and for this to be his initiation back into that sphere was truly, well, it was beyond words.

"I'm Samantha. Sam for short."

Darryl kept a hold of her hand far longer than he probably should have done, but she didn't seem to mind. At last, he released it, albeit reluctantly. "Pleased to meet you, Sam."

"Same goes for me. So?" she said.

"So?"

"You were saying about my ceasing to exist, not that anyone would ever notice if I did." Now, there was the biggest clue. That was the Samantha of yesterday talking, her personality, her true feelings surfacing. A clue as to what her motivations had been.

"Come and sit down a minute," said Darryl, easing himself onto the wall of the bridge. "I want to tell you a story."

"I'm not sure I've got time for this. I should be...I should be somewhere. At least I think I should."

"A job? With your family? Trust me, this is where you're supposed to be right now." Darryl hadn't had anyone to explain it to him. He'd figured things out for himself, on all those long, lonely days wandering around. There was no reason why Sam should have to do the same. Not with him here.

She joined Darryl in sitting on the bridge, one knee delicately raised. "Okay. So you're going to tell me a story. Is it a good one?"

"Not really. It's pretty sad, especially the ending. But you need to hear it anyway. Are you ready?"

Sam nodded. "What's it about?"

"It's a love story."

"Oh. One of those. Do you mind if I don't."

"Please," said Darryl, patting her arm – more to touch her again than anything else. To convince himself that the handshake hadn't been a fluke. He was relieved to find that it hadn't. "You *have* to listen to it."

Sam nodded again, giving him the cue to proceed.

"Where to start…"

"Stories usually begin at the beginning," said Samantha.

Darryl gave her a half-smile. "The beginning of this one is also the beginning of the end, though." Samantha narrowed her eyes, intrigued. "It's about a friend that I once knew, let's call him Sean for the sake of argument."

"So Sean isn't his real name?"

"No, it *wasn't*. But that's not really relevant. Anyway, this Sean grew up an only child. He got plenty of attention from his parents, but it tended to make him a bit isolated when it came to mixing with other kids. He was shy, awkward. You know the kind I mean?" Sam said that she did. "And it was the same thing at school. Never quite fitted in, couldn't interact properly, was excluded from all the usual gangs and cliques. Was made fun of and taunted, right up to leaving at sixteen. Those kids at his school made him feel like he was nothing; *less* than nothing. That he'd never amount to anything. And the teachers weren't much better. They could see what was going on, but never did anything about it.

"No wonder he turned out so insecure about himself. He wasn't much to look at really, not what you'd call a catch, but they convinced him that things were even worse. And the loneliness, man, you wouldn't believe it. Having to watch as they all made friends, formed bonds, and later on split off into couples. He had the same feelings as everybody else there, in fact if anything his feelings ran deeper than most. While the rest of the youths were only bothered about a quick fumble or screw with the girls, he just wanted someone he could connect with. Someone to love; someone who would love him back. It didn't happen, of course. What girl would be stupid enough to hook up with a loser like him, right?"

Sam shrugged. "Sounds all right to me. Nicer than a lot of guys I've known."

"Oh, he was *nice*. But then nice guys always finish last, don't they? Or at least that's what he thought until he moved on to college. He was a fairly okay painter, you see, Sean. Had real potential, so the art teacher said: she was the only teacher in the entire school he ever thought anything about, and he liked to think the feeling was mutual. Mrs Kenworthy, her name was. Nice lady. She was the one who arranged for him to do the course at the local tech. He was really nervous at the interview, having to show them his work. His 'portfolio'. Looking back, most of the stuff in there was complete rubbish, amateurish. But they saw the same potential as Mrs Kenworthy. Saw what Sean might accomplish after being trained properly, after living and breathing art for two years. And they were right, his skills improved no end – not that Sean would ever admit to this. He always saw his work as poor, second-rate. Couldn't understand why anyone might be interested in it. But still, he enjoyed what he was doing, that was the main thing. He was allowed to express himself creatively; hell, it was encouraged. Something that hadn't really happened before outside of Mrs Kenworthy's lessons.

"But it wasn't just his painting that improved when he went to college. Thrown into a situation with a bunch of complete strangers who knew nothing about his background, he found that he could relax a little more and be himself. Sean came out of his shell, made friends with these like-minded teenagers – some of whom would remain mates with him for the rest of his life. Or what was left of it."

Samantha inched closer on the bridge, now obviously hooked by the tale. "So Sean died?"

"Not yet. I'll get to that bit in a little while," said Darryl. "First comes the love story bit... Like a lot of really deep and meaningful relationships, the one Sean got involved in started out with a friend. Her name was Ruby. She was an artist, too; well, an aspiring artist. He fell in love with her work first, and then with her. They used to stand next to each other in class and pass comment on one another's work, usually in a complimentary way – although if criticism were needed it was always given and accepted graciously. Ruby was different to the girls he'd known before, more mature, perhaps, and certainly more open. She was the only girl who'd ever shown an interest in him, who looked beneath the surface and saw into his very core. Her upbringing had been similar as well, so they also had that in common. They were like soulmates, thought Sean. Kindred spirits. Their friendship blossomed into something more over those two years and by the end of the course, by the time they came to exhibit their final pieces at the college, they were never really out of each other's sight. Ruby even helped Sean through the unexpected death of his mother from a heart attack."

Samantha's bottom lip was trembling. "So...So they had something really special together?"

"Oh yeah. So special there was even talk at one stage of them maybe renting somewhere when the time was right. But..."

"But what?"

"Well, people change. Circumstances change. And long-distance relationships never, *ever* work."

"Long distance?"

"Ah, sorry. I'm skipping ahead. While they were still at college, they both applied for fine art courses at the same university. It would have been perfect, another three years doing what they really loved. Together. An extension of their time at college really, putting off venturing into the real world for a little while longer – where they knew they'd have to get 'proper' jobs to supplement their incomes. Hardly any artist can survive on what they make from sales of their work, you know."

"Go on," said Samantha, eyes wide with anticipation.

Darryl sighed. "The problem was they didn't get into the same university, did they. Ruby ended up at her first choice, but Sean didn't do as well in his interview this time. Had to settle for his back-up university. Not a bad university, you understand; just not Ruby's university. So, *she* went down south and *he* headed off to the Midlands. For their last week together at the end of the summer holidays they journeyed down the coast and stayed at a campsite near a little fishing village. It was the best week of his entire life. They walked along the cliff-tops, ate fish and chips, went on the fairground rides and messed about in the amusements. And they tried to forget that the fates were conspiring to keep them apart. On the final night, though, they slept out in a cornfield in sleeping bags, underneath the most beautiful starry sky you've ever seen. And there and then they pledged themselves to each other, said that the distance wouldn't interfere. That their love *would* last the distance, against all the odds. And Sean really believed it. He *had* to believe it because Ruby was his world now."

"So what happened next?"

"What do *you* think?"

"It can't be good, because you've already told me it's not."

Darryl looked down at the bridge wall. "They each went their separate ways, and got on with two separate sets of lives. But whereas Ruby was in her element at uni, Sean found himself regressing back to his school years. He failed to fit in again, made hardly any friends, and couldn't seem to get into his painting. All his pieces were flat – or flatter than usual in his eyes – lacking feeling and emotion now that Ruby wasn't by his side. To begin with they called each other all the time, messaged saying how hard it was being apart; they even met up briefly in the holidays. But after a while the messages and calls started to dry up. And because Ruby was ever present in his thoughts, Sean felt as if his whole life was drying up, too.

"The final straw was when she cancelled their get-together at Easter, saying she had too much work to do – this being one of the most important terms and everything. Sean sensed that something was wrong and had to know what was going on. It was eating him up inside. He had to travel down there and speak to Ruby. It was a mistake, he knew that afterwards. Should've left well enough alone and continued hoping... At least that way his dreams might have stayed alive. And perhaps he might have, too. But Sean went there anyway, checking out the train timetables and using the last of his grant money to buy a ticket, trekking through city streets to find the university and then getting lost inside it. Until finally, at last, he came to the arts and humanities section. And who should be walking out of the canteen in there but Ruby, a tall, handsome guy with his arm around her shoulders, pulling her in to kiss and slobber all over her. Ruby never complained once – she was enjoying it, in fact. A classic case of out of sight, out of mind. And that's exactly what Sean did. He went out of his mind."

Samantha let go of a held breath. "Can't say as I really blame him. If I'd been in that situation…" She paused, thinking.

If she'd been in that situation…what would she have done? What did *she do?*

"Sean *was* in that situation. And he did the exact opposite of what anybody else would've done. He didn't confront Ruby, didn't beg for her to return to him, didn't take a swing at her new 'boyfriend' with the model looks. Maybe if he had, he might've felt better about things. Instead, he just walked away and never contacted her again."

"Oh my God. Why?"

"I think for a couple of reasons, really. For starters there had always been a part of Sean that couldn't understand why Ruby was with him in the first place, let alone why she'd stayed with him for so long. Somewhere at the back of his mind he'd always been expecting her to find someone new, someone *better* than he was. It was inevitable. Another reason was that he cared *so* much about Ruby he just wanted her to be happy – even if it was with another boy. He'd back away graciously, because that's just who he was. He didn't have the authority to make claims on anyone, didn't feel he had the right. And he certainly couldn't force Ruby to love him anymore if that's not what she wanted. Of course, none of that stopped it from hurting.

"If Sean thought his life *before* Ruby had been rough, then the next few months, the next year, certainly proved him wrong. And if that week away had been the best of his life, Sean paid for it in spades with weeks that seemed like the very worst – although there was always another one to top it just around the corner. When he returned home in the summer, Sean spent most of his time in his room, doing absolutely nothing. He didn't paint, didn't read, couldn't sleep half the time. All he could do was think about Ruby and what might have been, Ruby with that guy." Darryl paused a second to wipe the corner of his eye. He looked up to catch Samantha watching him. "Like I said, sad story," he offered in his defence. Clearing his throat, he began heading for the home stretch. "You can imagine what that kind of thing does to someone, when they're stuck in the past and can't move on."

"Yes," said Samantha, now also crying. "Yes, I can."

"It doesn't matter what anyone says to you, you just can't dig yourself out of that hole. Your life doesn't seem to be going anywhere and sometimes you just feel like taking off. You might even do it, just like Sean – worry your father and the rest of your family to death when you vanish into thin air. And on your travels you have even more time to think, to wallow in self-pity and depression.

"Then, one night, you see what you think is a way out. You're sick of feeling like this, sick of existing in a world that's done you wrong. Your perspective is warped and you can't see past the next day, the next hour, the next minute. Can't see that if you just hold on then things might come right again."

"And that way out is..." Samantha tapped the bridge.

Darryl nodded.

"And you're Sean, right?"

Again a nod.

"You saw the bridge and you went to the edge. Looked down at the drop, the water rushing past. And you thought to yourself how good it would be just to jump in, to lose yourself in that water and never have to—" Samantha wept freely now, the tears coming thick and fast. "*I'm* down there, aren't I? Somewhere. Down there just like you?"

Darryl moved closer and put his arm around her. "I think so, yes."

"Nobody's ever going to find us, are they?"

"Probably not." He held her, placed her head on his chest. "But...But at least we found each other."

"His name was Andrew," she mumbled.

"Who?"

"The boy who was *my* world. Who tore it apart."

"Oh," said Darryl. When she was ready, Samantha would tell him *her* tale, he knew that. They had time, all the time in the universe.

A dog's barking growl shook them from their reverie. Its owner, an overweight man in a raincoat, was pulling the lead back, assuring his pooch that there was nothing on the bridge. The black Labrador knew differently.

Darryl lifted Sam's chin up and wiped away the tears – these too felt incredibly real to him, their wetness on his fingertips. "Okay?" he asked.

"I will be, I think. So what happens now?"

"I don't know." Darryl paused for a beat before speaking again. "Could I maybe take you out for a drink sometime?"

In spite of herself, Samantha laughed. It was a heart-warming thing to watch – or it would have been if Darryl possessed a heart to warm.

Had she, for whatever reason, been sent to him? Was it possible that even a man in hell deserved some companionship? Was Samantha a true kindred spirit, maybe even the bona fide soulmate he'd been searching for all his life? It would certainly explain how he could see her, and she him. How ironic, then, to stumble upon her in death.

To find out for sure, they would have to walk, and they would have to talk. Build bridges of their own and let the water carry on flowing underneath.

But that, the ghost reminded himself, looking into her deep green eyes again, eyes no longer as sad as they'd once been...

Now that would be another story entirely, wouldn't it?

THE GOAT

I've never really liked that word.

Not the animal, don't get me wrong. I *love* animals, I've watched my fair share of cute cats and puppies videos. NBD, they cheer me up. My heart! Nothing against the actual OG goat as such, tho they don't really do anything, do they? I don't think. It's more the term I have probs with.

Greatest. Of. All. Time.

When did it change from 'The Bomb' to 'The GOAT' exactly? Must have missed that memo, lol. I guess bombs have a more frightening meaning in this world, at a time when we're closer than ever to blowing everything to shit, amma right? Least the letters don't stand for something else, or I don't think they do. Best of the motherfucking best? Naw, can't see it, lol. Whatevs.

It's not short for anything, either, I can't stand those names like STAN. Superfan, that's okay I guess, because it means you're good at it. Brilliant, in fact. Totally. Super, lmao. But Stan? *Stalker*-fan? I don't care for that. I'm not a stalker, not like all those others. Sounds like when that comedian Mum used to like, the small sweaty one, was talking about a made-up foreign country at the Olympics walking around the track at the opening ceremony, holding their flags. Saying it was all the same guy called Stan – "E's-back-is-Stan!" Lol.

What was I talking about? Oh yeah, I don't like those terms describing fans. Negging them. Where would some of those so-called celebs be without them, eh? They're the ones who put them in *Brother's Big House*, *Ballroom Dancing on Ice* or on *Get Me the Hell Out of Here* with Ant or Dec. Most of them don't deserve that kind of status, anyway, were on some talent show or other – 'no-talent' show more like – or created a video that went viral like that one about the potatoes. Were on *Amour Island* shagging. I guess it's a kind of performance, isn't it. Totally whatevs.

Not like *Him*. He's a proper star, when you get right down to it. Has real talent, not a wannabe. Never has been. Auditioned to get into The Band when he was only very young, a baby really, teenager. Same as I was, we're more or less the same age – give or take. I've seen the footage, and I mean, yeah, none of them are that co-ordinated or anything, some of them aren't in tune, but you can see how they'd go on to do big things. Be absolutely massive. Especially *Him*. Even back then, you could see it. Star quality and all that.

And, TBF, it *was* like a bomb had gone off when I saw him for the first time. Went off inside me, in my head. In my heart. IDK. I didn't just see a star in him, I saw *stars* – real ones. Sparks or whatever you want to call it. I guess I knew, even then all those years ago, I knew we were going to be together at some point. You can feel it, can't you? You know when something just *feels* right... More so when you see someone in person, not just on your TV screen. I mean, they can't see you, can they? Through the screen. But when you share that special look IRL, that's when you really, *really* know.

Everyone was into them back then, when I was at school. I wasn't the only one. They were the talk of the classroom, the playground. I sometimes wished they weren't. Weren't as popular as they were, because then it would just be my little thing. I mean, it kinda was anyway, but not. IDK. I wouldn't have joined any fan clubs for exactly that reason. I *was* his fan club.

I collected all the stuff, not just the albums and singles – this was before streaming, y'know? You actually had to collect it all. Posters on every bit of wall in my room, Mum'll tell you – *would have* told you. The annuals, all the memorabilia. His biography, even though he wasn't really old enough to have one. Told you more about him, though, like his favourite colour and what he liked to eat when they were on tour. Proper obsessed, I was. No, not *obsessed*...

Then that day, the night when we got to see them live. All right, so they were miming, but all the bands did it. Some still do. Didn't mean they couldn't sing, He definitely could. I'd listened to some of his acoustic music, wasn't that easy to get hold of, either. Showed you what was to come when he finally parted ways with the other members of The Band. His solo stuff.

But I'm getting off topic again, aren't I? I do that. IDFK.

The concert. Mum only let me go because Shelly Bradley's dad was taking us, the whole responsible adult thing, which was back before anyone found out what he was actually doing to Shelly at home. Oh no's. Urgh. El creepo! I can't even... Least she had a dad, tho, I guess, so there's that.

The concert was okay, but I couldn't really enjoy it for all the screaming around me, not just Shelly, but Jane Roberts and Hilary Tench. OMFG, she was the *worst*! Going nuts she was. I tried to shut it out, all of the noise – retreat into my own little bubble like I tend to do. Wasn't easy, not until he came up towards us on that little stage. Dancing in those baggy trousers The Band always wore, pointing at people in the audience.

Pointing at me.

I tell you, at that point (ha ha!) I just died. I literally *died*.

And that look...That wink, meant specially for me – I was the only one he did it to. That was when I truly felt it. What I've felt every time since, waiting outside the back doors for him to leave after performances, or appearing on chat shows or wotnot. He always looks for me, has done ever since that day.

I'm not gonna lie, it's been hard. There have been times over the last ten years when I've almost given up. I used to pray every night that he'd come to me, that we'd start dating. Praying, like Mum told me to do, not in a selfish way, but, well, when things are meant to be like that, surely—

And when that didn't work, when the...when doing those things to myself just didn't cut it. Hah...*cut* it. I've just realised what I said. OMFG. Times when that didn't help at all, to take my mind off the fact that I couldn't have him. Not then, anyways. Times when I thought I never would get him, so it'd be better just to not be here anymore.

Glad I didn't tho. So glad now I've figured it out. Figured out a *way*.

The lyrics in his songs defo got me through some dark times. The way they'd speak just to me, y'know? If I listened closely enough, I could hear my name being whispered between the guitar riffs. All that longing, those words about wanting...wanting...I wished there was some way to just let him know. That I was doing the same, waiting for him. Longing, wanting. OMG, the *wanting*.

But it wasn't the right time. I know that now. Just like he suffered for his art, I had to suffer for our...our love. I knew all those flings wouldn't last. The ones with those models or TV personalities. You could just tell. As for that bitch who used to do the weather, she was just using him to further her career. To get presenting gigs. Ha! FFS. I can't even. She couldn't present a bag of dicks. Was everywhere for a little while, but then people woke up to her – how false she was – and stopped liking her. Cow. Didn't she realise what she had? I would've killed to have what—

I *will* kill, if that's what it takes. But we'll get to that in a bit. I haven't finished quite yet...

All the stuff on the 'net, it's made it easier to keep tabs. I'm not sure that's been a good thing or a bad thing. You had to put the effort in before, really go out of your way to *follow* people – not just hit a 'like' or a 'friend' button. Most of the time you can't tell what's real and what's not, on Instatok or wherever. IDK. Like, I don't get why there are so many people pretending to be the 'real' James Blunt. Or Keanu or somethin'. Even their mothers, sometimes…

Mum, I really miss you. I. Can't. Even.

Why? Why do that? Pretend? They message you, reaching out to 'fans'. As if those people would do that! I pity the idiots that reply, I really do.

Actually, I used to know someone who'd engage with those kinds of 'bots or whatever they're supposed to be. Liked to mess with them, when they were just trying to get your information. Your money, really, LBH. They'd talk for hours to them, trying to get a rise, LMFAO.

And don't even get me started on those clips those whores put up there, just to get attention. Your 'work wife' or 'office distraction'. Sweetheart, anyone would be distracted by those inflatable boobs bouncing down the hallway, or you bending down to pick up a pencil or wotnot. Bimbos holding up underwear and slapping it repeatedly against themselves just to give the frustrated viewer a two-second flash of them wearing it. Don't flatter yourself. It's really NBD.

Thirst traps, to get you obsessed. Obsessions… One I remember seeing was a beautician, hairdresser – her clips were just an excuse to flash everything she had. You could see what she'd eaten for breakfast in those skimpy outfits. Cosplays of superheroes and anime characters, dressed in lycra – grown-ups playing dress up like they used to do as kids, but for different reasons. IDFK.

Women, just girls most of them, reaching off screen and pretending – least I hope they are! – to be jerking someone off. FFS! Is that what they think *love* is? Because it's really, really not. They should listen to some of *his* songs if they want to know. Those hit different, go hard – and I'm not talking about that kind of *hard*, either. What's wrong with them? Pandering to men... Men are actually disgusting, when you think about it. Most men, that is. Not *him*.

It's why I never really bothered with them, apart from the fact who'd live up to my soulmate, my one true love? Who'd compare?

And they used to say I had probs. What was it they called it? Parasocial something or other... That's right, said I had a parasocial relationship, just because I felt proud of all his achievements. I mean, OMG. Can't the love of someone's life be proud of things like that, supportive?

Like with the acting, when he moved into that. Sometimes, DGMW, I wished he hadn't, because it brought him into contact with all those actresses, like that bottle-blonde one with the big lips, or the brunette who had those legs that went on forever, or the redhead who had those eyelashes. FFS. I've got news for you, ladies, *real* women don't look like that. We don't walk around with a shit-ton of plastic in our faces or our bums. Fillers, implants...Jesus. Who wants that? It'd be like having sex with a blow-up doll or something. I'd imagine, lol. Not that I've...I mean, I haven't— I don't think doing what I do counts, does it? Not the cutting, the other stuff. Although sometimes I imagine I can connect to him when I do those things to myself. Like perhaps he can *feel* it. I really, really hope he can. Like, I only do that because of what he means to me, the way he makes me feel. I just want to be able to do that for him too. Reach off the corner of the screen and—

I'm getting myself all worked up again and I really need to concentrate, get on with this. Where had I got to? Oh yeah, the acting. He started out doing a few bit-part roles, on big movies mind – don't think that they weren't! – and that got him some attention. I was proud anyway, but the critics, well, they did what critics do. Pull things to pieces, called him wooden as a tree. YMMV. Fuckers! I'd like to see them do any better, but then again those who can do, those who can't... No, that's not right. That's teachers, isn't it? But I'm sure the same's true of folk who slag off things they couldn't possibly do themselves.

And for the record, just because you put money into something – executive produce it – that doesn't make it a 'vanity project', dickheads. He just happens to really, really like spy capers. So what if he got someone to write one with him in mind as the lead, then took it to a director friend and got them to make it? That doesn't take away from its worth, does it? FFS.

That doesn't mean you can't be proud. Supportive. Go and see that movie twenty times in its opening weekend. Try to help bump it up. Cost of living crisis? What about my cost of lovin' crisis, eh? Lol. Didn't make a difference in the end, drop in the ocean. It didn't do that well – and let's face it, a movie's got to make so much now, what with advertising and publicity budgets. That's what he said in all the interviews, that was the reason, and I for one believe him. Doesn't mean it wasn't a success in all the ways that count, right? I've seen it so many times now, I should know.

Acting...Acting the goat. That's something Mum used to say when I was little. Stop. Acting. The. Goat. Or "you're getting on my goat", have you heard of that one? Might have been a local thing...

Obsessions. Me and my—

Oh, but he's such a great actor, almost as good as he is a singer. Songwriter. It's hard to say which he's best at. Of. Best of the motherfucking…

Mother…Mum.

She was the one who went with me all those times, even though she should have been at work. Took me to see those people, got me to talk and talk and…I do like talking, you've probably noticed, but not about stuff like *that*. FFS. In front of Mum. Not when they look at you that way. Wasn't the way he looked at me and pointed that first time. Winked. When I *died*.

It's how I knew, even then. Like I said, that we were always destined to be together. Good actor, that's what he is. So good at pretending. At making out that he doesn't really recognise me, know me, know my heart – when he absolutely does. My *heart*. He just can't let on, has to keep up appearances, be fair to his fans. He didn't mean it when he took…when he took out the court order, I know that. I forgave him. There was nothing *to* forgive. Not really.

Made it harder, of course. But then nothing that's worth having is easy, is it? Lol. The restraining thing, the 'not coming within' whatever it was, however many miles of him. I didn't even read it, TBF. Had no intentions of doing what they said, what they wanted. Don't get what you want, what you need in life by following the rules. Rebels all the way, FTW! Yeah!

It's not like I have to anymore, not like anyone's breathing down my neck watching everything I do. Every move I make. Tho I really wish she was sometimes, that she was still around. She was only doing what all mums do, what she thought was best, looking after me. A different kind of love. Keeping me on the 'straight and narrow'. IDFK. Didn't want to see me get hurt, when at the end of the day I was being hurt more by not just going for it. Not just acting on my – *our*

– feelings. Because they're mutual, *of course* they are. Nobody's going to tell me, convince me otherwise.

I really wish she could have been around to see how all this works out, tho. To be at the wedding, then maybe even grandkids… I'm getting ahead of myself again. Haven't even—

It's amazing what you can find on the 'net. Horrible stuff, and all that toxic crap on social media, yes. Yeah, that's true. But also *incredible* things, how to do certain things. OMFG…God…gods, plural. Who'd have thought there were so many of them? So many that could help you with so many different problems. If you prayed every night, just prayed differently. If a certain set of tasks were completed, a ritual, a sacrifice.

Didn't help with Mum. The tumour still got her in the end. But I think it will with this.

I know we're going to be together, I'm going to make sure. You know when something just feels right. Amma right? Lol.

Funnily enough, the final act involves an animal. Guess which one, LMFAO. It's all to do with the entity I've been asking for help. And I love animals, don't get me wrong. Nothing against the actual…that particular one as such, tho they don't really do anything, do they? I don't think. It's cute and all, I guess. But would I watch a video of it to cheer me up? Maybe…if there weren't any cat or dog ones available. Whatevs. Ah well, it'll have to be done. I have to kill it.

'Course there's a slight chance I might end the world; not just my little bubble, but the *whole* world, if I do it wrong, say it the wrong way. May not just be me who dies. Literally dies, IRL. But if I can't have *Him*, my world has no meaning anyway. And it might as well all get blown to shit for a good reason, yeah? Least I'll have explained myself, I think. Kinda. Tho if everything ends, then I guess nobody will be around to read this, will they? *Oh no's!*

Anyways, I'm doing it. So wish me luck and all that. Got the bowl ready. The knife's pretty sharp, same one I use on myself. So it shouldn't feel a thing. I don't think. The goat. To get the… No, *for* The GOAT.

Ha! I've never really liked that word.

Not until now.

IT'S ALL OVER...

They were the words that had haunted him for what seemed like years.

Words he'd said, tumbling from his lips before he could stop them. Words he'd wished – so much later, after everything had gone to shit – that he'd never even heard of. That he didn't know the meaning of.

He'd known it after the fact; God, how he had then. Knew it now, even though circumstances were conspiring to trick him – to *convince* him things were far from over. Because it wasn't only the words that haunted him.

It was the person he'd said them to.

"Brandon." He heard her now, in spite of having his fists pressed up against his ears. "Brandon, it's so cold out here, baby."

Cold? You bet it's fucking cold, he thought. *But you shouldn't be able to feel it. After all, you've been dead six months, haven't you?* You're *cold as well.* Beyond *cold, or at least you should be.*

A vision of a decomposing corpse floated into his mind: laying there in the coffin, buried so deep (an image he might once have taken great delight in). The face a virtual skeleton, that hazel-coloured hair still splayed over the satin lining, as it had done the morning after they first made love.

Brandon focussed on that instead: watching Hannah sleeping, her eyes flickering beneath the lids as she dreamed. That beautiful face, so young and innocent. Mouth full and lips a deep red even without the aid of make-up. Had there ever been such a perfect moment as that one? He couldn't remember another like it in his life, not even his wedding day.

(As a contrast his mind flicked suddenly and without warning again to him grunting and sweating – another woman below him; jet-black hair this time, her moans in perfect unison with his thrusts. Perhaps a little too perfect? A hotel room surrounding him, instead of the college digs he'd been in when Hannah first opened her eyes. "Oh Brandon, yes! Please, oh my God...*Yes!*")

"Brandon." There it came again. "Brandon, please... Please, baby. Why won't you let me in?"

He'd let her in once. All the way in. Hannah couldn't have been more a part of his life, sharing those student days with him when he'd first started setting down his stories. Had he known she was the one when their eyes met across that lecture theatre? Clichéd crap, the kind some other writer might infect the page with. But not him. Not his kind of thing at all. And yet—

"Brandon? Why won't you just answer me? Say something, *please!*"

Because you're not fucking real! You can't be! I saw them bury you, Hannah. Shit, I was the one who had to identify you after—

For about the millionth time since this all started, Brandon shook his head, trying to gather his thoughts. There were too many, all mixed up and fuelled by emotion: sadness, regret, fear, anger, loathing – of himself more than anything. And, of course, the guilt.

Now that last one. That was a biggie.

It was probably the cause of this whole damned thing. Did he somehow bring her back, even if it was only in his imagination? Some grief-crazed hallucination that he was doomed to see and hear every single night? He often wondered if *he* was the one who'd died all along, maybe killed *himself*, and this was his punishment in Hell?

Crazy. It was like something out of one of his books. Precisely why it *could* be a blurring of fantasy and reality, the stress of everything that had happened mixed with plots and characters from—

"Brandon, please."

Shut up, shut up, shut up. Just shut the fuck up!

The words inside his head, or coming from that figure out there? They were too loud, surely, to be emanating from those deep red lips. Brandon got up, about to go to the window. Then froze.

You've seen her. You've seen what's out there. You know all too well, without having to look again.

But maybe tonight would be different. Maybe tonight would be the night there'd be nothing there. At least then he could get some kind of handle on what this really was: him losing what little sanity he had left.

Brandon recalled the first time it had happened. The first time he'd foolishly looked outside when he heard the voice calling to him. Telling himself – although he knew each and every inflection, knew the timbre like he knew the intro to his favourite song – that it wasn't her. *Couldn't* be Hannah. It was someone else out there shouting his name at eleven o'clock, interrupting his late-night drinking session with old Jacky Daniels. Maybe some fan of his work who'd managed to get hold of this address (he'd kill whoever was responsible); this isolated farmhouse they'd chosen and overseen the conversion of together.

(A sideways slip again, to one Sunday when they were alone and putting those final touches to the place. Picturing Hannah painting the walls – pushing the roller up and down, that old shirt of his covered in paint splatters, but clinging to her torso. The jeans she was wearing fitting tight against that perfectly-formed bottom of hers, moulded to the denim. He'd crept up behind and wrapped his arms around her stomach. She'd pretended to fight him off, but when his hands reached higher, cupping both breasts beneath the shirt, Hannah had relented, turned and kissed him full on the mouth. Eagerly, they'd undressed each other and rolled around right there on the floor. It wasn't as if anyone was going to see them, not out here. They were completely cut off, completely—)

Cut, severed – just like the flesh she'd opened up, opening her veins in the process and allowing the blood to pour out onto that bed, in yet another faceless hotel room (the police told him that it was a common place for suicides, and that made sense – for fuck's sake, he'd even written stories about that before. Hannah had read them, too).

No, don't think about that.

Okay, his mind seemed to say – taking him back to his original nightmare. The one where he'd gone to the window to peer out into the darkness, wondering why that state-of-the-art security alarm they'd had installed hadn't kicked in. Only *he* knew the codes for it at the gate. Only him and—

There was the figure, shades of black on black. Standing in the middle of the yard, about twenty, thirty feet away from the door. He couldn't make out much, so his hand reached instinctively for the floodlights they'd also had installed. Floodlights which would have snapped on automatically if 'she'd' been just a couple of inches closer.

"Brandon," came the voice once more, chilling his blood. "Brandon!"

His fingers were quivering as they reached for the switches, as they brushed the edges but didn't flip them yet.

"Brandon, answer me, baby."

Christ Almighty! Brandon's fingers either slipped, or his subconscious decided that he'd had enough of this and was going to chase away these stupid suggestions, brought on by too much booze and not enough sleep these past few months.

But suddenly it was too late.

There she stood, the shadows no longer providing any comforting doubt. It was her, or at least a damned good look-a-like (he hadn't dismissed that notion, especially back then; there were enough people who knew what Hannah looked like to pull something like this, photos of them out together at launches and parties; what had happened was a matter of public record, in the papers – even mentioned briefly on the local evening news – though hardly the *big* topic of conversation that day).

Brandon blinked. *Got to get a grip – just get a grip!* The rational part of his mind told him that he was imagining this. That Hannah was dead, and when you're dead...you're fucking dead! A line from one of his favourite flicks back in the eighties – the one with the guy with all the nails banged into his head.

A film, a novel, a fiction. But this was happening, right now, out there. The woman he'd loved, his wife. The woman he'd spent more than twenty years with. The woman who was in the ground, buried because of what he'd done. Because of what he'd said. Those words:

"It's all over..."

She looked pretty sprightly for a corpse, it had to be said. Pretty sexy, too. The more Brandon stared out at this vision of his deceased spouse, the more details he took in. The flowing hazel hair, more lustrous than it ever had been in life. Those piercing eyes, framed with thick lashes – which she was batting against the sudden glare of the lights. The figure she'd always had, shown off in a flimsy nightdress (that, even more so than the shirt and jeans she'd worn when they'd been decorating, clung to her curves in all the right places). She must have been frozen out there, judging by how hard those nipples were jutting against the fine material. And, Heaven help him, he was getting turned on by it.

"Brandon," she said again, holding out her arms in a pleading gesture. "Please answer me, baby. It's Hannah. Your Hannah."

He closed his eyes this time, squeezing them shut. Knowing that when he opened them again she would be gone. Knowing that it was only the stress, the sleeplessness, the bourbon, the—

"Brandon?"

He opened them again.

Still there. Still. Standing. There.

More details now, like the fact that there were scars at her wrists, the blood congealed and scabbed over. She was so pale – *wouldn't* you *be if you'd died half a year ago?* he said to himself. He shook his head. Make-up, that's all. You could do all sorts these days, special effects and stuff. He'd seen enough evidence on the fleeting visit to that set, the one turning his short story into a movie – before it had been consigned to DVD oblivion.

Not that again, not now. No time for that bitterness. The set visit... He'd seen extras walking around with their arms hanging off; those effects guys were brilliant. They could make you believe *anything*.

Make you believe that your wife hadn't really killed herself at all. A bad dream. She'd returned to him, just like he'd prayed for all those nights he'd cried himself to sleep. After the rows with Melinda, after she'd fucked off because she knew she wasn't going to get anything more out of him. Out of this...whatever it had been.

("Oh God. Brandon. Yes. Harder. Please. *Yes!*")

It had started out as just a drunken fumble one night after a convention up North, where Brandon had been Guest of Honour. Just two nights away from home. Was it his fault Hannah had been called away to go and see her sister again? "She's sick, Brandon. I *have* to go and help look after the kids while she's in hospital."

He'd sighed. "The first fucking time I've ever been asked to do something like this, all expenses paid. Can't that waste of space ex of hers do something to help?"

"You know she doesn't want him going near the kids, Brandon. And now Mum and Dad aren't around—"

"I wanted you there! You know how nervous I get about doing the public stuff. This is important to me."

"Yes, I know," she'd said, looking down.

"I'm not cancelling."

"I don't want you to," Hannah had whispered meekly. "I wouldn't expect it."

"Well I'm not. It's too late to back out now, anyway."

"I don't know what to say. I'm sorry, baby."

"Ah, forget it!" he'd snapped. "Go on then, fuck off and go."

Hannah had recoiled as if slapped, then gone and packed her bags. She'd tried to get around him before leaving, but he was having none of it. He'd sat sulking as the taxi came to collect her. The following day Brandon had travelled to the convention alone, but he hadn't stayed that way for long.

Melinda had been there at the live onstage interview, in the very first row. He vaguely recognised her as someone who'd attended his last couple of signings. She was young, her raven hair in a bob, extremely pretty; such a sweet expression. Black mini-dress and tights. As Brandon sat uncomfortably on stage, thinking of interesting answers to give the fawning interviewer, he'd looked out and caught her eye.

(Had he known then, when he'd caught her eye?)

From that moment on he'd been talking to *her*, and her alone.

Afterwards, once the handful of people who'd lined up to get their copies of books like *Poisoned Chalice*, *Mayhem's Match* and *Undaunted* signed, drifted off, she'd been waiting to have a word with him.

"No books?" he asked.

"Already signed – personalised to me." She'd smiled. "I was wondering if you fancied a drink at the bar?"

Brandon smiled back. "That sounds like a great idea."

Over the course of the next few hours, they chatted on one of the sofas in the lounge area. Others had come and gone, pulling up chairs to ask him about this and that, usually how to get into the industry, whose arse to kiss, if he'd give them a quote. Brandon took it all in good nature, knowing he wouldn't bother using any of the email addresses being handed to him. And all the time there was Melinda. Laughing at his crap jokes, listening intently again as he gave her pearls of wisdom about the writing game accumulated over many years (so many years, and who had stood by him when he'd almost given up, when he was hardly making a bean from his stories? Hadn't been Melinda, that was for damned sure). She admitted she'd had a go at some shorts, but they were nowhere near ready for sending out anywhere.

"I don't mind having a look," he'd said, as the wine flowed and they'd got closer and closer on the couch.

"Oh, you don't have to do that."

"Don't be silly, I'd love to read them," he was saying before he realised he was doing it.

He'd walked her to the lift that night, but nothing else happened – apart from a peck on the cheek.

When Brandon got back to his room, he checked the mobile he'd kept switched off all day and found a message from Hannah wishing him good luck with the interview, and another one sent later wishing him well for the panels tomorrow. Both were signed: 'luv u v. v. much, baby xxxxxx'.

For a moment that had got to him, even in his drunken stupor. But then he thought to himself that if Hannah loved him so much, why wasn't she here? With him? Why wasn't she the one who'd been on the front row at his interview, and in the bar celebrating afterwards? Not that it was her thing, being around crowds. She'd always said she preferred it to be just them.

He didn't surface until it was almost time for his first panel, the panicked runners looking for him when he reached the convention level. "This way, Mr Slater," the pimply twenty-something had said, trying to keep the annoyance out of his voice. Melinda had been there again, sitting waiting for it to start.

And she'd been there again at the next one, and at his final appearance. He felt more than a little embarrassed and guilty about the night before, so slipped out without saying a word all three times. But, when Brandon spotted her again in the bar, now chatting to some other guy, he'd felt more than a pang of jealousy.

Turning to make his way out of the hotel, off for dinner at the Con's expense – making the most of his last evening – she'd caught up with him.

"Brandon...Brandon? I've been trying to grab a moment all day. About last night, I hope you don't think I was being too, well, you know," she said. Today she was wearing a short, flared skirt with leather boots and a halter-top. "It's just that, I've never really met a man like you before."

He cocked his head.

"You're so clever, you know so much about loads of things. You saw what you wanted and just went for it, you know? Are you all right? You haven't said a thing."

("Why won't you answer me? Why won't you talk to me, baby?")

"Look, I'm just heading out for a bite to eat – on the organisers." *Slick, Brandon. Slick.* "Would you like to join me?"

"Oh, I'd love a bite, thanks."

So they'd headed off for a meal in a swanky French place – a little beyond the 'reasonable expenses' the con had stipulated – and ate, drank, laughed, and talked again. Really *talked* this time.

"...So that's what I'm doing here on my own," he finished explaining to her after the second bottle of Merlot.

"Poor Brandon. If that had been me, I would never have let you go to something as important as this alone. I'd be proud of you."

"Exactly," he slurred. "Exactly. But then she's never really been into the genre that much." Wasn't strictly true: she used to read it a lot, but got bored of it around the time his work started taking off. Found other interests, like her genealogy, delving into the past. Who bloody cared where people came from? All that mattered was the present.

That night, when it came time to say goodbye at the lifts, neither of them had been able to. Nothing was said, but Melinda took Brandon's hand and led him inside the lift, then led him to her room on the third floor.

He hadn't been able to remember that much about what happened next, but he knew he'd had a bloody good time. A better time than he'd had with Hannah lately, the rolling around on the floor at the farmhouse a distant memory these days.

They said their goodbyes sheepishly the next morning and Brandon had returned home to find Hannah waiting. She'd organised for the local authorities to help with her sister, telling her that she was needed back at home. That her husband needed her.

(Jesus, how he needed her *right now*. How he'd give anything to know if this was real or just–)

Though he'd barely been able to look her in the eye when he got back, and he suspected she knew *something* had happened on that trip, he'd fooled himself into thinking it was just a one-off. Hannah seemed happy to ignore it, so life went on as usual.

Except it hadn't ended there. Melinda sent the first text a fortnight later, saying that she couldn't stop thinking about him. If Brandon was honest, she'd crossed his mind more than once as well.

They hooked up every time he could get away, using the excuse of meeting his agent Ken, or his publisher, or his PR person. Hannah was content enough working on her family trees. It got to a point, though, where Brandon was looking at his home life, looking at his secret life with Melinda (oh, some of the things they'd done over those months!), and wanting more than just a few stolen hours here and there. Actually, he wanted to swap. Wanted Melinda at home with him so he could have her anytime he wanted – first thing in the morning, in the shower, over the kitchen table if he so desired, smearing pancake syrup all over her.

And for Hannah to be gone.

It wasn't as if they'd ever had kids, was it? Though not for the want of trying in the early days. Maybe that might have changed things – maybe not. Neither of them wanted to be tested in case it was their fault. Didn't care to play the blame game.

Should have been a clean break, in theory. Ah, who was he kidding? After so many years, how could anything like that ever be clean?

Brandon resolved to tell her when he got back from one of his 'business' trips, fired up at the prospect of sex with Melinda on tap.

"Look, it's just not working out, Hannah."

"What are you talking about?" He could see tears welling in her eyes already, the first of many that afternoon. She'd run the gamut of emotions: from misery to anger; from resentment to denial.

"It hasn't been good for a while, surely you've seen that?"

"Please Brandon, please don't do this to me."

("Please, baby, why don't you let me in?")

His turn to look down at the floor. "I have to, don't you see?"

"Who is she?"

"What do you mean?" Brandon replied, looking up again.

"I know you, Brandon. You wouldn't throw away what we've got without there being someone else involved."

"You're crazy."

(You're going crazy. It *can't* be her.)

Hannah grabbed him by the arms. "I can still smell her on you!" she'd screamed into his face.

He'd shrugged her off, pushing her back at the same time. That's when he'd said it. Those three little words; not the three he'd said to her for the first time the morning after they'd slept together. But just as powerful. "Hannah. It's all over."

But it wasn't, was it? That was just the start.

When he wouldn't speak to her anymore, Hannah packed and left – as far as he knew going back to stay with her sister. Melinda moved in about a week later.

Next there came the phone calls, pleading at first – "Why do things have to change? I want to come home." – and later accusatory. "I know she's there with you," Hannah would say bitterly. In the end he began to hang up as soon as he realised it was her.

Then the calls stopped.

A good month went by and he didn't hear anything from his wife, though he was expecting to hear something from a solicitor at some point. Tying up loose ends. (Is that what she'd become, Hannah, a loose end?) Divorce proceedings would be starting soon – yet strangely he wasn't in any rush to initiate them himself. Probably because the shine was wearing off his fling with Melinda. Because that's all it was, that's all it *ever* had been. In the end he understood that, especially when she was going out and spending his money on expensive clothes and jewellery. Brandon had made a rod for his own back there, buying her presents in the first place, leading her to think that what was his was hers. While at the same time she was trying to muscle in on those real meetings with his agent, publisher and PR person.

"I can see what you're up to, you know," he said to her after coming out of one such session.

"I don't know what you mean," Melinda answered, her sweet expression long since replaced with the hard as nails one she wore most of the time around him.

"Come off it. 'Oh Ken, don't be silly, you don't have to look at my stories – just because I'm shagging one of your biggest clients'." He fluttered his eyes then, mocking her, and she slapped him.

"Fuck you, Brandon."

Things hadn't gone so well after that. But they'd gone from bad to worse when he got the call. A couple of weeks on his own with no Melinda, flipping through old photo albums (who exactly gave a shit about the past, now, eh?), and he'd started to realise what he'd thrown away. What a bastard he'd truly been to Hannah.

When the phone rang, he snatched it up this time, praying it would be her, praying they could work things out. It hadn't been Hannah, though. It had been *about* her.

"You're listed as her next of kin," the voice down the line informed him. He dropped the receiver. No, not Hannah. She wouldn't do something like that! Except...except, he'd driven her to it, hadn't he. While he'd been making up his fucking mind and coming out of the other side of this...this what? midlife crisis?...she'd been going through Hell.

(He often wondered if he was the one who'd died all along, maybe killed *himself*, and this was his punishment in—)

Fast forward several months. Months after identification, months after putting her in the ground. Just when he'd got to the point where he would give anything to see her again.

Then came the first visit. The first of many. In all kinds of weather, out in that sheer nightgown. Brandon recalled the night of the rain; she hadn't moved as the water saturated her, causing the wispy material to stick to her body, making it see-through, making him hard again.

(And another time, another place, out walking when they were young – not caring about the torrential downpour because they had each other. "We've been in this rain, feels like for hours," she'd said to him. "So?" he replied, clearing a wet strand of hair away from her eyes.)

Hannah was out there in the rain alone that night, and this time she *had* been there hours. "Please, Brandon. Why do things have to change?"

Because you're dead, Hannah. Things change when you're dead – or at least they're supposed to. You don't just carry on with your lives – ha! – as if nothing's happened. Doesn't work that way.

Night after night, time after time. Yet he told no-one about it. What would he say? "Hey, Ken, I think my dead wife's coming to see me every night. I think I'm being haunted or maybe I'm just going nuts, y'know?"

"Understandable. Now, when are you going to get that new manuscript to me?"

That wasn't going to happen any time soon. He could hardly focus on existing, let alone working. Now it was Ken's calls he was ignoring; his knocks at the door when the agent came out to visit.

Because there was Hannah, and only Hannah.

Here again, tonight. "Brandon? Brandon, *please!* Won't you answer me? Won't you let me in?"

Tonight might be different, he told himself again. *She might not be there when you look, when you flip on the lights. Then that will prove you're okay.*

Dammit! He pulled the curtain back and looked. There was the figure. He didn't need the lights. It was her, same as always.

But something *was* different tonight. Hannah was turning; leaving.

Christ, do something. This is what you wanted – the chance to be with her again. You've hesitated all this time, frightened of what you might find if you just went out there and...touched her. Remember the feel of her, remember what it was like to hold her?

("Oh God Brandon, please!")

To really hold someone you love and care about. You wanted this and now you're about to let it slip through your fingers. If there's a chance, just a chance that she could be real...

Brandon ran to the door, undoing the locks and bolts, flinging it wide open. "Wait! Hannah, please wait!"

The dark figure, in the process of walking away from him forever, paused and turned. He could see the outline of her head. Feel her gazing at him – and though he couldn't see her eyes he knew it was a longing look.

"Baby?" she asked.

"Yes. Sweetheart, is it really you?"

There was a slight tip of the head.

"I didn't dare hope. I thought I was going mad."

Hannah walked forwards, passing through the floodlight's invisible boundary. He saw her clearly now as they flicked on, more clearly than he ever had before – coming closer and closer as she did so. "It's me, baby. It's *really* me."

There were tears welling in Brandon's eyes. "I'm sorry, Hannah. I'm so sorry for what I did, what I said. Sorry I didn't believe. I—"

"Shh. It's okay. Let's go inside and we can talk."

She'd covered the distance between them quickly, obviously as eager to get to him as he was to reach out and touch her – make sure she was actually there (and God, did she look good in that nightdress, the way it clung to her, just like his shirt had once done...ignore the slashes on her wrists...). But she was just out of reach near the doorway. Just come a little closer, a little closer.

Now it was Hannah hesitating. *Don't just leave her out there in the cold, she wants to come inside. She's* always *wanted to come back home.*

Brandon pulled back, into the hall, and beckoned for Hannah to follow him. "Come in," he told her. "It's all right."

Hannah smiled, then crossed another boundary.

She approached him, reaching out her own hands. Letting him touch them. She was real – as solid as anything Brandon had ever felt in his life. Hannah took one of his palms and placed it on her breast.

"That's it, baby." She smiled again. "I know what you want."

Brandon couldn't help grinning. It had been so long since he'd made love to his wife, even before her death, before the split.

"Yeah, that's right," said Hannah as he kneaded her. "Please, baby. *Please.*"

"Oh God, Hannah. God, I love you so, so much."

At that, Hannah tensed up. "Love?"

"Yes," said Brandon, looking deep into her eyes. "I love you."

She smiled again, but then the smile grew organically into a laugh. "You don't know the meaning of the word."

Brandon frowned. Suddenly this whole situation – this whole situation which shouldn't really be happening at all – was turning sour. Had Hannah come back just to tease him, then point out the error of his ways? The 'ghost' of dead wives past? He didn't need *her* to do that! He'd felt bad enough without.

"Fortunately, *I* do. Now," she told him.

"What—" he began, but she placed a finger to his lips.

"Don't speak, Brandon. You've done all I needed you to do. Now it's my turn." Hannah grabbed him by the arms and swung him around into the wall. It shouldn't have been possible to even lift him, let alone do this, but his wife was incredibly strong suddenly. Stronger than she ever had been in life.

And when she smiled again, he saw her teeth.

"No," said Brandon. It couldn't be possible, he'd seen her corpse. Couldn't be possible that she'd become something he'd written about – albeit only a few shorts, as it didn't do to overuse the classics...unless you had a new twist.

But, as he was about to find out, Hannah was exactly that. "You didn't think I'd actually topped myself because of you?" She laughed once more, cocking her head right back. Still no bite marks.

Except why did they always have to be at the neck?

"You think while you were having fun with that slut, I wasn't out looking for someone else, too? Someone who could stop the pain, someone who could make me feel wanted again?"

There was a shadow at the door, just beyond it in fact. The figure of a large man shrouded in darkness.

"We're going to be together for a long time, he and I. He promised and...I believe him. His family history's fascinating, Brandon. His *heritage*. Oh, the things we've done together this past year. But I just couldn't stop thinking about you. I knew I had to come back." She grabbed him by the shirt and shoved him against the wall again; hard. It was now that he saw it – the cuts at the wrists, easily mistaken for razor slashes, but too jagged. Too much like—

Panicking, Brandon tried to push his wife back, but he couldn't shift her. "Please, Hannah, please don't do this to me."

"I have to, don't you see? Please don't struggle, Brandon. You'll only make things harder on yourself."

"No—"

"*Yes!—*"

("Yes! Please, oh my God...*Yes!*")

"I've waited all this time for you to drop your guard. But I can be oh, so patient. Especially now. It was also sort of fun, given your line of work." She tutted. "You really should have known better than to let me inside."

There was another noise from the doorway and Brandon saw more figures emerging from behind the broad-shouldered man. Oh, Hannah *had* friends now. So many friends. Crowds didn't bother her in the slightest.

"But now it's time, Brandon. Time to tie up loose ends." Her incisors grew longer than ever, her face altering, contorting, brow furrowing. He had to admit, there was a part of him that had always wondered if stuff like this existed. He'd never wanted to find out this way, though.

("Oh, I'd love a bite, thanks.")

"There's just one last thing I have to say to you," Hannah managed through her new teeth, pushing against those lips, now a deeper red than ever. "And I think you know what it is, don't you?"

In spite of himself Brandon nodded.

"It's over," he whispered eventually.

"It's all over..."

BENCHED

He likes to get there early, that way he can watch them as they walk in.

Same as he waits when it's over, sits and waits for them to get up first so he can follow them; he should be a gentleman and offer to get their chair, but most don't want that these days: a gentleman, or to be patronised. Those aren't the only reasons, though. It's so his eyes can trail over their bodies: observing the way their shoulders move – the swaying motion of the form – the muscles in their thighs and, of course, the way those buttocks go up and down with each step. Doesn't really matter what they're wearing, it's all still there. He can't help the way he is, men are visual; it's programmed into them...most of them, right?

That's why he doesn't feel guilty about any of it, hasn't since he arrived on the scene in his teens – university a revelation for a young boy from an isolated village. Why he feels no shame about the way he looks at them, the way he treats them. Back then it was like a conveyor belt, his love-life having more in common with a revolving door than anything. And the girls seemed to be into it as well, didn't mind that policy – trying to 'out lad' the lads. One-night stands? Not a problem. Meaningless encounters time after time with a string of faceless blokes? Sure, why not. Some even seemed to prefer being treated like pieces of meat. Or at least they acted like it, told him as much, when he could be bothered to listen. And that was fine with him.

He'd calmed down a lot in the decade or so since then, but that didn't mean he was ready to *settle* down. Didn't think he'd ever be ready for that.

He wasn't like those couples he'd passed walking through the park on his way here, sitting together holding hands, feeding the ducks or whatever. Monogamy? That was a kind of wood, wasn't it?

Each to their own; he just couldn't imagine doing that. And don't even go there with the 'M' word. Just the thought of the 'E' word was bad enough, brought him out in a cold sweat. Or even simply the 'R' word. Wasn't as if his relationships were what you'd call normal anyway; they changed depending on his mood. There were some girls he knew who were up for partying till the morning, would dance all night and still have the energy for you know what – usually all day the next day. Sally was like that, and he thought of the last time he'd been with her. Thought about the way her golden locks swished from side to side when she was riding him, occasionally dipping her head so that the tips tickled his chest, or throwing that head back accompanied by screams of ecstasy. What did he care if they were real or not?

Should stop before he became too aroused, focus on the here and now. On what he was doing. Get his head in the game, this new game. It's all this was when you got right down to it, a game, and he was the best player in town. In any town, he liked to think. It was a game, all about winning. All about power and control, as in who had it and was in it. That would be him, even on the occasions when he let them think it was otherwise.

Another reason to get there early, to be around when they arrived – it sent the message right from the get-go that he was one step ahead, so they might as well get used to it. Submit to it and go with the flow.

Like some of them did who were into the rough stuff, even if they didn't know it. Those were his favourites. He could usually gauge it, when to bring that up – and only a handful in all the years he'd been doing this had said no, walked away. Or tried to, anyway. Then there were the ones like Natalie, who were so into it the things she suggested made him blush sometimes. Good old Nat; he could always rely on her not being tied up when he got in touch, though that situation wouldn't last for long.

And of course there were those times when all you really wanted to do was just chill. Netflix and chill, that was. When you really couldn't be bothered to make much of an effort and just needed a relaxed evening in with a take-away, a bottle of wine and... Joanne was perfect in that respect, her agoraphobia meaning that she couldn't really leave the house anyway. She'd explained it to him one time, some sort of trauma from when she was younger. Who the hell knew? He hadn't been listening to her, had been too busy thinking about the things he was going to do to her once they'd finished that particular season of some popular box-set they were watching. Who the hell knew, who the hell cared? Those tears as she'd poured out her heart and soul to him had meant nothing. "I know a way of making you feel better," had been his response.

Some were proper talkers though, really went for it, and to be honest he liked to avoid those wherever possible – unless he enjoyed the conversation, like say they knew what the offside rule was, or could list their favourite Statham movies. He'd talk forever about the highs and lows of *The Fast and the Furious* franchise, and especially the merits of the spin-off with Mr S and The Rock. That might segue nicely into talking about that bloke's movies, too. Would be another couple of hours right there with the likes of *GI Joe* (sequel, not original) and *Jumanji*.

But sometimes you just weren't into talking, or listening, and there were girls like Brenda for that.

Girls who barely even spoke, were so mousey it was hardly even fair to take advantage like he did. Might as well have neon letters over their heads announcing how shy or vulnerable they were. Some were pretty messed up as well, like something quite serious had happened with Brenda, hadn't it – some sort of abuse? A family member? She hadn't talked much about it, because she didn't talk much *at all*, and that was good, that was okay with him. It had taken some work to even get her there – trust issues, see? – but it had been *so* worth it. She was used to being abused, and he'd worked with that. There had been no complaints, at any rate. Would she have even dared, he wondered? Now there was a girl who knew who was in charge, and once she'd put her trust in someone...

Like he said, though, she hadn't been a pushover; not at first, anyway. There was something to be said for earning it. For having to outsmart someone. It gave you a bit of a thrill, made the hairs on the back of your neck tingle.

If he was being honest with himself, as much as he was disappointed by the fact that there this new prospect was – sitting down at the table already, waiting for him even though he was early – wasn't there a part of him feeling that shiver of excitement? Still, it was a pity, because he would have loved to have seen this one enter and walk over to where *he* was sitting instead. On their first date, at the coffee shop – where he'd made up his mind right there and then that he wanted to see her again (she didn't get a say in the matter) – she'd been pretty well covered up. Trousers (not even figure-hugging jeans), raincoat, which she'd only shrugged off once they were sitting in the comfy chairs by the piece of modern art made out of open books, and a baggy jumper underneath.

But hadn't there been a huge part of him that loved trying to work out what was beneath it all? What she was wearing under that angora? Under those slacks? Maybe it was just comfortable underwear, after all she wouldn't have been expecting anything other than coffee on a date like that one – nice and public, made sense. Sometimes women like this, though, hey, it was all going on under the surface. She might have had *anything* on under there. Or nothing. That sense of mystery was so tantalising.

They'd arrived at more or less the same time on that occasion, practically bumping into each other at the door when he'd turned around and she'd been there. "Let me guess," he'd said, clicking his fingers, "Lauren?"

She'd laughed, nose crinkling slightly, light-brown hair tied back in a ponytail. "And you must be Tom."

"I suppose I must be." Lauren had laughed again. He'd known exactly who she was, though, the same as she had; their profile pictures weren't totally off like you got with some. An old photo: sometimes really, *really* old. A photo back when they were thin, before the comfort eating had kicked in. Not that he wasn't averse to women who had a bit of meat on them, especially in the chest area. Usually they were quite grateful for anything they could get. Look at Tracy, she was willing to do just about anything to make him happy, to make sure he didn't run off with a much thinner alternative. On the back foot all the time.

Lauren was pretty much how she looked in her photo, and that was what had caught his attention originally. Just the right amount of make-up, lipstick, eye-shadow. Nothing over the top; that would come later, and at his behest if he wanted the easy look, say. Mouth full, but not overly so; not blubbery, slimy. Definitely kissable. Eyes a gorgeous green colour and wide, but not too wide. Not anime character wide. You got some of the best porn in those Japanese cartoons, mind.

His type, certainly, but then some might argue that you only had to have a pulse and be female to be his type. They'd be wrong, but not far off. He wouldn't just shag any old bird (though there had been that one time when he was really desperate and he'd gone off home with a woman who'd been pushing forty, practically ancient; that had only been the once, though, he didn't do the whole toyboy thing – toy*girl* maybe, but not the other way around, which was more than could be said for that particular evening).

He'd offered to buy Lauren a latte, but she said she'd get her own – and he understood, it meant that she didn't owe him anything. Not yet, anyway. Another form of control. When they'd sat on those comfy chairs, the conversation had been nice and casual: a bit about her (she worked in life insurance, kinda boring but...); a bit about him (artist – yeah, right, piss-artist...a sort of free spirit, and it helped here that the family was well off, though he didn't tell her that bit – didn't want a gold-digger hanging around). He'd been on his best behaviour, as always at the start. Hadn't even checked out the waitress when she'd come to clear away their stuff, regardless of the fact she had that really low-cut blouse on so that when she bent down...oh man! Obviously hoping for a terrific tip, though she had a couple of those already – *badum tish!* But, anyway, he hadn't looked out of respect for Lauren being there, and what might end up happening, with a bit of luck.

The only warning sign had been when she'd talked about a few of the creeps she'd been on dates with in the past. "I mean, you wouldn't *believe* some men, Tom." Oh, he would. He *was* some men.

"Scum of the earth," he'd replied with a nod, seeing that she was fed up with that kind of treatment. Also getting more than the faintest whiff of 'long term' from her. Looking for something more permanent, though she was hardly going to come right out and say it on their first meeting. No girl wants a bloke to think she's got the wedding dress waiting in the car and the registry office booked for 2 p.m. that afternoon. Didn't mean it wasn't on her mind.

Nevertheless, that was a problem for some other time. If it looked like it was going that way, she wouldn't see him again for dust. She'd see just how much of a free spirit he was then! Wouldn't be able to trace him, either. Well, Tom? Seriously? You couldn't get more generic than that. Good luck! Wasn't a vast amount on that profile, apart from the picture: that *was* the truth. No, he'd tackle that when he came to it – and when he'd done with Lauren, naturally. For now, though, she had potential. Definite potential. Who was he to put her off if she wanted to rub his sleeve between her thumb and forefinger and think to herself: *boyfriend material.*

After all, weren't there others who thought that about him? Were still thinking it even as he was sitting in that hipster coffee place paying four times the amount he should for something he could get in MaccyD's for pennies? Still thinking that he was theirs?

He wasn't anybody's. He was *his.*

Not that Lauren knew that, she still thought there was a chance she'd be his one and only and he'd be hers. Even as they'd made that second date, moving up from coffee to dinner, she'd probably been thinking this was heading in the right direction – the peck on the cheek confirming it. He thought it was heading in the right direction as well, it was just that his direction was the bedroom.

Only, when he'd arrived tonight, Lauren had been here before him. There was no need to panic, though – probably just that she'd wanted to make sure she wasn't late and the bus or taxi or whatever had cut through the traffic quicker than she expected. She wasn't driving because, look, she had a glass of wine on the go already. Was here and was already ordering wine. Wine he'd be paying for tonight, if he wanted to get control. He shook his head, then told himself it was a good thing; alcohol was always a good thing. Helped to grease the wheels. As did other things if they were necessary, slipped into drinks when they weren't looking.

She was waving at him, had seen him come in – was rising actually to greet him. And it was now that he felt more of a pang at not being here soon enough to observe her entering the restaurant (nothing too swanky, just an Italian place he knew but she didn't, really – out of the way so it wouldn't be too busy). Because she was dressed up tonight, still not in a dress-dress or even a skirt – still favouring trousers, so there was no chance of dropping a knife or fork and seeing if he could catch a cheeky look under the table, confirm what she might be wearing underneath – but this time at least leggings, which clung to her and gave him more of an idea how shapely these were (even better than he expected, as it happened; perfectly proportioned, not too long, nor too stumpy). In addition to this, she had on an electric blue silk blouse which again showed off more of her curves than the jumper had done, and he wasn't disappointed in that respect, either. She'd also slung a short black jacket over the back of her chair.

But, if he was being frank (not Tom, ho, ho), it was her face that made him want her more than anything. The way she'd done her make-up tonight was very different, not too slutty but— He realised he was holding his breath and released it. The way she'd crimped her hair as well, so that it fell over that face on one side, falling in waves. If he hadn't been in such a public place, surrounded by other diners, he might have whistled – and he would have been right to do so.

He noticed her looking him up and down as well, once he started to move across to the table. He'd gone for smart casual, suit-jacket and trousers but without the tie, leaving the shirt open at the top; a halfway house of dressing up. He'd put on his most expensive cologne, so that when Lauren was close enough she could smell it. Indeed, even now as she gave him another of those pecks, one hand on his shoulder, another at his waist, she couldn't fail to miss the scent. He had no idea whether all that kind of crap worked, but women seemed to appreciate the effort in his experience – and his experience was far-ranging.

"Tom!" she exclaimed, as he made to pull away and sit down. Then found she still had her hands on him, was reluctant to let him go, it seemed – to release him (again, he was thinking should he be worried here?). Suddenly Lauren did let go, and he was free again, could finally put in his order for his own drink: a lager, he told the waiter who'd been hovering around *waiting* for him to get settled.

"Hey," he said. "How've you been?"

"Fine, fine. How're you?" She beamed at him.

"I'm…" He studied that face again, was so surprised by the transformation from the coffee shop Lauren; so what if she ended up being a bit clingy, he could handle that. It would be worth it to be in bed with *that* tonight. Still not really a person to him, he couldn't let himself think that way or he wouldn't do the things that he did. 'Tom' smiled back. "I'm good. Really good, thanks." Then he looked at his watch and frowned in mock irritation, attempting to get back some of that power from her – she'd have none by the time he was finished, and that made the hairs on his neck prickle even more. The notion of victory. Of conquest. "I thought we said quarter to…?"

Lauren flapped a hand. "I know, I know. But well, I figured… Truth is I've really been looking forward to tonight, Tom. You know what I mean?"

He did, though probably not for the same reason she had. Whatever, that gave him back a degree of the control. Lauren had been looking forward to this, would definitely not want to mess it up – which put him right back in the Captain's Chair.

The waiter delivered his lager and he drank a couple of gulps in one go, then spotted her looking at him. What? did she think he was an alky or something? He was thirsty, had walked it from the tube station to get here. Besides, *she* was the one who'd had a wine clutched in her mitt when he got there! How did he know she wasn't the addict? If she was, that was another no-no with him; he was nobody's sponsor or cold turkey buddy. Just didn't have the empathy. She smiled again, though, and it was all good.

He twisted and noticed the waiter was hanging around, for the order presumably, and he took the lead there as well. "Do you trust me?" he asked without even glancing at Lauren. "They do a fantastic antipasto to share here. You know, slices of meat, that kind of thing." He hadn't even waited for her to agree before ordering it; he rarely waited for that with anything. "And before you say anything, this one is definitely on me." Including the damned wine! Then he was delighted to find when he ordered his spaghetti carbonara for mains, she'd plumped for the same. Already it was working, she was mirroring him – accepting he was in charge.

Conversation as they waited for, and ate, the starter had revolved around work, mainly. He'd initiated it, but soon wished he hadn't when she began to go on and on about a life insurance policy she'd been wrestling with that day. Who gave a shit? "Have...do you have life insurance, Tom?"

"I..."

"Because it's important, you know." *To you, maybe.* "You shouldn't put it off, you never know what's around the corner." Was this a pitch, was she trying to sell him some? She must have noticed his expression, because she asked him next: "How about you, what have you been working on today? Something artistic? Drawing, perhaps?"

"Only drawing a few breaths," he told her and she laughed.

"No, of course, silly me. I don't know anything about the creative side of things. I'm more on the practical side." Then she looked up sharply, clearly worried she'd said something wrong, something that might put him off. "Not that— I mean, I do appreciate art. I just— But then, they do say opposites attract...don't they?" And was there more than a little pleading in that sentence?

"Sometimes," he told her, not wanting to give her too much – but not wanting to lose her, either. Now the fish had taken the bait, it was time to begin reeling it in, pulling that line taut. "Who knows? The night is young!" he'd said with a chuckle.

Now, as the mains arrived and she complimented him on his choice, Lauren moved on to talk about the minefield of dating again. That oh-so fascinating topic! How she was looking for something different – those warning bells once more – something other than the usual bastards you found in modern socialising. "You really wouldn't believe some men, Tom."

I know, you said that before in the coffee shop. This time he just nodded.

"They're just so... I mean, there are even names, terms for the kind of thing they do. Take ghosting, you ever hear of that?"

He had. He'd done it, any number of times. But they were calling it cloaking these days. "I...No, I don't believe so."

"That's because you're one of the nice ones, Tom. It's where the bloke cuts all contact with you, sometimes without any warning. Across the board, like email, messaging. Happened to a friend of mine after a few months of going out with someone, she was in pieces. Guy got what he wanted, I suppose – *all* he wanted. She was looking for something more long term, the man wasn't." She shrugged.

He nodded, then caught the waiter's eye and held up his empty glass for another pint.

"How could someone just do that, pretend they don't exist anymore? Coward's way out of a relationship, if you can call it that. A relationship, I mean."

"Staggering," he said.

"I know, right?" She fell into silence and he thought for a moment she was done, then started when she suddenly blurted out: "*Breadcrumbing* as well, that's another one!"

"What's that?" he asked, knowing full well and trying to keep the boredom from his voice.

She pursed her lips before continuing. "It's when you lead a romantic interest on, dropping little nuggets so that they'll follow and get taken in. Like *Hansel and Gretel*. Did you ever read that when you were younger? The witch trying to eat them?"

Wait till later, I'll be eating you *then*, he thought. *With a bit of luck.*

"Cuffing, uncuffing," Lauren went on, and he thought for a moment she was talking about something sexual, because he hadn't heard of that one. But no, it was another one of those – yawn – dating terms. She explained it to him at length (thank Christ the beer had arrived) that it was to do with only wanting someone for the winter, for those long, snowy evenings, and then cutting them loose so you could have your fun in the summer. Sounded all right to him.

"DTRs," she continued unabated. It was obviously a topic she enjoyed more than her work, even. "Defining The Relationship. Putting a label on it. I mean, can you imagine? In our parents' era, you went out and you were boyfriend and girlfriend. Simple as that. Like, here, now, second date...You'd be my boyfriend!"

His left eyebrow shot up before he could stop it. That warning bell, that ringing was getting louder by the second. He'd only ever had a handful in the past who'd talked about stuff like that by this stage, and they hadn't lasted long. No longer than a quickie, at any rate.

Lauren took another sip of her wine. In contrast to him, she'd actually slowed down, which really wouldn't do. Drunk in this case would definitely be better, her in particular. "Would you like another glass of—"

"Benching. Now there's one not many people have come across. Like in sports, so you can imagine it was some guy who came up with that horror! You know, where you have substitutes on a bench, rest a player and then call on another one. Some guys have ten, twenty or more women on their benches at any given time. I mean, *come on!*"

He smiled awkwardly.

"Fucking maggots!" she said abruptly and he winced. It was the first time he'd heard her swear and it didn't sit right with Lauren's personality. "I'm...I'm sorry. I just get so...I mean, I'm not talking about people like you here. Not even talking about men in general, just those guys who treat women like cattle, y'know? Who get rough and think we like it, or just treat us like shit. Half of them don't even use their real names on sites, Tom." Lauren said that in a really strange way, a way that made him want to down his beer in one. "Makes you wonder why more of them don't come to grief, doesn't it? I know what I'd do to them."

He laughed nervously. "Good job I'm not like that, then."

"That's right." She gave him a smile. "Mind you, you hear stories, don't you? They think they're being so clever these people, think they're like shadows or something. Untouchable. But eventually they get sloppy, leave their phones lying around unlocked. Talk in their sleep sometimes, things like that. Muttered names. Imagine, *just imagine* Tom, if any of those women on those benches ever found out about each other. Swapped war stories, that kind of thing. I wonder what they'd do."

He swallowed dryly, took another large gulp of the lager and held up the glass to show Lauren. "Oh dear, too much of this damned stuff. I should really…"

She smiled sweetly again, watching him. "Sure," said Lauren. "No problem."

Getting up, he made for the direction of the loos. He hadn't been lying, he really did need to pee, but instead took a right turn and out through the front door of the restaurant. He drew in a few deep breaths, thinking about what to do – head a little fuzzy from necking that last pint. It was obvious this Lauren had a bee in her bonnet about all that shite, was some kind of feminist, probably. Not his type at all. Had the makings of someone who could be trouble. But then there was her face, her body. He almost went back inside, braving it.

Instead, he found himself heading away from the restaurant, getting out of there – and getting out of paying at the same time. Putting it down to bad luck tonight; not being careful enough. Although nothing in that first encounter had screamed nutter, had it? Mind you, they were very good at hiding it, sometimes. He'd fallen foul before, or almost had. No, he'd make himself scarce – ghost, cloak or whatever the fuck it was called now!

Night had fallen while they'd been drinking and stuffing their faces, and the streets had taken on a different air. As he made his way up one, down another – weaving a bit from the beer, though he could usually hold it better than this – he found there were less people out here now. Which was okay, he still needed to relieve himself and would find a nice quiet alleyway to do it in.

He'd turned one corner, then another. Only to find someone standing there. A figure all in black. A shadow amongst the shadows: no face, nothing.

He blinked, shook his fuzzy head.

It took a step towards him and he backed off, saw that actually it was a dark cap the figure was wearing; head kept low, obviously to avoid being caught on any CCTV cameras. This was all he needed, to get mugged on top of everything else. But, yes, that was quite obviously the intention because there was something glinting in this figure's gloved hand. They'd been waiting for their next mark.

"Shit!" he hissed through his teeth, then half-ran, half-loped off in the opposite direction – jamming his hand in his pocket for his phone to call the police. Only…where was it? The shitting thing! It had been in his jacket pocket earlier, he could have sworn it had. He looked around for a phone box, trying to focus, but of course those were as rare as hen's teeth now that everyone was so connected.

Breathing quickly in and out, he looked over his shoulder – then breathed a sigh of relief to find the figure wasn't following him.

Think, think! Get to the subway, to a train. Get somewhere where there are some lights, for fuck's sake!

Of course the quickest way was the one he'd taken to get here in the first place, ignoring all those couples sitting hand-in-hand; what a load of bollocks! He made for the park and was glad to find the gate still open. It would only be a quick walk – stumble? – through here and the subway entrance would be in sight.

His bladder was protesting though, and he couldn't hold it much longer. There was nobody around here, either, so he ducked sideways to go behind a hedge. Fiddling with his fly, he dragged out his manhood and waited for that familiar tingling sensation to ease.

A noise caused him to tense up, putting an end to the stream of urine before it could even start. Something rustling not far away, on his left, no, his right? Was it the mugger? Had they followed him here? That was ridiculous.

But he crashed out of there anyway, backing away from the noise. Those shadows looked alive, though, didn't they? Were *becoming* alive. Too much to drink, definitely!

Backing off again, he almost slipped on the path, falling.

Staggering...

As it was, he took a few steps backwards and ran into something – something that took out the backs of his legs. He found himself falling, but was caught, his spine supported; and suddenly he was sitting down.

"What the—" He was reaching out with both hands, had already started doing that because he thought he'd have to brace his fall. They were flat though, on the seat he'd found himself on, wooden slats underneath his palms. It was only now that he registered the pain from his back and his arse hitting that wood, from falling so sharply.

The rustling continued in front of him and he held his breath...as a duck waddled out through the foliage. A bloody *duck!* Quack fucking quack! One of the ones that those couples had been feeding. It came towards him, probably thinking that he had bread as well. He kicked out a foot and it scrabbled backwards out of the way, terrified. "That's right, piss off Donald! I'm not in the mood," he slurred. No, he'd been in the mood for something else and denied. Right now, they should have been getting the bill – on the way back to her place, or his, whichever. Maybe even an alleyway, just not the one with the mugger in it.

"Do you have life insurance, Tom? You never know what's around the corner..."

He had to laugh. But couldn't sit here laughing for long. He still needed to pee, and then get to the tube and then—

Someone was behind him. He hadn't even heard them, sensed them, until it was too late. Then the line was there, around his throat, pulling, tugging. Tight, thin, like—

Now the fish had taken the bait, it was time to begin reeling it in, pulling that line taut.

Cutting off his airway, making it hard to breathe. Choking him. Two-handed at first, because he reached back and tried to pull them off. Then, as he got weaker, began to struggle less, the wire was held with one hand, twisted, and the other reached down, holding a knife. A knife in its gloved hand. So, the mugger *was* here! He tried to say they could take his money, just leave him be, but there was still not the breath. There'd have been more than a little pleading, if he could speak.

Then, even before he heard the voice, he saw a flash of blue satin at that sleeve – poking out of the black jacket that had been hanging from the back of her chair. Along with those leggings, it would only have taken that cap – pulled out of a pocket – to cover up completely. To be that shadowy figure.

Should he be worried here?

"Let me guess...Lauren?"

"It's not my real name, you know. Same as Tom isn't yours," she whispered. "I have a few, but she's my favourite. After the woman who played one of the best femme fatales, Bacall. Some people even say I look a bit like her." He twitched, but she had him held fast; he was usually stronger than this. That bloody lager...

Other things if they were necessary, slipped into drinks when they weren't looking.

Like when a waiter suddenly appeared?

"They send their regards, by the way: Sally, Natalie, Joanne, Brenda, Tracy...I could go on. The girls from the sidelines, the ones you've been switching between recently. Though God knows this is for all the poor women you've ever messed with, fucker!

"They clubbed together, see? Weren't that crazy about what you'd been doing, wanted revenge. And one of them had a friend of a friend, one of those unsavoury types, you know what I mean? They knew someone who did dirty jobs, for a price. But you know what, when I listened to them, I decided to waive the fee. This one's on me."

It was all going on under the surface...Very good at hiding it.

Warning bells once more.

*That ringing was getting louder by the second...*in his head.

He tried to move, struggle, then, but she pulled again on the wire. "Oh, what's the matter? I thought you liked it rough? Now, I can make it fast, I can make it slow. Do you trust me?" She tapped his still exposed and flaccid penis with the knife.

"They do a fantastic antipasto...You know, slices of meat."

Being treated like pieces of meat.

Not good, not okay. Not fine with him!

More struggling, but she was reluctant to let him go (he was *hers*); and he had hardly any strength left anyway. Just enough to piss himself and she pulled a face at that when she came round the front, eyes narrowing under that cap. Then she was tying his hands and legs, gagging him, slapping him. "Hey, hey, not yet. The night is young, remember? No ghosting yet! Just submit, go with the flow. You still need to find out what I'd do to people like you, when I'm in control."

"The truth is I've really been looking forward to tonight...You know what I mean?"

He wasn't getting out of paying *at all*.

Next she took out his phone – the one she must have lifted when she hugged him back at the restaurant – and took his picture, said she was sending it to her clients; before tossing it on the ground, crushing it underfoot. "It's all just a game when you think about it, and you just lost big time, 'Tom'." She turned him sideways, laying him down and gleefully setting to work while he grunted in agony. "Like I said, practical. But I do appreciate art!"

And then, suddenly, he was drawing a few breaths. Drawing his last ones.

Right there and then on that park bench.

YIN & YANG

The end of the world, the end of the universe, began with a kiss.

Not a war, not a bomb exploded by people too blind to see the consequences of their actions, nor a deadly disease genetically engineered or originating from birds. Just a kiss: that most simple expression of emotion. But, as many have discovered in the past, it is often the simplest of things that can cause the most devastation.

And whole empires have been known to crumble because of a 'simple' thing called love.

*

Stanley Bennett never listened.

He'd never listened as a kid, when his parents had told him not to hang around with Darren Walters and his crowd – who smoked like exhaust pipes, drank like long-distance swimmers, and eventually weaned him on to a hundred a day and multiple cans of lager a night. Never listened when his mates told him not to touch Rita Hepworth with a bargepole, and had regretted that night of messing around in the back of his dad's Ford when Rita announced she was pregnant and they were bloody well getting married or she'd tell her brothers about it (who'd rearrange his limbs and break his face – or vice versa, whichever he preferred). Never listened to Rita when she told him to cut down on the fried foods, all those burgers and chips and kebabs that were bloating him up to almost twenty stone. "You work all day at a desk and don't get any exercise," she moaned at him, but he was usually too busy tucking into a curry and watching the match on TV – that was when he could hear a thing over the bawling of their three-year-old. He never listened when she told him they needed a smoke detector in the house, and then one weekend he dropped to sleep on the couch with a lit cigarette in his hand and set fire to the living room. Rita and little Michael barely escaped with their lives and left him not long afterwards, once her brothers had given Stanley a good kicking.

He took no notice, either, when he'd collapsed at work and the doctors had told him that if he didn't stop drinking he'd almost certainly be looking at liver failure and then who knows? The sick leave just gave him more time to eat, drink and watch telly. Stanley never listened when his son, now eighteen, visited to announce that Rita had been diagnosed with breast cancer and was asking to see him. Never listened when Michael returned to let him know she had passed away and that he never wanted to see Stanley again as long as he lived.

Never listened *ever* in his entire life: except once.

Only once, in the urinals of the *George and Dragon*, did Stanley listen. He'd just finished his sixth pint of the evening and felt the sudden urge to empty his forty-five-year-old bladder. That urge turned into a desperate need, and as he was at the urinal pissing as many toxins out of his system as his body could eject in one go, the need became a sharp pain that spread throughout the whole of his body, sending him rigid.

It was at that point Stanley felt a hand on his shoulder. He was about to turn and say something like, "Can't a fella get a bit of privacy around here?" when he realised the hand didn't belong to anyone even remotely human. It wasn't the hand of Death, of that he was certain: for one thing he wouldn't listen to Death even if it walked up to him sharpening its scythe and beckoning a bony finger. Stanley Bennett would tell the Grim Reaper to just fuck off because he was going to live for a long, long while yet. For another, it wasn't cold like Death's hand should be. It was warm, and it squeezed tightly.

But Stanley Bennett did listen: he listened as the figure just behind him leaned in close to his ear and said these words in a deep, rich voice: "It is your time."

And Stanley nodded his head sagely as if it made all the sense in the world to him.

*

It was dark in that place. Dark and wet and...safe.

Though Jenny had seen nothing of the outside world yet, she knew much. Somehow, she knew that her mother and father loved her and wanted her, more than anything in the entire world. They had been waiting so long, trying so hard. They had even been visiting the hospital so that the doctors could help them. Years and years, and then finally, at long last, the news they had been hoping for. Jenny knew how happy this made them: how proud her father Kyle was, how complete her mother Helen now felt. She knew she would be cared for and given as much love and attention as anyone could ever want.

So why was she hesitating?

Why, after months of hearing them talk to her, play music to her, having the proper scans and tests, and Helen eating just the right foods that should make Jenny healthy and strong – apart from when her mum had gone through that early phase of scoffing Marmite and Salad Cream sandwiches – should she now want to remain exactly where she was? Perhaps it was because, along with the knowledge that these two people would give her the best home she could possibly wish for, came another awareness: that there were things out there beyond her parents' control. In spite of the many times they would promise never to let anything bad happen to her, they wouldn't be able to stop it. Because along with the good things she was about to experience would come so many bad things, too. It was inevitable, and Jenny knew this, also. That was the way things were, the way they always had been.

So she dug her heels in, steadfastly refused to come out – ignoring the struggle that was going on not far away, the clamour of voices, the quakes that shook the small space where she was curled up with her eyes closed tight. She was being evicted from her temporary home and there wasn't a thing she could do about it. But more than anything she was frightened, of what was out there awaiting her. Of the unknown.

Then the voice spoke to her, soft and low. It told her not to worry, that everything would be all right. "It is your time," whispered the voice.

Jenny let go, allowed herself to be dragged unceremoniously out of Helen's womb, accompanied by the amniotic fluid she'd been 'breathing' for nine months. It was then Jenny realised that she would forget all of this, forget everything she knew, and start over from scratch. She would not simply *know* things anymore, she would have to learn them, as she grew, as she lived…and wasn't there something a little bit exciting about that? More exciting than scary? For her the adventure was just beginning. It *was* her time, it—

Jenny was struck on the back; hard. It forced the last of the fluid out of her lungs and she took her first breath, screaming loudly. As she opened her eyes – her vision blurred, hardly able to see at all – she felt sure she caught a glimpse of the figure that had been in the room standing beside her mother, on the opposite side to her father (who was now crying tears of pure joy).

But then the figure was gone and Jenny had other things on her mind, like the sensory overload of being wrapped in a blanket and passed over to Helen.

"There we are," she heard one of the nurses say, "a gorgeous baby girl. Any idea what you're going to call her?"

"We were thinking of Jennifer," said Helen.

"Why, that's a lovely name," replied the nurse.

*

She found him on the hillside, overlooking the graveyard.

He sat on the back of a peeling green bench, looking down on the small group gathered around one particular grave: a handful of figures dressed in mourning black. She knew all of them instantly. One in particular, a young man in his twenties, with his hands clasped in front of him, head bowed solemnly. His name was Michael.

Yang was staring at them intently, his single black eye set deep into his bleached face like a nugget of coal on a snowman. The light breeze was blowing his creamy fringe and the loose alabaster robes he wore, his silken belt flapping as he leaned forward, one hand rubbing his chin.

"Hello Yin," he said on her approach, without ever taking his eye off the scene.

"I thought I would find you here," she said, walking towards him and sitting down on the lower part of the bench. Yin straightened out her own dark robes, pushing a rogue strand of ebony hair back over one ear. "You're getting sentimental in your old age."

"Hardly," replied Yang. "Just seeing the job through to its proper conclusion."

A man walking a dog went past. The Collie stopped and looked at them, barking playfully at Yang, then growling at Yin. The man looked right through them, frowned, and tugged on the lead. "Come on, Triton, stop playing silly beggars."

Yang grinned and returned his gaze to the funeral.

"You still never think about it, then? Not even after all this time?" asked Yin, looking up at him with her one milky eye.

"About what?"

She nodded. "About them. About what we do."

Yang shook his head. "Why should I? What purpose would it serve?"

"About what we do *to* them?"

"As I said, what purpose—"

"We interfere in their lives, every day. Don't you think we should take more time to understand them?"

They locked eyes, then. "We have a task to do; we do it. We serve a function."

It was Yin who looked away first, though she could still feel his eye upon her. "You never question any of it?"

"Never. And we have had this discussion before."

A tomcat appeared then and curled itself around Yin's leg, brushing its head against the delicate pumps that she wore. When it looked up and saw Yang, though, it hissed at him. Yang flapped his arm and the cat ran off, terrified.

Yin's eye narrowed.

"You know the rules just as well as I do, Yin," her opposite said. "We're here to ensure balance. Without us—"

"Without us, what?" she demanded. "The truth is we don't know, do we? Without us things might just go on the same as always."

"Or not. Do you really want to take that risk?"

Yin didn't answer.

"Did you not enjoy your last assignment?" he asked her.

"I feel," she said, "that you may have enjoyed yours a little too much."

He snorted. "Where one brings light, the other must bring darkness, where one brings summer, the other winter."

"Where one brings death, the other brings life," Yin said quietly.

"You should study the *I-Ching* more often. It's really quite fascinating." There was a hint of sarcasm in Yang's tone, but she didn't rise to the bait. Just because they had chosen, long ago, to adopt the names given to the opposites of the Tai Chi simply because they were tired of not being able to address themselves, and they had chosen forms to more readily reflect their function, didn't mean that *all* those ancient words of wisdom were correct. A perceptive few had definitely tapped into something, but they were off about a number of facts. For one thing, Yin was far from the passive force she was said to be; although Yang would probably have preferred it if she had been. Nor did Yin oversee endings, and Yang beginnings – sometimes it was both simultaneously, although they'd found the opposite played to their strengths more often than not. Perhaps that was only to be expected, given their female/male roles.

It wasn't, as the Emperor Fu Hsi proclaimed, necessary for Yang to be dominant over Yin for balance to be obtained. They were true equals, and always had been throughout time, since the first 'adjustment' had been made: the creation of a universe where once there had been nothing. They had been busy ever since. Every day, billions of changes to be made, billions of tiny details attended to, from the smallest opening of a flower to the biggest natural disasters; from the delivery of a bill to the winning of a lottery.

"We maintain the equilibrium," Yang informed her, repeating a speech he knew by heart. "We are not here to judge, to get involved, or to feel pity for them. They are a means by which we do this."

"They are people," said Yin.

He let out a breath. "It was all so much easier before they came along."

As if on cue, a woman walked along their path pushing a pram. She paused on the brow of the hill, no doubt considering whether to rest on the bench. She, too, looked down at the funeral – the mourners dispersing, leaving only the young man behind. Yin got up and looked into the pram; the baby inside giggled.

The woman, wearing only a thin dress and cardigan, shivered. "Come on, Jenny, let's get you home. There's a bit of a chill in the air." Deciding against sitting on the bench, she walked off down the path – never looking back once.

Yang smiled. "You see?"

Yin ignored him. "I have to go. There is work to be done."

"Yes," said Yang, climbing down. "As always."

And with that they both winked out of the scene.

*

The atmosphere in the flat was so thick that anyone entering unannounced would have needed diving equipment to breathe properly.

Dave Parkinson had only really returned to get his stuff. Some of the clothes he'd forgotten, his CDs, books, his DVDs. He'd been hoping that Anna wouldn't be there, that she'd be at work by now in the advertising agency, cooking up more ways to sell fridge freezers using cartoon characters and campaigns to turn the humble potato into the next cookery fashion item. But she wasn't. Anna was on the couch, curled up under a blanket, wearing a vest and her tracksuit bottoms, an empty bottle of Pinot Noir upended on the wooden floor, the drained glass not far away next to an empty box of tissues.

She'd stirred as soon as she heard the key in the lock, then sat up when Dave entered the living room. Her cheeks were puffy, eyes red and sore; and her long blonde hair was sticking out at odd angles. Anna looked at him hopefully, then her eyes travelled down to the suitcase he was carrying.

He didn't know what to say, so he started with, "Hi."

Pouting, Anna replied, "Not changed your mind, then?"

Dave's eyes dropped to the varnished floor. "I'm sorry."

"No you're not." Anna swept the blanket aside, sitting up on the maroon cushions. "Just tell me one thing."

"I-I'll try," said Dave. He really didn't want to get into this again.

"Were you ever happy with me? Did you *ever* love me?"

Dave looked at her now, but it was like looking directly into the sun and his eyes soon found the floor again. "Of course I did. How can you say that? You know I did."

"I don't know anything any more," said Anna, starting to cry once again. "I thought I did, but then...but then everything..."

"I did, Anna. But people change." Sounded like some shit line out of an afternoon drama on Channel Five: it's not you, it's me, and all that bollocks. But he didn't know what else to say. Sometimes the clichés are right. Sometimes they're clichés for a reason.

"*I* haven't changed," she blurted, sniffing.

"That's just it; maybe I have." He couldn't help himself, he looked at Anna for the third time: and this time she wouldn't let him go.

"So tell me – tell me what you want. Anything, I'll do anything."

Dave's eyes were welling up. "It's too late for that now. I'm sorry, Anna. I never meant to hurt you."

He watched as those soft, tearful eyes suddenly turned hard and cold. "Well you have. Look, just take what you want and get out."

"Anna—"

"I said *get out*, and leave me alone!"

Dave hung his head and walked into the bedroom. He went through the wardrobe, finding everything just as he'd left it. Taking out clothes, he folded them and put them in his case. Then he went back to the living room and started to go through the CD and DVD racks, before turning his attention to the bookshelves. Anna now stood in the corner; she'd been to the kitchen and poured herself a fresh glass of wine.

His eyes caught a framed photo of them both on holiday, some foreign place he couldn't for the life of him remember the name of. Somewhere hot, somewhere they'd been happy – as the smiling faces on the picture testified. A long-lost moment in time. Dave laid the picture down.

He turned.

"Got everything now?"

"I-I think so. I left the things we bought together, you know, the stuffed monkey in the bedroom and—"

"Cheers," said Anna, taking a gulp of the wine. "I'll get the charity people to come and collect them. I don't want anything in this place that reminds me of you."

"Anna, don't be like this."

She scowled. "You've got your stuff, you bastard. Now piss off. You wouldn't want to keep *her* waiting."

He went to the living room door, carrying his case.

When she heard the front door slam, Anna backed up against the wall and slid down it. Her body started to wrack with sobs, and she let go of the glass in her hand. It shattered on the wooden floor, the mixture of red wine and glass resembling the aftermath of a suicide attempt. Anna held her head in her hands and sat on the floor, rocking backwards and forwards. After a little while she brought up her knees and folded her arms on top. Resting her chin on them, she stared out into space.

Yang got up from the living room chair, where he'd observed the whole performance with his cyclopean eye, and walked across to her. "Let him go," he said, bending down. "You'll be better off on your own."

Then he was gone, and there was nothing left to fill the void but silence.

*

Andrew Croft had been staring at the blank canvas all day, one of many he'd stacked against the far wall.

Brush in hand, oil paints poised, he'd approached the white rectangle several times, only to step back again and look at it from another angle, like a hunter sizing up its prey or a boxer dancing round his opponent. In the end he simply sat down on the hard wooden chair in front of it and sighed. Nothing was coming, no inspiration, no motivation: nothing. Not since—

Andrew lifted his head and looked around at canvases he'd finished before Kristy left just over a month ago, walking out of his life and taking a large chunk of it with her. All were so full of energy, colours blending into each other with ease, circles, squares and stars forming the backdrop to surrealistic vistas populated by semi-naked human figures. Kristy herself had cropped up in several of these, but he'd had to put those away in the attic space of his studio as he couldn't bear to see her face looming down on him while he worked. No longer was she the inspiration she'd once been, now she was an unwelcome distraction – one who worked her particular brand of mayhem through the ceiling, as well as from thousands of miles away.

Kristy had been a force of nature, entering his world like a red-headed tornado and leaving the same kind of devastation in her wake. Ruined farmhouses, trees and fences scattered the landscape of his heart, and he'd been left behind to watch this twister carry on its destructive path over the horizon, no doubt to batter the next poor guy she encountered along the way. He'd been swept up in the moment and had ignored all the warnings his friends had given him about her, so he supposed he asked for all he got. But there had just been such a mystery about Kristy he couldn't resist.

The phone rang and the noise echoed all around the studio. Andrew went over and picked it up. "Yeah?"

"So?" asked the voice at the other end. It was direct and to the point, but he'd learned to expect nothing less from his agent over the years. Wendy Douglas was a good person to have on your side and a very bad person to rub up the wrong way. "Any progress with the rest of the pieces for the exhibition?"

Andrew looked over at the untouched canvas. "It's...getting there," he said.

"You haven't done a thing, have you?"

"No," said Andrew honestly.

"Look, you need to get that harpy out of your system. We haven't got long now to finish up and people are expecting big things."

"Maybe if the last one hadn't been so successful I wouldn't feel under so much pressure."

"You're complaining about success?" She sounded very close to being annoyed. "If you knew how many artists would kill to be in your position—"

"I'm sorry Wendy. Really. That came out wrong." Andrew sat back down on the chair.

"Listen, darling," she said, the edge leaving her voice, "why don't you reconsider about coming to the party tonight. It might do you some good."

"I..."

"No arguments. You'll be there or I'll come over and make you even more miserable by telling you the story of *my* turbulent love life; then you really will have something to complain about."

Andrew laughed. "All right, all right. You win."

"Good," said Wendy. "See you at eight."

Andrew put down the phone. He had no idea why he'd just agreed to that. He hated parties, especially ones that Wendy wanted him to show his face at. They were usually full of superficial people from the world of the arts and the media, all talking rubbish and expecting him to join in. Andrew shook his head; still, he supposed he'd better go and start getting ready. He pulled off his sweatshirt as he headed towards the door that connected his apartment with the studio.

Yin smiled as she watched him go, the words she'd spoken still lingering in the air around her. "You might just enjoy it, and you never know who you'll meet."

Andrew hated it.

He glanced at his watch. It was only nine o'clock and already he was bored out of his mind.

He'd spent the last twenty minutes discussing the pros and cons of whether Magritte should really have left those bowler-hatted gentlemen out of his 'otherwise magnificent' paintings with some pre-pubescent researcher for an arts programme on a satellite channel, and had only managed to extricate himself by saying he had to get some air out on the balcony because he felt sick.

It wasn't a lie. He did.

On his way through the throng, he bumped into Wendy for the first time since he'd got there. The short, fortyish lady, dressed in a man's suit with a streak of Elsa Lanchester grey at each temple, had been busy talking to a potential sculptor she wanted to place on her lists by the name of Ellis Blare.

"I think I've died and gone to the musical hell," said Andrew, "only without the light relief of the birds with legs and the giant egg man."

"You're not enjoying yourself, sweetie?" said Wendy, genuinely surprised.

"Oddly enough, no."

"Give it some time to liven up. Here." She handed him a glass of champagne, and he drank half of it in one go.

"I'm going out to get some fresh air," said Andrew, remembering his mission.

He pulled the huge glass door open and wandered out onto the capacious balcony of the penthouse suite where the party was being held. Who it belonged to, he neither knew nor cared, and probably wouldn't even bother to ask. It was one of those sorts of parties.

Andrew was alone for the first time in over an hour. He rested his arms on the balcony rail and drank some more of the champagne. The moon was full and round tonight, hanging over the city like a single, giant eye against the dark sky. *No wonder all the nuts are out*, he thought.

"Excuse me," said a voice from behind him. Andrew almost dropped his champagne glass into the street below.

He pivoted, ready to tell whoever it was to get lost – but then he froze. Standing before him in a black evening dress was the most captivating woman he'd ever seen. Her chocolate-coloured skin was smooth, her raven hair falling straight down her back with only a strand or two breaking on her shoulders. Her lips were full and the whites of her eyes sparkled brightly. Around her slim neck she wore a string of pearls. Andrew opened his mouth and closed it again.

"I'm sorry," said the woman, "am I disturbing you?"

"What?" Andrew shook his head. "No, I...where did you..."

"I just needed an escape. This really isn't my kind of thing."

"No," said Andrew. "Mine either."

"In fact," she continued as she joined him at the railing, "I'm sort of new to all this."

"New?" asked Andrew.

"I mean, new to the area."

"I see. Oh God, look, where are my manners?" Andrew switched the glass into his left hand and stuck out his right. "I'm Andrew. Andrew Croft."

She smiled, and her teeth were even whiter than her eyes – which Andrew could now see had perfectly circular black irises. He'd never seen a woman quite like her, and somehow he knew he never would again. Shaking his hand gently she said, "Yes, I know who you are. I've seen some of your work."

Usually this would be a signal to back off; he could smell a hanger-on from a mile away. But something was different here. "Well, it would seem you have me at a disadvantage," he said.

"Ah..." said the woman. "My name."

"That would be a good place to start." Andrew laughed softly. *But to start what...?*

"I'm Yvonne," she told him. "But some people...some people call me Yin."

"Yin." Andrew turned the name over on his tongue as she looked up at the moon.

"Beautiful tonight, isn't it?" said Yin.

"Yes," said Andrew. "It is. It really is."

*

"You're late," said Yang from his position cross-legged on top of the traffic lights.

The traffic on the roundabout was particularly busy this rush hour, the drivers racing around, none of them sure which lane they were supposed to be in. Yang reached down and flicked the lights to turn them green.

Yin pointed at the lights on the junction to make them red and halt the traffic's progress there. The cars Yang had let go travelled relatively safely around the bend. "I apologise. I had...matters to attend to."

"Such as?" asked Yang.

"Matters of balance," said Yin, climbing onto her own traffic light and wobbling slightly.

Yang thought about questioning her further, then said, "I haven't seen much of you these past few days."

"As you always say, time is on our side."

Yang flicked his lights to red. Yin turned hers green.

"I was present at the birth of a new strain of HIV today," said Yang. "Faster acting, deadlier than ever before; no drugs can help. You..." he let the word settle before carrying on, "were supposed to initiate a cure for cancer."

"That is where I have just been," said Yin defensively. "That is why I am late."

"You're quite sure?" asked Yang.

"I am. Why, do you have something you wish to say to me?"

Yang shook his head and clicked his lights back to green. Yin matched his movements again. "Only that I would hate to see you lose your focus."

"I am just as focused as I ever was," countered Yin.

Yang changed his lights once more. Yin followed his lead. Yang changed them back, Yin did the same. The traffic stopped and started and stopped again. "Enough of this," said Yin eventually. "I will leave you to your games."

She disappeared, leaving both sets of lights on green. The cars from each direction ran into each other, and all the drivers got out to protest that *they'd* had the right of way. Yang looked down on the chaos, like a bird on a perch, his white robes spread about him. It meant nothing to him but a ripple in the symmetry of order. He felt nothing for the people now getting into arguments and fistfights.

All he could think about was Yin. And why his partner had been lying to him.

*

"It's superb," she said as he showed it to her.

The painting was indeed exceptional. A night sky, picture perfect, with a large moon illuminating a couple on a balcony. The pair, barely an outline, had their arms wrapped around each other. "In honour of our first meeting," explained Andrew.

Yin, still dressed in black, now a dress suit rather than robes or an evening gown, and boasting two eyes again, where usually there were one, beamed brightly. "I love it," she said.

"And I love *you*," said Andrew, then instantly wished he could take those words back. He saw the fear in Yin's eyes, the panic. What had he been thinking, to tell this woman he'd barely known a week that he was in love with her! Ridiculous. It was how he felt, of course – he'd loved her from the first moment he'd seen her. Then, as they'd spent these last few days in and out of each other's company, having lunch, talking: two lonely people who complemented each other so well... But why spoil it all now by blurting that out? Him and his big stupid mouth!

She couldn't even look at him. "I-I think I ought to be going, Andy."

"No, please, wait," he said. "I'm sorry."

"You have nothing to be sorry for. This was all my doing. But I think it was a mistake. I should never have—"

Andrew covered the distance between them, placing his hands on Yin's shoulders. "Please."

"We don't belong together."

He tipped her chin up to look in her eyes. "No?"

"No," she whispered, but there was little conviction in her voice.

Andrew pressed his lips to hers, held her close to him. Yin gave in to what she'd been feeling, what she'd wanted to feel all this time but couldn't allow herself to. Her hands clutched his shoulders, urging him on, pleading with him for more. Eventually, sadly, the kiss ended. She smiled when he pulled back.

Taking her hand, Andrew guided her through to the door that would lead them to his apartment, that would lead them to his bedroom. It was all like a dream, but it was a dream from which neither of them wanted to wake.

As the studio door closed, one of the blank canvasses stacked against the far wall blinked with a single black eye. And as the canvas stretched and bent into the shape of a man, that single black eye shed a tear.

Then Yang, seeing all he needed, all he *wished* to see, took his leave of that place.

*

Yang's skin boiled hotter than the sun with jealousy.

How could she! How *dare* she! After all that she had said to him in the past – and with a mortal! Yang winked himself into existence at the base of a dormant volcano and set it off. He caused a tidal wave that killed thousands overseas, and an earthquake that killed many more. He had not felt such rage since the sacking of Troy, when they had first spoken of this subject; not felt such a need for sheer, unadulterated violence since Hiroshima, when last it had cropped up.

"Oh Yang," she had said then, with genuine regret. "We are alike in one way, but different in so many more."

Yet none of this rampage made him feel any better. Nothing could sate his anger and there was no way to dull the pain he felt inside. This was the final straw: he had put up with Yin's rejections time and again because he knew it was the way things were meant to be. For if Yang should love her, then the only thing Yin could ever feel for him was hatred. It was the way of all things, necessary to maintain the balance. He had accepted that and lived with it for so long.

Except now she had crossed the line: and with one of them!

As Yang walked the streets he felt the heavens open and he let the rain fall on him in the hopes it might cool him down. It did no good.

At some point he found himself back in Anna's apartment. She was in bed, asleep, dreaming of Dave. Sneaking inside, a ghostly apparition, Yang covered her mouth with his hand and yanked down the sheets. Anna's eyes were wide with terror, but he ignored it. "It is your time," he growled fiercely.

There would have to be balance, Yang told himself.

There would have to be restitution.

*

The sun was shining brightly through the window when Yin woke up in Andrew's bed. She had never experienced such a thing as this before. Her whole being quivered when she thought of him, and the night they'd spent together had passed all too quickly. She had observed other humans engaging in such rituals of course, often wondered how it might feel to be held, to be kissed, to be this close to someone. Now she knew.

Yin propped herself up and watched Andrew sleep, his head against the pillow. There were a billion things she should be doing right now, a billion things that demanded her attention, but they all seemed inconsequential to her right now. She'd blanked out everything but him. Finally, at long last, it was *her* time.

Andrew woke then and smiled. "Now that's a sight I could get used to in the mornings. Hello you."

Yin smiled back.

"Sleep okay?"

She nodded.

"Feel like some breakfast?"

Yin shook her head. "Later," she said, kissing him.

"You're...hmmn...you're the boss..." mumbled Andrew in-between kisses and pulled the sheets up over their heads.

As Andrew fixed them toast, Yin sat at the kitchen table in one of his shirts, drinking a glass of orange juice. It was what you were supposed to do after a night such as the one they'd just spent; she'd seen it many times.

Andrew switched on the TV and the news blared out: "...disasters the likes of which have scarcely been seen on this scale."

Yin rose to her feet. "Turn it up."

"What?"

"Turn up the television," she said in a voice he wasn't about to argue with.

"Relief funds have been set up for the survivors," said the newscaster grimly, "but already governments are saying there might not be enough money to cover all of these and help the countries involved."

"Jesus," said Andrew.

Yin had a hand to her mouth. "No. This is— It's all my fault."

"What are you talking about?"

"Andrew, I've got to go." Yin turned to head back into the bedroom.

"Go? Go where?" asked Andrew, following behind her. But when he got to the bedroom he found it completely empty.

"In other news," carried on the TV from the other room, "the body of a woman was discovered this morning by her ex-boyfriend, who had apparently gone back to her flat to check on her after an argument. The woman, who we are not able to name at this time, had been brutally attacked and police are now questioning the man about this incident."

*

She found him, this time in the graveyard itself. Yang was gaping at one of the headstones, tracing the words with his single, black eye.

"How could you?" she said.

It took him a moment to answer, then Yang said, "I did what I had to do."

"No you didn't. This has got nothing to do with them – it is to do with you and I. Look at me!" she shouted.

Yang turned. "There is no order anymore. There is no balance."

"Yes, yes there is!" Yin told him. "I can undo what you have done. There is still time—"

"No!" spat Yang. "Time is irrelevant. You will leave things be."

Yin shook her head. "I know how much this must hurt you. But you and I...we can never be."

"I know," said Yang. "But you have abandoned who you are."

"No," she told him. "You took away a love. I gave a love."

"*Your* love!" he screamed at her.

"I redressed the balance."

Yang sloped towards her; for once in his very long life he looked his age. "It was not meant to be like this."

"It *has* to be," she told him.

"And you think you have a future – with *him*?"

Yin knew better than to answer such a question.

Yang laughed. "I don't think so. He doesn't have long." There was something she didn't know, something that would put a stop to their little romance.

"What do you mean?"

"Even now the poison spreads throughout his body, only he doesn't know about it yet."

Yin frowned. "What have you done?"

"His former partner had already passed it on to him. I simply added my twist." Yang grinned maniacally. "But look on the bright side, Yin – he will never get cancer."

She slapped him hard across the face. "I can undo this unjust thing."

"I said *no!*" Yang grabbed Yin, but she struggled to free herself, raking his face with her nails. Yang's jaw locked tight and his black eye became a slit. He took her by the neck and squeezed. Her cold body heated up. Laughing, Yang said, "There is one more balance that has yet to be redressed. It is something that has been...overlooked right from the beginning. If I live, Yin, it follows – naturally – that *you* should not."

Yin's milky eye bulged in the centre of her ebony forehead. She choked, batting his arm, clutching at his fingers. But Yang was the stronger of the pair that day. She spasmed once, twice, there was a cracking sound like broken twigs. Then her whole body went limp. He let her lifeless form drop to the cemetery floor.

Moments passed and Yang did nothing but stand there looking at her corpse, wondering how she could even *be* a corpse. Then, backing away, he suddenly realised the enormity of what he had done. In his mad rage he had not only destroyed the one thing he had ever truly cared about – he had also killed the Yin to his own Yang. There could never *ever* be balance again.

"Without us things might just go on the same as always."

"Or not. Do you really want to take that risk?"

Yang wept as the ground beneath his feet began to tremble: the earthquakes he'd initiated were spreading, becoming more powerful than anything he could ever produce. Even now seas and rivers were rising higher than anyone could ever have thought possible. Without order, everything was in disarray. No night would follow day, no summer to follow winter. No moon to reflect the sun's energy. No life, where there was once death. Now it was this world that didn't have long, and the universe thereafter.

It was their time.

But, as it had always been, the only thing Yang could think about was Yin. As he disappeared for the last time, putting up no resistance. As the whole of existence imploded, then promptly followed him. One final adjustment, one final act of redress:

To create nothing where once there had been all.

And peace where once there had been none.

'Love is of all passions the strongest,
for it attacks simultaneously the head,
the heart...
and the senses...'

Lao Tzu, Founder of Taoism.

BIOGRAPHY

Paul Kane is an award-winning (including the British Fantasy Society's Legends of FantasyCon Award), bestselling writer and editor based in Derbyshire, UK. His short story collections include *Alone (In the Dark)*, *Touching the Flame*, *FunnyBones*, *Peripheral Visions*, *Shadow Writer*, *The Adventures of Dalton Quayle*, *The Butterfly Man and Other Stories*, *The Spaces Between*, *Ghosts*, the British Fantasy Award-nominated *Monsters*, *Shadow Casting*, *Nailbiters*, *Death*, *Disexistence*, *Scary Tales*, *More Monsters*, *Lost Souls*, *The Controllers*, *The Colour of Madness*, *Traumas*, *Darkness & Shadows*, *The Naked Eye*, *Tempting Fate*, *Nailbiters – Hard Bitten*, *Zombies! Even More Monsters*, *Dark Reflections* and *The Roads Less Travelled*. His novellas include *The Lazarus Condition*, *RED* and *Pain Cages* (a #1 Amazon bestseller). He is the author of such novels as *Of Darkness and Light*, *The Gemini Factor* and the bestselling *Arrowhead* trilogy (*Arrowhead*, *Broken Arrow* and *Arrowland*, gathered together in the sell-out omnibus edition *Hooded Man*), a post-apocalyptic reworking of the Robin Hood mythology. His latest novels include *Lunar* (which is set to be turned into a feature film), the short YA novel *The Rainbow Man* (as PB Kane), the critically-acclaimed and award-winning *Sherlock Holmes and the Servants of Hell* from Solaris, the sequels to *RED – Blood RED* and *Deep RED*, all recently gathered together in an omnibus edition – *Before*, *Arcana*, plus the sellout novels *Her Last Secret*, *Her Husband's Grave* and *The Family Lie* from HQ/HarperCollins (as PL Kane).

He has also written for comics, most notably for the *Dead Roots* zombie anthology alongside writers such as James Moran (*Torchwood*, *Cockneys vs. Zombies*) and Jason Arnopp (*Doctor Who, Friday the 13th, The Last Days of Jack Sparks*) and as part of the team turning *Clive Barker's Books of Blood* into motion comics for Seraphim/MadeFire. His stand-alone comic *The Disease*, published by Hellbound Media, was also a 2016 Ghastly Award-nominated title in the 'One Shot' category. Paul is co-editor of the anthology *Hellbound Hearts* (Simon & Schuster) – stories based around the mythology that spawned *Hellraiser* – *The Mammoth Book of Body Horror* (Constable & Robinson/Running Press), featuring the likes of Stephen King and James Herbert, *A Carnivàle of Horror* (PS) featuring Ray Bradbury and Joe Hill, *Beyond Rue Morgue* from Titan (stories based around Poe's detective, Dupin), *Exit Wounds* – a crime anthology featuring the likes of Lee Child, Val McDermid, Dennis Lehane and Jeffery Deaver – *Wonderland* (a finalist in the Shirley Jackson Awards), the bestselling *Cursed* and its sequel *Twice Cursed, The Other Side of Never, In These Hallowed Halls* (the first ever Dark Academia anthology) and *Death Comes at Christmas*, the last seven also from Titan.

His non-fiction books include *The Hellraiser Films and Their Legacy, Voices in the Dark* and *Shadow Writer – The Non-Fiction. Vol. 1: Reviews* and *Vol. 2: Articles and Essays*, plus his genre journalism has appeared in the likes of *SFX, Fangoria, Dreamwatch, Gorezone* and *Rue Morgue*. He also co-wrote the afterword to the PS edition of Stephen King's *Night Shift* collection. He has been a Guest at Alt.Fiction five times, was a Guest at the first SFX Weekender, at Thought Bubble in 2011, Derbyshire Literary Festival and Off the Shelf in 2012, Monster Mash and Event Horizon in 2013, Edge-Lit in 2014, HorrorCon, HorrorFest and Grimm Up North in 2015, The Dublin Ghost Story Festival and Sledge-Lit in 2016, IMATS Olympia and Celluloid

Screams in 2017, Black Library Live (Warhammer 40k) and The UK Ghost Story Festival in 2019 and 2023, delivered the keynote speech at the 2021 WordCrafter conference, as well as being a panellist at FantasyCon and the World Fantasy Convention, and a fiction judge at the Sci-Fi London Film Festival. He is a former Special Publications Editor of the British Fantasy Society, has served as co-chair for the UK arm of the Horror Writers Association, and was co-chair of ChillerConUK 2022 in Scarborough.

His work has been optioned for film and television, and his zombie story 'Dead Time' was turned into an episode of the Lionsgate/NBC TV series *Fear Itself*, adapted by Steve Niles (*30 Days of Night*) and directed by Darren Lynn Bousman (*SAW II-IV* and *Spiral*). He also scripted *The Opportunity*, which premiered at the Cannes Film Festival, *Wind Chimes* (directed by Brad '*Hallows Eve*' Watson and which sold to TV), *The Weeping Woman* – filmed by award-winning director Mark Steensland, starring Tony-nominated actor Stephen Geoffreys (*Fright Night*) – *Confidence*, directed by award-winning Mike Clarke (*A Hand to Play*, *Paper and Plastic*) which stars Simon Bamford (*Hellraiser*, *Nightbreed*, *Starfish*), and *The Torturer* directed by Joe Manco of Little Spark Films, now streaming in over 100 countries. Loose Canon/Hydra Films have just turned Paul's novelette *Men of the Cloth* into a feature called *Sacrifice* (aka *The Colour of Madness*), starring *Re-Animator* and *You're Next*'s Barbara Crampton. His work for audio includes the full cast drama adaptation of *The Hellbound Heart* for Bafflegab, starring Tom Meeten (*The Ghoul*), Neve McIntosh (*Doctor Who*) and Alice Lowe (*Prevenge*), and the *Robin of Sherwood* adventure *The Red Lord* for Spiteful Puppet/ITV, narrated by Ian Ogilvy (*Return of the Saint*), plus his plays have been performed at FantasyCon and by Hideout Theatre in London. His books have been translated into many languages, including French, German, Spanish, Ukrainian, Turkish, Czech, Bulgarian and Polish. You can find out more at his website www.shadow-writer.co.uk which has featured Guest Writers such as Dean Koontz, Charlaine Harris, Robert Kirkman, Olivie Blake and Guillermo del Toro.

ADRIAN BALDWIN (COVER DESIGNER)

WINNER of INDIE NOVEL OF THE YEAR 2016 (Readers' Choice) at Underground Book Reviews

Adrian Baldwin is a Mancunian now living and working in Wales. Back in the Nineties, he wrote for various TV shows/personalities: Smith & Jones, Clive Anderson, Brian Conley, Paul McKenna, Hale & Pace, Rory Bremner (and a few others). Wooo, get him.

Since then, he has written three screenplays, one of which received generous financial backing from the Film Agency for Wales. Then along came the global recession to kick the UK Film industry in the nuts. What a bummer!

Not to be outdone, he turned to novel writing - which had always been his real dream - and in particular, a genre he feels is often overlooked; a genre he has always been a fan of: Dark Comedy (sometimes referred to as Horror's weird cousin).

BARNACLE BRAT (a dark comedy for grown-ups), his first novel won Indie Novel of the Year 2016 award (see above) - his second novel STANLEY McCLOUD MUST DIE! (More dark comedy for grown-ups) published in 2016, and his third novel: THE SNOWMAN AND THE SCARECROW (another dark comedy for grown-ups) published in 2018.

Adrian Baldwin has also written several dark comedy short stories, some of which he has published himself, whilst others have appeared in anthologies published by a variety of indie publishers.

His latest project, DEVIL'S ACRE, is a horror/sci-fi/period drama; it's basically Victorians vs 'aliens' vs zombies! What's not to like. The unfolding story will be released in a series of novellas/novelettes – with Episode 1 The Great Stink already out there.

Adrian cites his major influences as Kurt Vonnegut, Monty Python, Stephen King, David Bowie, Christopher Moore, David Mitchell, Robert Rankin, Galton & Simpson, Colin Bateman, Bruce Robinson, Jasper Fforde and Irvine Welsh.

For more information on the award-winning author, check out: www.adrianbaldwin.info (*You can read the beginnings of all his works there.)

Previous Publication History

A Suspicious Mind (*Cemetery Poets: Grave Offerings*, Double Dragon Books, 2003)

The Cursed (*The Naked Eye*, Encyclopocalypse, 2021)

Guilty Pleasures (*Demonology: Grammaticus Demonium*, Double Dragon Books, 2004)

The Anniversary (*Tourniquet Heart*, Prime Books, 2002)

Lady (*The Butterfly Man*, PS Publishing, 2011)

Baggage (*Un:Bound* website, September 2010)

Sin (*Nailbiters*, Black Shuck Books, 2017)

The Cave of Lost Souls (*Terror Tales* Issue 4, Christmas 1998)

Remote (*Redsine* Issue 10, October 2002, Prime Books)

Pleasures of the Flesh (*Traumas*, published by Black Shuck Books, 2020)

Kindred Spirits (*Darkness Rising Volume Seven: Screaming in Colours*, Prime Books, July 2003)

The GOAT (Original to this Collection)

It's All Over (*Scenes from the Second Storey*, Morrigan Books, 2011)

Benched (*Grievous Bodily Harm*, Zombie Pirate Publishing, 2019)

Yin & Yang (*Peripheral Visions*, Creative Guy Publishing, 2008)

Other Books by Paul Kane:

Novels
Arrowhead
Broken Arrow
Arrowland
Hooded Man (Omnibus)
The Gemini Factor
Lunar
Sleeper(s)
The Rainbow Man (as PB Kane)
Blood RED
Sherlock Holmes and the Servants of Hell
Before
Deep RED
Arcana
The Red Lord
Her Last Secret (as PL Kane)
The Storm
Her Husband's Grave (as PL Kane)
The Family Lie (as PL Kane)
The Gemini Effect
The RED Trilogy (Omnibus)
The Wet

Novellas & Novelettes
Signs of Life
The Lazarus Condition
Dalton Quayle Rides Out
RED
Pain Cages
Creakers (chapbook)
Flaming Arrow

The Bric-a-Brac Man
The PI's Tale
Snow
The Rot
Beneath the Surface (with Simon Clark)
Blood Red Sky
Confessions (as PL Kane)
Corpsing (as PL Kane)
Coming of Age (as PB Kane)
Murder on the Golden Sands Express (as PL Kane)
The Communion (as PL Kane)

Collections

Alone (In the Dark)
Touching the Flame
FunnyBones
Peripheral Visions
The Adventures of Dalton Quayle
Shadow Writer
The Butterfly Man and Other Stories
The Spaces Between
Ghosts
Monsters
The Dead Trilogy
The Spirits of Christmas
Shadow Casting
Nailbiters
Death
The Life Cycle
Disexistence
Kane's Scary Tales Vol. 1
More Monsters
Lost Souls

The Controllers
White Shadows (as PB Kane)
The Colour of Madness: Official Movie Tie-In
Traumas
Darkness & Shadows
The Naked Eye
Tempting Fate
Nailbiters – Hard Bitten
Zombies!
Even More Monsters
Dark Reflections
The Roads Less Travelled

Editor & Co-Editor
Shadow Writers Vol. 1 & 2
Terror Tales #1-4
Top International Horror
Albions Alptraume: Zombies
The British Fantasy Society: A Celebration
Hellbound Hearts
The Mammoth Book of Body Horror
A Carnivàle of Horror: Dark Tales from the
Fairground
Beyond Rue Morgue
Dark Mirages
Exit Wounds
Wonderland
Cursed
Twice Cursed
The Other Side of Never
In These Hallowed Halls
Beyond & Within: Folk Horror
Death Comes at Christmas

Non-Fiction

Contemporary North American Film Directors: A Wallflower Critical Guide (Major Contributor)

Cinema Macabre (Contributor)

The Hellraiser Films And Their Legacy

Voices in the Dark

Shadow Writer – The Non-Fiction. Vol. 1: Reviews

Shadow Writer – The Non-Fiction. Vol. 2: Articles & Essays

Leviathan – The Story of Hellraiser and Hellbound: Hellraiser II (contributor)

Hellraisers

War is Hell: Making Hellraiser III: Hell on Earth (Contributor)

Stuart Gordon: Interviews (Conversations with Filmmakers Series) (Contributor)

Hellraisers: Italian Language Edition

DEMAIN PUBLISHING

To keep up to-date on all news DEMAIN (including future submission calls and releases) you can follow us in a number of ways:

WEBSITE:
www.demainpublishing.org

TWITTER:
@DemainPubUk

FACEBOOK PAGE:
Demain Publishing

INSTAGRAM:
demainpublishing